THE SPY WHISPERER

A Ben S

Matthew Dunn

CHAPTER 1

No one at the Moscow dinner gathering knew their guest's real name was Ben Sign. And only one of the other eight Russian attendees knew the guest was a senior MI6 officer.

Today the forty nine year old British Intelligence officer called himself Tobias Harcourt. He'd chosen the nom-de-plume because it sounded posh and matched his fake backstory. He was posing as an aristocratic arms dealer; somebody who purportedly was looking to do an under-the-counter illegal weapons trade with Russian oligarchs. His real intention was to lure one of the men to Vienna, where that man would be snatched and interrogated by Austrian intelligence officers. Sign didn't care which of the men took the bait. His Russian agent at the table had set up the dinner. Both agent and Sign knew that all of their invitees were members of the FSB, the domestic successor to the KGB. With the help of the Austrians, Sign wanted to grab one of the FSB men and make him talk. Sign had advised his Russian agent that someone in MI6 was passing secrets to the Russians. Sign needed that name.

Some considered Sign to be too tall to be a spy. *We need grey men who don't stand out*, his MI6 recruiter had told him twenty seven years ago. Sign, back then a graduate student with a double first degree from Oxford University, had replied that in order to play the grey man one needed to stand out. His answer had made the recruiter smile. After extensive tests and interviews, his intelligence career began. Now, he was tipped to be the next chief of MI6. What he was doing in Moscow was his last official oversees assignment. After this, he'd be kept in London, ring fenced in order to protect him, so that in one year's time he could be interviewed for the post of one of the most prestigious roles in Western intelligence.

As he sat at the table, Sign thought of today as his last dash at the cut and thrust of the spying he so enjoyed. He was making the most of the job. Wearing a hand-tailored Gieves and Hawkes suit whose charcoal colouring matched his clipped hair, silk tie bound in a Windsor knot over a cut-away collar shirt from Saville Row, immaculately polished black Church's shoes, and a Rolex watch he'd borrowed from MI6's props department, he was ready to do business. Often Sign had to playact wholly different personas with very different attires. But today he was as close to his real image as possible.

And he kept the family backstory of Harcourt identical to his own. His parents were academics, but not eminent professors who could be easily traced. Plus, they were dead. He had no siblings. His wife was an NGO worker who'd been shot in El Salvador. They'd never had children. He was alone.

Sign opened his napkin and delicately placed it over his lap.

They were in the private dining room of the restaurant, sat around a solitary circular table that was adorned with a starched white cloth and accoutrements befitting of one of the city's finest eateries. The walls were draped with purple Mongolian sashes. The subtle glow from ceiling spotlights were enhanced by candles that were cleverly positioned around the room. Paintings were French and Dutch. And a small iron bowl of smouldering coals and rosemary was in the corner – there to produce an aroma that complimented the plat du jour of roast poussin, sautéed potatoes, winter vegetables, and Domaine aux Moines Savennieres wine from Roche aux Moines.

Sign's Russian agent, Peter, was a roguish businessman of many trades but with links to the FSB. Sign had been running him against the Russians for five years. Peter was ex-Spetsnaz, built like a prize fighter, a womanizer and heavy drinker, and had a permanent grin on his face. His attractive jet-black hair and green eyes were offset by his calloused and scarred hands. But like Sign, he was immaculately dressed. Sign had put him up for this job.

The MI6 officer had said, "Tell your FSB pals that there's a British arms dealer you know who wants to do business with Russia. Tell them the trade he's offering is worth billions. But also tell them that you can't verify if the weapons he's selling are of value to Mother Russia. Plant hope and doubt in their minds. Encourage them to meet me with suspicion in their minds."

Sign looked at Peter and the others. "Gentlemen: shall we begin." Sign's demeanour and tone of voice was as cool as cucumber. He spoke in English, even though he was a fluent Russian speaker.

Peter poured himself wine. Addressing the FSB men, he said, "I've known of Mr. Harcourt for years, but to my knowledge he rarely attends business meetings in person. In the past, I've spoken to him on the phone and corresponded with his office. Yesterday was the first time I met him in person. He has an interesting proposition for you."

"And if you like the deal, Peter will take a one percent cut of the trade." Sign paused, looking at each of the men in turn. "Peter vouches for you, saying you have access to serious money."

"And what do you have to trade?" asked one of the FSB men.

"Technology that Russia doesn't have." Sign smiled. "Blueprints of Britain's latest prototype EMT weapons, Polaris submarine communications systems, and satellite interceptors."

"But they are just prototypes."

Sign shook his head. "Not anymore. The trials have been completed and approved by the British military and the COBRA committee."

The Russians glanced at each other. One of them asked, "How did you get these blueprints?"

Sign folded his hands. "I stole them via two generals on my payroll." He laughed. "I hope Peter didn't tell you I was a legitimate businessman."

"And your price for these blueprints?"

"That's for you to decide and for me to agree or disagree on." Sign took a sip of wine. "My business is a tricky one. Trust is non-existent. Proof of concept is the bane of my life."

"Meaning – how does a buyer know the technology works?"

"Yes." Sign's heartbeat had dropped by ten beats per minute. "So, here's the conundrum: how do I show you what I have; how do you decide if you like it; and how do I ensure that I'm not royally fucked over?"

The men looked at each other.

Sign waited.

The oldest FSB officer at the table said, "It is an impossible problem."

This was the moment Sign had been waiting for. The moment to lure in one of the FSB officers. He looked at Peter. "Who do you trust the most around this table?"

Peter glanced at each man. "I trust them all."

"I suspect that's not true but it doesn't matter. Regardless, pick one who can view the blueprints."

Peter said, "Boris. Simply because his forename is first in the alphabet of the men dining with us. But any of them would be up to the task."

"Boris it is." Sign stared at Boris. "You have a huge weight of responsibility."

Boris looked like a rabbit in headlights. "I'm not a scientist or engineer. How can I verify the blueprints?"

"You can't, but you know business. I will meet you in Vienna. Bring which ever experts you deem fit for the analysis of the prints."

Boris looked confused. "Vienna?"

"Neutral territory."

Boris shook his head. "My experts will memorise the blueprints and return with me to Russia. No money will be exchanged. Your theft will have been a waste of time."

Sign clapped his hands. "Bravo Mr. Boris." His demeanour turned serious as he analysed the men. "Just because Russian men play chess doesn't make you all chess masters." He tossed his napkin onto the table, his food uneaten. "Boris; expert analysts; Vienna; three days' time; a hotel of my choosing. You'll have one third of each blueprint. A supercomputer might be able to recall the data of each one-third. A genius or photographic mind or anyone on any form of spectrum will most certainly not be able to recall a trace of what I show you. You pay me ten million pounds for the traces. You take them home. You make a judgement call. Do you move your queen to take king? Or to do you walk away? If the former, you get the rest of the blueprints for a serious price. If the latter, I have ten million quid for wasting my valuable time. What say you?"

The senior FSB officer in the room touched Boris' arm. "This could be a trap."

Sign snapped, "Gentlemen – if this was a trap, I wouldn't be in Moscow. On my own. I'm giving you the ability to neutralise what Britain, France, and America can throw at you." He stood and looked at Peter. "If I've wasted my time, do let me know. I have a private jet to catch."

Peter waved his hands up and down. "No need for any of us to get annoyed. I think Mr. Harcourt's strategy is sound for all sides."

Sign swivelled and said in a loud voice, "So, what's it to be?"

The door swung open with sufficient force to make it bang against the wall. Five policemen rushed into the room and grabbed Sign. Peter and the FSB men stood. The intelligence officers had grins on their faces. The senior officer said, "You talk of chess. Well, you've just been outplayed. We knew all along that you were an MI6 officer."

Sign looked at Peter. "Tut tut, Peter. Only you could have done this. And I thought we were friends."

To Peter's surprise, Sign laughed as he was led away.

For forty eight hours, he was interrogated by the FSB in its headquarters in Lubyanka Square, Moscow. He wasn't tortured – to have done so would have been a catastrophe for Russia, given Sign had diplomatic status and the FSB was fully aware that maltreatment would be dealt in kind by the Brits if they caught a Russian spy. But, for two days he was given no food or water, and in between harsh questioning he was made to stand while distorted noise was blasted from speakers. Sign was a thinker, not a man of action, yet he told them nothing.

On a road in Russia's north western border with Finland, Sign was guided to British authorities who were flanked by MI6 paramilitary operatives. It was dark; snow was falling.

The senior FSB man who held Sign's arm was the man at the dinner who told Sign that he'd been outplayed. Ten yards from the British men, he released Sign's arm and said, "Never come back to Russia."

Sign turned to him. His exhausted face was highlighted by the headlights of the FSB and MI6 cars that were fifty yards apart from each other. Sign said, "You forgot the rule. Because you play chess doesn't make you a chess master. I've been running Peter for five years. I always suspected he was a double agent, though had no proof. So, for five years I've been feeding him crap. It was time for me to flush him out at our lovely dinner two days ago. You did the heavy lifting, for which I'm very grateful. Send my regards to Peter. He was my pawn. Don't be too hard on him. And don't be too hard on yourself that you've been sucker punched."

Sign smiled and walked to the British men.

CHAPTER 2

The morning after Sign was delivered over the Finnish border, Tom Knutsen and Helen Pope were in a stationary transit van in Unwin Street, Elephant & Castle, London. The two undercover Metropolitan Police officers shared the vehicle with hardened criminals who had concealed pistols. A shotgun was beside the driver. In front of them was another van, containing three more criminals. They were here to do a bank heist. Knutsen and Pope's role was to witness the crime. The gang lord who'd planned the heist wasn't present in the vehicles, instead monitoring the job from afar. The protocol was simple: he called them with the location of the robbery; they mobilised; the bank was assaulted. And he'd given them strict instructions that the assault was to take place with speed and absolute aggression. The guns were not here for show.

Knutsen and Pope had infiltrated the gang from different angles and timeframes.

With the permission of the Met, one year ago Knutsen had held up a post office in Canterbury. He was brandishing a disabled WW2 Luger pistol. He tried to fire a shot at the ceiling, knowing the gun wouldn't work, but hoping his theatrics would draw the attention of the Kent Police. He was arrested and incarcerated in Parkhurst Prison for nine months. The sentence was lenient because he'd not pointed his weapon at anyone, nor had he committed ABH or GBH on any of the customers in the post office. In fact, the witnesses declared in court that the medium-height, muscular, thirty seven year old seemed desperate and kind. He'd sat on the floor after his gun failed and told everyone around him that he was a good man from the wrong tracks. He gave no resistance when the police came. But his real ploy had worked. In prison he was in the A-list, because he was an armed robber. Serial killers are viewed as weirdos; paedophiles are killed if left alone with other inmates; teenage knife crime is viewed as kids brandishing weapons they don't know how to use; drug dealers are considered useful because they might get substances into the clink, but otherwise they're labelled parasites; and petty criminals are simply ignored. But major gun crime equals prestige. Quickly, Knutsen came to the attention of other armed robbers. His target was a criminal boss who was due for parole shortly. The Met and Knutsen knew the gang lord was pretending to be a reformed member of society. Once out, the gang lord would go back to his old ways. Knutsen had to stop that from happening. Knutsen assaulted guards and inmates in prison, but not to a pulp, even though he could have done so against the most hardened members of Parkhurst. Many times, he was put in solitary confinement. Eventually, he was summoned to the gang lord who gave him a simple command.

"You're a man who should be working for me."

When gang lord and Knutsen were out of prison, Knutsen had achieved his Met mission to infiltrate the gang. Now, he was about to commit a heinous crime, all in the name of queen and country.

Pope had different instructions, though no less arduous. Fifteen months ago she married Knutsen in a Brixton registry office. The plan was they'd divorce as soon as their undercover objective was complete. She visited Knutsen in prison, bringing contraband secreted in her private parts. Her visits were welcomed by many inmates, because Knutsen distributed the contraband to prisoners. Plus, Pope always dressed to kill during her visits. Other inmates in the visitors' reception gawped at her. She put a smile on their faces. Playing a bimbo was hard for her because in reality she was anything but. Prior to her undercover work, she'd had stints in the Met's firearms units, hostage negotiation, had been a detective in the serious crime unit, and had worked as a scuba diver, pulling bloated human carcases out of rivers and lakes.

When the gang lord had asked Knutsen to work with him, Knutsen replied, "Only if my wife is there with me on every job. She's a looker. She distracts people. Plus, she shoots guns better than any man I know. And there's one other thing. She works at a bank. You know the adage: if you want to rob somewhere, work there. Eventually you'll spot the cracks."

The gang lord replied, "Which bank?"

Now, Knutsen and Pope were brandishing pistols. Pope looked nothing like a bimbo. She was wearing jeans and a puffer jacket. Knutsen and Pope exchanged glances. They were married. And they now felt it was real. Knutsen nodded at her. She smiled.

The team leader got the call from the gang lord. The gang lord said, "Royal Bank of Scotland. 29 Old Brompton Road. But don't tell the others until you're there. Just get them to follow you. And make sure your route to the target is circuitous."

"Circuitous?"

"Don't go the most direct route."

"Why?

"Just move."

The team leader looked over his shoulder. "We're on." Via his mobile, he relayed the instruction to the other van and drove out of Unwin Street, the other van on his tail.

Pope held her mobile phone out of view of the others and sent a text message to the Met's head of the Specialist Firearms Command. The message was *MOBILE TO TARGET*.

Clad in fire-resistant black overalls, Kevlar body armour, helmets, boots, communications sets, holstered pistols, and Heckler & Koch submachine guns strapped to their chests, eight members of the Met's elite SCO19 firearms unit waited fifty yards from the Royal Bank of Scotland branch. They were in a decrepit white van that had insignia on its exterior declaring the vehicle belonged to a plumbing firm. The bank knew they were there. Its staff had been replaced by plain clothed detectives who'd been given a twenty four hour crash course in how to run the branch until the heist took place. Only the branch manager remained on site, to ensure business was efficient and unsuspicious before the attempted robbery.

The Met paramilitary officers had rehearsed the drill twenty two times. The robbers arrive. SCO19 wait. The robbers enter, alongside Knutsen and Pope. The SWAT team still waits. Only when one of the robbers brandishes a gun and tells the fake bank staff to hand over cash or die will Pope run out of the building and wave her hands. That will be the trigger and the end of Pope and Knutsen's undercover assignment. SCO19 knew they could get to the building in six seconds flat. They'd deploy flashbangs. The criminals would be dead before their heads smacked the floor. Knutsen and Pope would walk away and vanish to their next job.

It took forty minutes for the vans to arrive in Old Brompton Street. The drivers remained in the vehicles. Alongside Knutsen and Pope, six armed criminals exited the vehicles, their guns hidden from pedestrians on the bustling street. The RBS branch was forty yards away. When the job was done, the vans would hurtle toward the front entrance and collect the robbers.

"This is the target," muttered the team leader.

Knutsen and Pope resisted every urge to panic. This wasn't the bank that Pope had allegedly worked in. That was two miles away. The gang leader who'd set up the heist probably didn't trust Pope and Knutsen, so had chosen a different target. They were fucked.

12

SCO19 waited. Knutsen and Pope would be in hoodies. No way of identifying them and the men around them. All SCO19 could rely on was Pope's signal to assault. The firearms officers were poised, breathing fast, their van filled with the musky scent of testosterone, their fingers on the triggers of their submachineguns.

Fifteen yards from the bank's entrance, Pope pulled out her mobile, desperate to inform SWAT of the change of plan. But the team leader spotted her action, slammed his hand on hers, and stamped on the phone after it hit the ground. He barked, "No calls now!"

Knutsen moved to her side and whispered, "Run. I'll go in with them."

Pope replied, "I'm going in."

"I thought you'd say that." They were by the front door of the bank as Knutsen pulled out his sidearm and pointed it at the criminals. "Police! Drop your weapons! You're under arrest!"

The team leader grabbed Pope, spun her around so that he and her were facing Knutsen, held a gun to her head, and shouted to his men, "Get out of here! I'll find my own way back."

His men sprinted to their vans. People in the street were screaming, some of them running, others ducking behind whatever cover they could find. Within seconds, the place had become chaos.

Knutsen was motionless as he kept his gun trained on the few inches that were visible of the team leader's head. "Attempted robbery is one thing. But if shots are fired, that puts you into a different league. Don't be stupid!"

The team leader laughed and walked back with Pope. "You set us up."

Knutsen was silent.

"That means you've got boys with big guns somewhere nearby. But I'm betting they're not near enough. The boss saw through you, I reckon."

No way could Knutsen take a shot at the criminal's head. The team leader's finger was on his pistol's trigger. A bullet entering his brain would most likely cause his finger to tighten and blow out Pope's brains. Knutsen lowered his gun and said, "Let her go and I'll let you go. I can't promise you that you, your men, and your boss will get away with this, but at least I can give you a breathing space."

"A breathing space. I like the sound of that." He shot Knutsen in the shoulder, causing the undercover cop to crash to the pavement and release his firearm.

Pope screamed and kicked her captor with her heels against his shins.

But the criminal held her firm. "Not my lucky day. Not your lucky day."

Police sirens were drawing close. And the van containing SCO19 was hurtling toward Old Brompton Road. They'd realised what was going on.

The robber said to Knutsen, "Time for me to go." He shot Pope in the head, killing her instantly. He spun around and ran.

Knutsen shouted, "No." He staggered to his feet and collected his sidearm. The criminal was twenty yards away, then thirty. Knutsen was right handed, but it was his right shoulder that had been hit and was now useless. He put his gun in his left hand and raised his arm. The action was excruciating. The criminal was now forty yards away, his head moving left and right as he was looking for side alleys to dash down and vanish. Knutsen wasn't going to let that happen. He took aim at the criminal's head, pulled the trigger, and hit him in the back. The team leader hit the ground and started crawling. Knutsen walked up to him, blood pouring down his chest, his breathing erratic. He pointed his gun at the robber's head and put two bullets in his skull.

He walked as quickly as he could back to Pope, knelt down, and cradled her head. It was a mess – nothing like the beautiful visage he'd admired since he'd worked with her. He doubted they'd have got divorced after this job. They were meant for each other, not just as cops, but also as civilians. He kissed her forehead, not caring that her blood was on his lips. He gently lowered her head and started sobbing.

CHAPTER 3

Two days' later, Ben Sign was in MI6 headquarters, Vauxhall Cross, London. He'd been summoned to one of the Babylonian-style building's conference rooms on the ground floor. The Chief of MI6, Head of Security, Head of the Russia department, and the service's senior legal counsel were facing him across an oak table. Sign felt like he was on trial by a kangaroo court.

All were silent throughout the meeting, save for the Head of Security; a man called Jeffery who alongside Sign was in the running to be the next chief of the service. Jeffery was a ruthless officer whose stint in operational security as a board director was merely a stepping stone up his career ladder.

Jeffery said, "At what stage did you suspect Peter was a double agent?"

Sign smiled. "From the outset."

"And yet you ran him against the Russians for five years."

"I ran him *at* the Russians. Your terminology needs to be more precise, Jeffery."

Jeffery flicked through a file on the table. "You had no proof he was a double, but you went on your gut instinct."

"Don't be crass. Gut instinct? Dear me. No – when I inherited him from my predecessor, I felt he was too good to be true. Plus, there was tangible evidence that the crap I fed him was being actioned on by the Russians. Everything I said to him was being passed by him to the FSB."

"And yet you failed to tell us about your suspicions."

Sign could see where this was headed. "It's always difficult to know who to trust at our level."

"Meaning?!"

"It's a statement, not an accusation." Sign smiled. "Sometimes senior MI6 officers use operational successes or failures to further their careers."

"You're suggesting I would have capitalised from the fact you were running a double agent?"

With sarcasm in his voice, Sign replied, "Heaven forbid, no. It had never occurred to me that you'd see this as an opportunity to better me in the application to be the next chief. You wouldn't stoop that low, Jeffery." Sign's tone hardened as he added, "I knew there was a mole in MI6. I thought it unlikely that the mole was cadre MI6. Most likely I thought it was Peter. But then again, it's always difficult to be certain. For all I knew, the mole could have been you, Jeffery."

The fury in Jeffery's face was obvious. "I have a distinguished…"

"Yes, we all have distinguished careers, blah blah. But some of us are not back-stabbing shits." Sign looked at the others, before returning his attention to Jeffery. "I'm not accusing you of anything untoward. But do I trust you? Not a fucking chance."

Jeffery composed himself. "Do you know what's happened to Peter?"

Sign shrugged. "I've been held in lockdown since I got to Finland. Most likely the FSB has promoted Peter and given him a medal."

Jeffery closed the file in front of him. "One day ago, a cardboard box was delivered to the British embassy in Moscow. Inside was Peter's head."

17

Sign digested the news, though showed no sign of emotion, even the he was shocked by the development. For all of Peter's treachery, Sign had liked him. "Peter's use to the FSB came to an end when he set up my Moscow meeting. But there was one more thing Peter could do – send a message to us that we must not spy on the motherland. Peter's head was that message."

Everyone before him nodded.

Jeffery smirked as he said, "Your actions got an agent killed."

It was time to take the gloves off. With an angry and strident tone, Sign said, "Jeffery – God knows how you've made it to the board of directors. You were never a good operator and your intellect is somewhat wanting. So too your compassion. Peter was deployed against us. I knew that and played along. No doubt, Peter hoped to receive Russian praise for what he'd done. He was many things, including being brave. Let's not be hypocritical. We deploy our agents against the Russians. And some of them are double agents. It's the endless game. I corrupted Russian Intelligence by using Peter. Read the Ukraine and Crimea files. What the Russians did there would have been one hundred times worse had I not planted the idea in Peter's head that NATO was about to strike." Sign stood and looked at the chief of MI6. "Your successor will be chosen by you and the Joint Intelligence Committee. I realize that this witch hunt today has smeared my name. Unfairly, I should add. But that matters not. May I suggest to you sir, that you choose your successor very carefully. Don't pick anyone in this room. And that includes me. Because as of now, you have my resignation."

"You executed a criminal!" The commissioner of the Met Police was sitting behind his desk. Standing to attention in front of him was Knutsen, wearing a police uniform that hadn't seen the light of day in years.

Knutsen said, "He killed my wife."

"Your fake wife."

"She was still my wife. Plus a fellow officer. What would you have done, Paddy?"

"You'll call me sir!"

"Okay Paddy sir."

"You're one of the best shots in the Met. You had a clean line of sight. Why didn't you shoot him before Pope died?"

Knutsen moved his legs apart.

"Remain at attention!"

"I can't. It's the shoulder. It hurts. Standing makes it worse for some reason. I'd like it on record whether you'd like me to stand to attention. I'm not saying it's torture by you or anything but I would like to hear your views on interrogations under duress... Paddy."

The commissioner sighed. "Sit. How is the wound?"

"They got the bullet out. Bit of reconstructive surgery and physio over the next few weeks. After that, I'll be punching above my weight."

"And how is your mental health?"

"Like most people, I get up in the morning and think, Not this shit again. What about you?"

The commissioner ignored the comment. "Why didn't you take the shot?"

Knutsen shrugged. "You give us elephant-stopper side arms. That's good if you're in an isolated field and chasing a guy with a bullet-proof vest. Bad if you're in Old Brompton Road with hundreds of people around you. If I took the shot, I'd have hit his head. He'd have involuntarily squeezed the trigger. Pope would have died. But it may not have ended there. The bullet could have exited his head, ricocheted off a wall or the street, and thumped into an innocent bystander. In fact, the power of these bullets is such that my shot could have gone through three or four bodies. Would you have liked that on your conscience?"

The Met chief hesitated. "No."

"I thought not. My wife's dead as a result of my calculated decision."

"Fake wife..." The commissioner held up his hand. "No need to correct me. I'm sorry."

Knutsen touched the arm of Britain's most senior cop. "Put me back in jail again if you want. I'll handle that. Put me in a noose if you want. I'll handle that, too." He bowed his head. "Helen Pope was more than a colleague. Least ways, I hoped it would pan out that way. I wanted to cook for her and take her to see me practise kendo."

The commissioner frowned. "That would have been an odd but endearing date."

"Yes, it would sir."

The chief drummed fingers on his desk and muttered, "What to do, what to do?" He looked at Knutsen. "CCTV has got you. Witnesses have got you. Point blank, you killed him."

Knutsen smiled, though his look was one of resignation. "In kendo, or at least the British version of it, we call it a death strike. When the opponent's on the ground, don't assume he won't get up. He will and he'll hit you with his bamboo stick bloody hard. Then you're down and he'll finish you off. I finished him off. I'll pay the consequences."

The commissioner walked to the office window and looked over the magnificent vista of London. With his back to Knutsen he said, "It is a shame. You were my finest undercover office."

"People come and go."

"They do." The commissioner swivelled. "But I don't want your life defined by this event. You deserve far better." He patted Knutsen on the shoulder. "I'll sweep this under the carpet. In return, you'll need to leave. I can't avoid that. My sincere apologies. You will be a serious loss to my team."

Knutsen rose and nodded. He held out his hand. "Thank you Paddy."

Paddy shook his hand. "Thank *you* Tom. Don't let the bed bugs bite."

Knutsen smiled and walked out of the room. This was the end of his career as a police officer.

CHAPTER 4

Two weeks later, Sign entered a small house in Mayfair that had been converted into a place of business. It belonged to a former MI6 officer turned head hunter. Sign had an appointment with the recruiter. The receptionist asked Sign to take a seat, phoned her boss and told him that his guest had arrived. She instructed Sign to proceed to the lower floor for his appointment.

The head hunter was Robert Lask. When in MI6, he'd been an expert on China, and spoke fluent Cantonese and Mandarin. Prior to joining the service, he'd been an inspector in the Royal Hong Kong Police. He was a bit of a throwback to colonial days, plus had been a fairly average MI6 officer, but he was a decent bloke. Sign trusted him, though did think that Lask thought he was more important than he actually was. It was his job that had made him that way. Lask specialised in finding jobs for former MI6 officers and other members of the British special operations community. That included interviewing former chiefs of MI6. It gave him power and a sense of self-importance, wherein the reality was that Lask would never have made senior management.

Sign shook the fifty five year old's hand and took a seat on the solitary sofa within the ornate room. Lask remained behind his desk, looking like a judge at the bench.

"How can I help you?" asked Lask.

"I'm on the *rock and roll*."

Lask laughed. "Of course. What other reason would you have for being here?" He frowned. "But you were tipped for the top. What went wrong?"

"I saw the writing on the wall and jumped before I was pushed."

"But you were the smartest man in MI6. One of the smartest men in the country. You could have outgunned them."

"If I'd had the will." Sign smiled with resignation on his face. "I no longer wanted to belong to an organisation run by buffoons."

Lask rifled through papers. "I can get you a job in a jot. For someone of your standing, you'll be snapped up. Head of Security at Price Waterhouse Cooper, senior advisor to the Prime Minister, professor at Oxford – the list goes on and on. You do realise how important you are?"

Sign ran a finger and thumb alongside the cuff of his shirt. "I don't care about that. I want something smaller. Something that matters."

Lask was confused as he reached the end of the CVs in front of him. "I don't have anything that matches that brief."

"I thought not." Sign crossed his legs, clasped his hands, and stared at Lask. "I'm not here for a job. I'm setting up my own private consultancy. I need to employ someone to help me. Someone special. You can help find me that person."

"Consultancy of what?"

"Crime, espionage, mysteries. That's what I do."

"Yes, yes. That is you." Lask pulled out a box file. "And what are the credentials of the employee you seek?"

"Someone who has an edge. Aside from that, I won't know until I meet him."

Lask rifled through his papers. "I have an ex-SAS sergeant who spent twenty years in the Regiment. Tours in Iraq and Afghanistan."

"Happily married with kids?"

"Yes."

"Dishonourably discharged?"

"No."

"Then let's move on. Next."

Lask picked up a CV. "This guy might interest you. Former MI5 and…"

"Boring! Next."

Lask went through his pile of CVs. "I have MI6 officers."

"I don't want MI6. I want someone different from me."

Lask picked up the last CV. "What do you think about cops?"

"They're a different breed to us. But there are exceptions. What's interesting about this man or woman?"

"It's a man. He was undercover for years. He spent time in prison as part of one assignment. Was shot. He…"

Sign held up his hand. "Don't tell me anything else. I want to meet him. Arrange that meeting. If I hire him, you'll get your introductory fee."

The next day, Sign entered Simpson's In The Strand. It was lunchtime and the restaurant was bustling with businessmen, government mandarins, and generals. One of the oldest traditional restaurants in London, Simpson's was renowned for its carved meats, brought to the table on trolleys by expert waiters. Sign had been here many times, but not because of the fare. Like many others, he enjoyed dining in the establishment because it had wooden booths that allowed privacy. He sat in one of the booths. Tom Knutsen was sitting opposite him.

"Mr. Knutsen. You know who I am?"

Knutsen was wearing a blue suit he'd purchased from Marks & Spencer. He looked immaculate. Knutsen said, "Yes, I know who you are."

"What do you know about me?"

Knutsen replied, "Senior MI6, until recently. Lask said you were destined for the top. He said your career was remarkable. Then he shut his mouth and said the rest of your background was classified."

Sign nodded. "I haven't read your CV. Lask gave me the briefest of thumbnail sketches. Beyond that, there's a lifetime of experience that I refused to hear about."

"Why?"

"Because I wanted to get the measure of you in person." Sign gestured at a nearby waiter. "Would you like a cut of beef or turkey? They slice it with razor sharp knives."

"I'm not hungry."

Sign summoned the sommelier. "But you'll have a glass of Sancerre." When the wine waiter was gone, Sign asked, "How is your injury?"

"Fully recovered. I'm back on my dojo."

"Dojo. The *place of the way*." Sign drummed his fingers. "I wonder what Japanese martial art you study. Karate? Aikido? Judo? Wrestling?" He stared at Knutsen. "The problem with those disciplines is they're street-fighting arts. I don't think a man like you – undercover for most of his adult life – would wind down by doing something so eminently useful in his line of work. I think you'd want something more romantic, noble, disciplined. You'd want the counterbalance to the grimy life you've led. You study kenjutsu."

"We call it kendo. Yes. You're right."

"Bravo, Mr. Knutsen. You are therefore a noble warrior."

Knutsen laughed. "Does everyone in MI6 talk like this? You sound…"

"Old fashioned?"

"Something like that."

"I can sound like many things, depending on the circumstances. You of all people know we adapt."

"Chameleons."

"Yes."

They sat in silence for a moment.

Sign broke the silence. "You're educated."

"How do you know?"

"Your eyes and your self-confidence."

Knutsen nodded. "I gained a first at Exeter."

"So why join the police, unless you wished to be on track to being a chief constable?"

Knutsen didn't reply.

"I posit that you wanted to escape something and join a gang; the gang being the police. But when you joined, you realized something – you were always destined to be a loner. Uniforms and allegiance were not for you. Destiny and reality is a cruel fate. Unhappy childhood?"

Knutsen shrugged. "Unlike you, I wasn't born with a silver spoon in my mouth. My father died when I was young. My mother turned to drink and had barely a penny to her name."

Sign took a sip of his wine. "My father was a merchant navy sailor. He joined the navy age fourteen after being flip-flopped between different foster carers. He came from a very poor family. His mother died when he was seven. He never knew his father. As a child, my father suffered problems in his legs. Doctors put his legs in irons for a year. They were different days back then. He failed entry into the army, when conscription was still around. His feet were too flat. So, he travelled the world on a boat. My mother was brought up in London's east end. She had a big working class family. They're all dead now. They had very little money. But they were brilliant people and stuck together. My mother educated herself and became a scientist." Sign pushed his wine away. "I am not as I seem."

"You most certainly are not." Knutsen felt like he was in the presence of a huge force of kinetic energy. "Undercover work is shit."

"It is, and yet we chose that life."

"For a reason."

"Indeed." Sign wondered how far he should deploy his mental prowess. He liked Knutsen. But, he had to test his metal. "Did you want her to be your real wife?"

Knutsen bristled. "That's none of your damn business!"

"Correct response." Sign looked at the other dinners. None of them had done what Knutsen and Sign had done. They were establishment, never having sacrificed their souls. Quietly, he said, "Dear fellow. You did the right thing. I did the right thing. The trouble is, the right thing eats us." He returned his gaze to Knutsen. "You are an expert shot, a warrior, a loner, a thinker."

Knutsen's chest puffed up with anger. "And I assume you have a healthy pension and a wife and kids to go home to somewhere near here."

"Actually, my wife was killed in Latin America. I have no children. I have very little money."

Knutsen's anger evaporated. "What is the job?"

"We become specialist detectives, operating in London."

"If you've got no money, how will you pay me?"

"By results." Sign leaned forward. "People want strange expertise that they don't like."

Knutsen smiled. "I'd never thought of it that way."

"Nor had I until now." Sign added, "It would be a fifty/fifty partnership. I'm too old for the dojo. You're not. But, as you know, on the dojo it's not about the fighting, it's about the analysis of the opponent. Together, we can do that analysis. But, if there's heavy lifting to be done, I'm not that man. You are."

"Where are your offices?"

Sign sighed. "I've looked around London. They're all too expensive. For now, we'd work from my home."

"Whereabouts in London?"

"West Square, Kennington. I recently bought the place off a superb former MI6 agent. He now lives in the States and is happily retired. Will Cochrane sold me his home for half its value."

"And this Cochrane character is no longer spec ops?"

Sign smiled. "He's done his time in the trenches. He's at peace." Sign tossed his napkin on the table. "We, however, are not at peace. Do you agree?"

"Yes." Knutsen was deep in thought. "Mr. Sign…"

"Ben."

"Ben – here's the thing. The Met commissioner got me off the hook for executing a piece of scum. But I had to resign, with no pension. I'm looking for a job with a salary. I'm broke. What you're offering sounds appealing, but it won't pay my next three months' rent."

"And yet, you could earn ten times that rent after just one assignment. I don't come cheap." Sign clasped his hands together. "I understand your predicament. Do you smoke?"

"No."

"Drink?"

"Yes."

"How much?"

"More than the British surgeon general recommends, but never to excess."

"Drinking is a man's prayer time. Doctors don't get that." Sign added, "I'd like to offer you the position of co-director of my business. You can stay at my place until the money starts rolling in. My bedrooms have en suite bathrooms. There is a sizeable lounge where we can conduct consultations with clients."

"Sir, I'm not..."

"Homosexual. Nor am I. This is business. You and I are out of work."

"Holmes and Watson?"

"Something like that, if you choose to draw parallels."

Knutsen asked, "Are you IT literate? Have you got a website? Twitter account? Facebook page? Advertising?"

Sign shook his head. "I have a black book. With your contacts in the Met, you'll add to that black book. Business will come to us. We don't need to prostitute ourselves by chasing petty divorce cases and the like."

"So, what would we be chasing?"

"Mysteries. But tell me something. Why should I go into business with you?"

Knutsen looked away. "You decide." He returned his attention to Sign. "Loyalty is key to everything, isn't it, Mr. Sign? If I join the business, I wouldn't do so half-hearted. As important, I don't have your abilities, but you don't have my abilities."

"True indeed." Sign held out his hand.

Knutsen shook his hand. "I can move in on Monday."

CHAPTER 5

The forty year old Englishman rang the bell of the Edwardian house in Godalming, Surrey. He'd watched the home for three hours and knew that the occupiers were at home. He was smartly dressed, an overcoat protecting his suit. His hair was cut to precision – shorter than a civilian haircut, longer than that of a military serviceman. This morning, he'd shaved with a cutthroat razor, after which he'd dabbed eau de toilette over his immaculate skin. Yesterday, he'd had a beard and his voice was that of a Belarusian artisan; the day before he was a Finnish drunk; today he was a gentleman. His true self.

A woman answered the door.

"Mrs. Archer. I'm sorry to turn up unannounced. I work with your husband. We have a crisis."

The wife looked uncertain. "My husband's at home. Who should I say is calling?"

"John Smith."

"Oh, it's like that, is it?"

"I'm afraid it is. My real name was buried a long time ago." He checked his watch. "I don't have much time."

She gestured him to enter the house while calling out, "Mark, we have a visitor."

Mark was a fifty one year old MI6 officer. He was reading a paper and was sitting next to a fire in a tastefully decorated living room.

Mark looked up as the man who called himself John Smith entered the room. "What do you want?"

Smith looked at Mrs. Archer. "I do apologise for asking this, but would you be offended if I asked you to give us some privacy?"

Mrs. Archer had been married to Mark for twenty three years. She'd accompanied him on four overseas MI6 postings. She knew what it was like to be married to a spy. She acquiesced and left the room.

The man sat opposite Mark and spoke to him for ten minutes.

Then he left.

Two days' later, the man who called himself by the fake name of John Smith waited in a hotel room in Mayfair's Duke's hotel. The senior MI6 officer wasn't wearing his suit jacket, but otherwise he was immaculately dressed. He was sitting in an armchair, two untouched glasses of beer were by his side. His fingers were interlaced while he was deep in thought.

Someone at the door knocked three times, paused for three seconds, then knocked again. It was the visitor Smith had been waiting for. He let the man in and locked the door.

The man was thirty six years old, wiry, of medium height, had shoulder-length black hair, and eyes that looked dead. He was wearing jeans, hiking boots, and a fleece.

Smith gestured to a spare chair and handed him one of the beers. "It's been two years. How have you been, Karl?"

Karl Hilt took a swig of his beer. "I've been doing private work since I left MI6. Pay's better."

Hilt had been a paramilitary officer in MI6, prior to which he was an SBS operative. He was an expert in surveillance, unarmed combat, weaponry, espionage tradecraft, and deniable assassinations. But what stood him out for Smith was he had no mercy. He was a highly trained psychopath who was kept on a leash only by virtue of the organisations he'd worked for. Now, he was off the leash. But Smith still needed him to have a master. For now.

"I want you to do a job for me. I'll pay you well. It will be UK-based."

Hilt nodded and said in his east London accent, "I'm between work at the moment. What do you have in mind?"

Smith didn't answer him directly. "Do you remember those guys you killed in Iraq?"

"Yeah. You were in a shit storm back then. They'd have cut your head off if I hadn't got into the house."

Smith nodded. "And you remember the last remaining member of that terror cell – the woman who came at you with an AK47?"

"I slit her throat."

"And you did so without blinking."

"She was a fanatical bitch. Wanted to put bullets in you and me."

"You could easily have disarmed her."

Hilt shrugged. "She could have been packing a secondary weapon, grenades, bomb vest, anything." Hilt smiled. "The point being – she deserved to die."

"Yes, she did."

"So, what's your point? Men, women, even kids who pick up RPGs and will one day soon be radicalised – I don't care who I've killed. Are you in or out of MI6?"

"Still in. But the money I'm going to pay you is mine and the job is private. Do you have a problem with that?"

"No."

"Good. There's a Metropolitan Police case that I have a particular interest in. I don't need to go in to details as to why the case peaks my interest. All that matters to me is that the case is open and is being investigated by a detective inspector called Katy Roberts." Smith handed Hilt a mobile phone. "That's deniable. It has one number stored in it. It's your link to my deniable phone. Keep tabs on Mrs. Roberts. Let me know of any developments."

"Where do I find her?"

"New Scotland Yard. I also have her home address." Smith handed Hilt a slip of paper. "For now, it's just surveillance and reporting back to me. But, if things develop in the wrong direction, I may ask you to up the ante."

Hilt smiled.

CHAPTER 6

Knutsen stood in Kennington's small West Square. The beautiful enclosure was surrounded by regal Edwardian terraced houses. Knutsen had a holdall slung over one shoulder. In his other hand, he held a small trolley case. Both bags contained all of his possessions. He pressed the intercom of the house containing Sign's apartment. The house had long ago been converted into four flats. Sign's dwelling was on the fourth floor.

The door buzzed and opened. Knutsen entered and walked up the stairs. He knocked on the door.

Sign answered and asked, "Did you bring your suit?"

Knutsen nodded.

"Good. We have a meeting this afternoon with New Scotland Yard." Sign showed Knutsen to his bedroom. "Unpack. I'm making a pot of tea. Let's convene in the lounge in fifteen minutes."

The bedroom was twice the size of the one Knutsen had been sleeping in within his former residence. A spiral staircase led to the attic that had been fully converted into a bathroom. He unpacked his clothes into a wardrobe and chest of drawers and examined the bathroom. It was state of the art – spot lamps in the ceiling, extractor fans in the shower cubicle and toilet area, and a heated towel rail. He exited his room, walked past the solitary toilet room that had come with the original layout of the property, and walked past Sign's bedroom. It too had a spiral staircase leading to a separate loft converted bathroom suite. Somebody had spent a lot of money converting this place. Sign was in the kitchen. By comparison to the other rooms in the property, it was tiny; no room even for a breakfast table. But it had an expensive gas oven and separate hob, a washing machine, dishwasher, Global knives on a wall-mounted magnetic strip, cupboards, and a wooden chopping board strewn with fresh vegetables sourced from Borough Market.

Sign handed him a cup of tea. "I guessed milk, no sugar."

"You guessed right." Knutsen followed him into the lounge. The place was twice the size of any lounge Knutsen had seen before. It was strewn with antiquities and other artefacts – a six seater oak dining table, a neo-classical era chaise longue, a sofa, gold-framed oil paintings on the walls, bookshelves crammed with out-of-print non-fiction historical and academic works, a wall-mounted Cossack sabre, Persian rugs, two nineteenth century brass miners' lamps within which were candles, a five foot high artificial Japanese tree with a string of blue lights around it, seventeen century Scottish dirks in a glass cabinet, a laptop on a green-leather covered nine drawer mahogany writing desk, lamps, seafaring charts, and so many other objects of interest it made the mind swirl.

On one of the shelves was a silk map that had been mounted between glass. It was the type worn under the garments of operatives working behind enemy lines. On its back were eight short paragraphs – in English, Dari, Pashwari, Tajikistan, Urdu, Uzbekistan, Turkmenistan, and Persian, together with the contact numbers of six UK diplomatic missions. The paragraphs asked for food and water, promised the reader that the bearer of the map wouldn't hurt him, and requested safe passage to British forces or its allies. On the front of the map was the title AFGHANISTAN & ENVIRONS, ESCAPE MAP.

Sign took the map out of Knutsen's hand and placed it back on the mantelshelf above the open fire. He said, "Different days for me back then."

The centre of the lounge was uncluttered. All it had was three armchairs facing each other, and tiny adjacent wooden coffee tables. Knutsen and Sign sat.

Knutsen looked around. The room seemed to him to either be an Aladdin's Cave or the result of an eccentric professor's penchants.

Sign followed his gaze. "I travelled the world. Many of these things are my purchases. But some were given to me. They remind me of good things." He took a sip of his tea. "This is our centre of operations."

"And we'll meet clients here?"

"I don't see why not."

Knutsen stared at Sign. "You could have been chief of MI6. Do you not worry that you could have done better than scratching a living with me?"

Sign replied, "No. I'd been thinking about resigning for some time. All my adult life I've worked alone or in small teams. As soon as I heard I was tipped the be the next chief of MI6, I feared that if I got the job I'd have to become a corporate beast – not just managing thousands of staff, but also liaising with all the other agencies, plus Whitehall and our overseas allies. I get easily bored with playing management and politics. Operating in the shadows suits me better."

That made sense to Knutsen. It was for similar reasons he'd gone undercover, rather than grabbing rank after rank until he headed up the Met or one of the county forces. "Tell me about the meeting with the Yard."

"I'll answer that indirectly and directly. Over the last few days, I've been making calls – to the chiefs of every police force in the UK, Interpol, the chiefs and directors of MI6, MI5, GCHQ, army, air force, and navy commanders, and twenty nine heads of foreign security and intelligence agencies. I've been setting out our stall; telling them that you and I are in business for any delicate work they need to outsource. Your former boss – the Met commissioner – has bitten. This afternoon he's sending a detective inspector to talk to us."

"What's the name of the inspector?"

"Katy Roberts. I don't know her. Do you?"

"No. But I do know *of* her. She's more than just a detective. She's Special Branch. And she's a rising star. What does she want?"

"I don't know." Sign checked his watch. "She'll be here in two hours. That gives us time for lunch. What say you to pan-fried guinea fowl, caramelised shallots, toasted carrots, green beans, and sautéed potatoes?"

"You've booked a table?"

"No, dear chap. I'm going to cook the dish myself."

Katy Roberts arrived on time after Sign and Knutsen had eaten and changed into their suits. Knutsen took her coat and asked her to take a seat in one of the armchairs. The men sat in the other chairs.

Knutsen asked, "How can we be of help, ma'am?"

"You don't need to call me ma'am. You're no longer a cop." Roberts had long hair that was dyed platinum. She wore no rings on her fingers, even though she'd been happily married for fifteen years. At first, Sign thought her elegant and beautiful demeanour was icy. He revised that assessment. No, she was an owl, he decided. She watches.

Sign said, "You know Mr. Knutsen is late of your service. I am Ben Sign."

"I know who you are." Roberts looked around the room, before looking at Sign. "You're a picky collector."

"*Picky*, yes."

"Why did you pick Tom Knutsen to work with you?"

"A raft of reasons, but in particular because he knows loss. I can't work with someone who doesn't understand emotional toil."

"Why?"

"Loss sharpens the senses and also allows us not to fear death."

Knutsen looked at Sign.

Roberts said, "An interesting perspective. And you think just because you were a high flying MI6 officer, you can help us out with difficult problems."

"I can but try."

Roberts huffed. "I didn't agree to this meeting. I told my boss it would be a waste of my time."

"I suppose, therefore, it could also be a waste of our time." His tone of voice was benign as he added, "I was recruited into MI6 because my DNA demands that I accurately read people. It's the key requirement of all MI6 officers. I've never arrested anyone, because I'm not law enforcement. But I have stopped covert nuclear programs, terrorist attacks, and wars. I wouldn't dare to presume I have your skills of detective work."

Knutsen suppressed a smile. He'd expected Sign to lambast Roberts, not flatter her. Then again, Sign was a gentleman when he needed to be.

Roberts said, "To my errand. We have the death of a senior MI6 officer. MI6 won't cooperate. It thinks it's simply a suicide. The victim has a wife. She has no idea why he'd have done something so devastating. We can't access MI6 or get in its head. You can."

"His name?" Sign was leaning forward.

"Mark Archer."

"Mark?" Sign was frowning. "He was ranked as an average officer, meaning he was exceptional by the standards of other special operations agencies. More importantly, he had a loving family and was a very stable man. Suicide makes no sense."

"That's what my boss thinks." Roberts tone softened. "He has a slush fund and is willing to pay you to do what he calls a *back channel investigation*. I thought he might be wasting his time. Maybe… I was wrong."

"It's a tremendous sign of intellect when one self-corrects." Sign was deep in thought. "Inspector Roberts – forget what your boss thinks. What do you think about Mark's death?"

Roberts had attended this meeting with a preconceived notion of what Sign would be like. She'd imagined he would be arrogant and condescending. But he was nothing like that. She knew he was treading softly with her. But that mattered not. What did were his impeccable manners and deference to her vocation. "The wife is hiding something. I've interviewed extensively. I applied every trick in the book. But I can't get through to her."

Knutsen asked, "What do we know about the wife?"

"Mrs. Archer has no criminal record. She has a daughter and son; both are at university. Due to her marriage to a spy, she's security cleared to the highest level. I saw no chinks in her armour." Roberts focused on Sign. "I'm told you can see things differently."

Sign waved his hand. "I'm an amateur, by your standards."

Roberts smiled. "Thank you for being so kind." Her tone hardened. "I'm out of my league. You, of all people, are not."

Sign stood and walked to the mantelpiece. "Your instincts may have been right. This could be a waste of time. Maybe it is suicide driven by any number of stresses – debt, marital problems, infidelity, the usual suspect list goes on. Or maybe he was murdered. If murder, then that is a police investigation. The only reason I should be involved is if the murder was carried out by a hostile foreign agency."

"It's not murder. He killed himself. Forensics is certain of that. So am I."

"How did he do it?"

"Fifty capsules of prescribed painkillers, washed down with a bottle of cheap vodka. He also slit his wrists in his bathtub for good measure."

"No bruising on the throat or blemishes on the inner mouth?"

"Meaning he was force fed the cocktail? No." Roberts elaborated. "The razor he used to slit his wrists was on the side of the bath. His, and only his, prints are on the razor. Mrs. Archer's prints and sole imprints are in the bathroom, as you would expect." She clasped her hands. "But even if a murderer was so ingenious to fake suicide without trace, he or she would not be able to eliminate their presence in the crime scene. Forensics is so good these days that a man in a disposable jump suit, face mask, and shoe covers would still leave traces of his presence. Mrs. Archer couldn't have killed him. She's not strong enough, plus there's zero evidence of forced death. It's suicide. But I don't know why. That's what I need you for."

Sign spun around. "Knutsen and I need to speak to Mrs. Archer. With your permission."

Roberts nodded. "You have my permission. The commissioner has authorised me to engage you both on thirty thousand pounds."

"Make it forty and you have a deal."

"Forty?"

"Try to find someone else who'll work for you and understands the secret world."

Roberts sighed. "My default position was forty. I can do that."

Sign strode up to her. "It's been a pleasure to make your acquaintance." He shook her hand. "We'll use our methods. But all formal communications will go through you. I don't want to liaise with anyone else in the police. Agreed?"

Roberts frowned. "Why?"

"Because I don't want to work with anyone I don't trust or respect. I can see into you. My evaluation is very favourable."

Hidden from view, Hilt watched Roberts leave West Square from the same position he'd seen her arrive. He called Smith. "During the last three days, she's either been at home or in the New Scotland Yard building. With two exceptions. I followed her to an address in Godalming three days ago."

"I know that address. What is the other exception?"

"She's just left a house in Kennington. She was in there for half an hour. The house is converted into four flats, but I know which flat she attended. Zoom camera. Saw which button she pressed to get into the communal entrance."

"Find out who lives there."

"Will do." Hilt ended the call and followed Roberts.

CHAPTER 7

Post dinner, Sign and Knutsen sat by the fire in the lounge. Sign said, "We are seeing Mrs. Archer tomorrow. When I called her she sounded understandably distraught. She can't believe her husband committed suicide, but she also knows that's what happened. She has two issues: one is grief; the other is bewilderment."

Knutsen asked, "You're certain it's suicide?"

"I'm inclined to believe the police know what they're doing, though I never discount anything until I'm on the ground. But if it is suicide, I can do something that the police can't. I can get into the minds of people, dead or alive."

Knutsen laughed. "Like a clairvoyant?"

"No. Like someone who knows the human condition, regardless of nationality, race, gender, age, religion, political beliefs, social status, or sexual persuasion." Sign look wistful as he added, "I like to think of the process as one of absorbing souls."

There was so much about Sign that Knutsen wanted to know. "Does it pain you to have that burden?"

"Absorbing souls?" Sign looked irritated. "It's like asking a shepherd if he's wracked with anguish because some of his sheep are mischievous or prone to stupidity."

"Fair point." Knutsen drank some coffee. "But you are a chameleon. I saw you change colours when Roberts was here."

Sign made a flourish with his hand. "Chameleon? Praying mantis. Whatever? You decide." Sign was distracted. "Thus far I have nine theories about Mark Archer's death. Eight are banal. One most certainly is not."

"You haven't even seen his dead body, or yet visited his wife."

"Body's don't talk and people lie. It is in the imagination that we begin to hypothesise." Sign added wood to the fire. "I need you to get a handgun. Something reliable. A Glock or similar. Can you do that?"

"Yes. Do you want me to get you one as well?"

"I don't carry guns unless absolutely necessary."

Knutsen frowned.

Sign elaborated. "We did things in the bandit zones of South Asia, Africa and Latin America that you wouldn't believe. I don't like those days. They stay with me. I held a gun when I was younger. Now I'm older. Let's leave it at that."

"But why do I need a gun?"

"In case my ninth theory is correct."

Knutsen said, "Okay." He paused for a moment before asking, "Are you religious?"

"No."

"Have strong political beliefs?"

"I've worked with too many politicians of different parties. They're all the same. All they want is power. No, I have no faith in one party versus another."

"Do you aspire to re-marry?" Knutsen expected a harsh retort.

But instead, Sign said, "Perhaps one day, but not for now. My wife's buried not far from here. I visit her grave when I can and talk to her. She's still my wife."

45

Knutsen wrapped his hands around his coffee mug. "There's a cold draft coming in to the room. We need to do something about that."

"I like the draft. I think of it as a messenger from the outside world, reminding me that all is not well." Sign smiled. "It comes from the extractor fans in the bathrooms. I suppose there might be one-way extractor fans on the market these days."

"I'll check it out." Knutsen checked his watch. "I've got to go out now."

"Excellent. It'll give me some peace from your questions. We're on parade tomorrow morning. Ten o'clock train from Waterloo to take us to Godalming. Then we'll see what we make of Mrs. Archer."

Forty five minutes later, Knutsen knocked on the door of a council flat in a high-rise tenement building in Brixton. A black woman, mid-forties, opened the door a fraction, but kept the security chain attached. When she saw it was Knutsen, she fully opened the door. Her eyes were bloodshot. She'd been crying.

Knutsen was worried. "Wendy. Is everything okay?"

Wendy couldn't stop the tears starting again. "He's not here."

"But the dojo starts at nine." Knutsen had driven here. Once a week, work permitting, he collected Wendy's son David and helped him with his martial arts training. It kept David off drugs and petty crime. "Where is he?"

"He'll… he'll be hanging out with those guys. You know the place. I thought he'd given up on all that. They're bad people, Mr. Knutsen. Tonight we had an argument. He laughed at me and told me he was going to see people who actually cared about him. He used bad language."

"Leave it with me."

Knutsen left and walked four hundred yards to a side alley off Brixton High Street. Wendy was right. Her eighteen year old son was there, hanging out with three men who were in their early twenties and had the physiques of basketball players. The older men were drug dealers. David was truly in the wrong company. Knutsen approached David and told him that he had to go or they'd lose their slot on the dojo. David feared Knutsen, though also highly respected him. But in front of the other men he tried to act defiant.

David said, "I'm not doing no training tonight. I'm working."

"With these idiots? And what are you actually *working* on? Construction? Taxi driving? Plumbing? Painting and decorating? Anything noble? Or are you just selling plastic wraps of hash, coke, and spice to kids? I don't call that work."

The tallest of the older men walked up to Knutsen and put his face millimetres from his face. "Back off, white boy."

David yelled, "Leeroy! No!"

Leeroy persisted. "You a cop?" His breath stank of fast food.

Knutsen held his ground. "I'm simply here to take David to his kendo class. He's improving. I don't want to see him fall behind."

Leeroy pushed him against a wall. "He ain't falling behind when he's with us, you cunt."

The two other older men pulled out knives. David looked terrified.

Knutsen said, "Calm down. I just want to help David. I'm not a cop.

"Yeah, all off-duty cops say that." Leeroy put his hand in his puffer jacket. "I got me a piece. Finger's on the trigger. If you fuck off, I don't put a hole in your gut."

Knutsen nodded, then head butted Leeroy, stamped on his chest and groin, advanced with lightning speed to the other men, dodged their knives, smacked one of them in the throat and jabbed the other with two fingers into his eyes. The men would live, though would need medical treatment. Knutsen said to David, "Let's go."

They walked out of the alley. Knutsen didn't care that the three men were writhing in agony on the ground.

Fifteen minutes later, they were in the Brixton martial arts gym. It entertained all sorts of fighting disciplines, including boxing, kung fu, and krav maga. But tonight was kendo night. Knutsen helped David get his armour on. He said, "Now we do a better class of fighting."

Knutsen geared up and stepped onto the dojo, facing David. Both were brandishing their bamboo swords. They bowed. Knutsen said, "Now, don't forget your feet and legs. The arms and sword are their slaves and are useless without them."

David lunged, trying to jab his sword at Knutsen's chest. Knutsen tapped David's sword to one side. Using both hands, David attempted to swipe his sword downwards. It was a move used by samurai to slice a man diagonally in half from shoulder to waist. It was also effectively used by Japanese soldiers against Americans in the Battle of Iwo Jima in WW2. Knutsen stepped sideways. David's attack didn't connect.

Knutsen discarded his sword and said, "First incapacitate, then execute. Show me where you want to strike."

David tried to slap Knutsen's abdomen. Knutsen stepped back, his hands behind his back. David dropped to a crouch and attempted to strike his ankles. Knutsen jumped, the sword cutting through air. David by now was angry and ill disciplined. He tried to hit Knutsen on the head. Knutsen dodged left, brought his arms in front of him, rushed forward, knocked David off his feet and punched his mask. "Now you've got a bloody nose and concussion. All I need to do is pick up my sword and cut you into pieces. Easy. Good job you're wearing protection."

David got to his feet. "Where did I go wrong, Mr Knutsen?"

"You had an argument with your mum and held on to the anger. Here we don't have anger. We have calm precision." Knutsen patted him on the shoulder. "You just had a bad night. I'll drive you home. But first there's something we need to do."

After leaving the gym, they stopped at a newsagent. "Why are we here?" asked David.

Knutsen walked David to a section containing cards. "Choose one. Inside you're going to tell your mum that you're sorry."

"Really, man?!"

"Do it."

David picked up a card. At the checkout, Knutsen gave him a pen and told him to write. After payment was made, they left.

Knutsen said, "One more stop."

Two shops next door was a florist. The shop was closed, but Knutsen knew the florist lived above the establishment. He pressed on the intercom. A woman answered. Knutsen said, "It's Tom Knutsen. I have a young lad with me. We need your help."

Inside the shop, the black woman kissed Knutsen on the cheek.

"How have you been doing, Maggie?"

The former meth addict smiled. "I breathe the free air. That's what you taught me to think."

"And it works." Knutsen pointed at David. "This gentleman went off piste tonight. He's now back on track and wants to make amends. Could you make us a bouquet of flowers? It's for his mother."

Maggie smiled. "My pleasure handsome. You want to stay here tonight?"

"Remember the rules. We always maintain parameters." Knutsen had killed Maggie's husband. He knew she was clean from drugs for two years. But like all addicts, her nervous system had been irrevocably changed by drugs. It meant she believed anything was possible, including sleeping with Knutsen. "Make the flowers pretty, Maggie. And find a good husband. Just avoid Internet dating."

Sixty minutes later they entered Wendy's house. Wendy was tearful as David handed her the card and flowers, hugged her, and told his mum that he was sorry.

Wendy made Knutsen a cup of tea, told David to go to his room, and sat with the former undercover cop in her tiny but pristine living room. "It's hard being a single parent."

"It is. Particularly when the child is a boy."

Wendy shook her head. "It makes no difference if it's a boy or girl. The challenges are just different, but equally hard. David needs a father. He's never had one. You're the nearest he's got."

The comment made Knutsen feel awkward. "I just want to help him out. In doing so, it helps me out. I have no children. You know that."

"What I know is that even when you can't move heaven and hell to train with him, you still lie to the probation service and tick the box that says he's been to the gym every week. You're a very good man."

"But David's not yet a man. He may look like one, but he's not."

"That's where you come in. You teach him." Wendy rubbed her eyes. "I couldn't bear it if he went back into prison."

Knudsen smiled. "I've eaten this evening, but I could do with a snack. Also, do you allow David to have a small, low alcohol drink?"

Wendy frowned. "Now and again."

Kendo is thirsty work. "How about I grab a couple of cans from the local off licence while you rustle up some crisps and salsa or whatever comes to hand. David and I will sit and have our beer and snacks. Alone, I'm afraid. It will be mans' talk."

"What will you talk about?"

"I will tell him about my father. He was conscripted into the army between '53 and '57. He served in Egypt and Libya. He wanted to know what makes the Japanese military thinking tick, particularly tactics and strategy in the medieval period. This brought him into contact with two experts in the arms and armour field. One was a curator of swords and spears at the V&A. The other was a representative of the Royal Armouries. My father's fascination about how swords and spears were employed in combat was underpinned by one thing: he wanted to understand discipline. He had a friend who he went to school with. The friend joined the merchant marine at the same time my father joined the army. Previously, they were inseparable. Both were highly intelligent. One stint of my father's tours was guarding the Suez Canal. My father spent hours there, hoping his friend would pass on a ship. His friend never did. But the possibility was there. They reunited after they were out of service. My father's friend had just got married. She'd died from malaria, age twenty two. My father taught his friend kendo. It saved his friend from depression or far worse." Knudsen smiled. "I want to tell David what I've just told you. And I think two thirsty men deserve a beer while I recount my history."

Wendy beamed, all traces of tears now absent from her glistening eyes. "You move your ass and get those beers, mister. And I'll do better than crisps and salsa. I do mean double fried chips and mayonnaise." She grabbed Knutsen's hand before he left. "Thank you for everything. And tonight will mean the world to my son."

CHAPTER 8

Accompanied by an icy wind, rain lashed the Surrey town of Godalming, as Sign and Knutsen walked from the train station to Mrs. Archer's house on Charterhouse Road. Both had umbrellas up and were wearing woollen coats over their suits. Due to the weather and the fact it was late morning, the pretty town was relatively quiet – London commuters had long since departed for work. Sign and Knutsen walked up the hill that took Charterhouse Road to the famous school bearing its name. The house was a detached four bedroom property, these days probably having a value of seven figures. There was no way that Mark Archer could have afforded that on his government salary.

Sign rang the doorbell. Mrs. Archer answered.

Sign said, "Mrs Archer – Ben Sign and Tom Knutsen. I believe you are expecting us."

She looked like she'd barely had any sleep during the night, though she was elegantly dressed, had applied makeup, and not one hair on her head was out of place. In a posh voice, she said, "Do you have any identification?"

Sign nodded and showed her his passport. "We're very happy to wait outside while you call Inspector Roberts to verify our credentials."

"That won't be necessary. Come in."

The men placed their umbrellas in a stand, hung their overcoats on a rack, and followed her into the lounge.

"Would you like tea?"

"That would be very gracious of you. Milk, no sugar." Sign sat on a sofa. Knutsen sat next to him, even though there were many chairs in the room.

When Mrs. Archer had left the room, Knutsen whispered, "Expensive gaff. Some of the furnishings and other stuff in here must have cost a fortune."

Sign placed a finger to his lips and shook his head.

Five minutes later, Mrs. Archer returned carrying a tray containing a teapot, cups and saucers, a small jug of milk, and a plate of biscuits. As she poured the tea, she said, "Inspector Roberts told me that you were advisers. She said you were to be trusted." She looked at Sign. "And she said you worked with my husband."

"I no longer work for The Office. And when I did, I knew of your husband, though our paths never crossed. We operated in different parts of the world."

After handing them their cups of tea, Mrs. Archer sat opposite them. She looked sorrowful as she said, "It's been an odd life. When Mark and I went on our first two overseas postings we made a mistake. In Kuala Lumper and Brasilia, like all newly-arrived diplomats, we were pounced on by the close knit expat community. They get so lonely and so bored. They want new friends. We thought it was great to meet new faces. The trouble is…"

"Postings last three years. Then people leave. We never see them again."

"Yes. You make a friend. But that friendship has a very short shelf life." Her hands were shaking as she sipped her tea. "So after that, on other postings, we kept our distance from expats and other diplomats. There was no point becoming their friends. For me, the only constant was Mark. He kept me sane."

Sign had a gentle smile on his face. "I'm so sorry for your loss. I'm also very sorry that we felt the need to meet you so soon after your husband's departure."

"Departure? Yes, he's gone. I'm not religious. I don't have a fantasy that I'll join him in heaven. What do you want?"

Sign gestured to Knutsen. "Tom is a former police officer. He's now my business partner."

"And what is your business?"

"To find the truth and then decide if the truth benefits good people."

"What an unusual remit." She raised a finger nail to her mouth, but quickly replaced her hand on her tea saucer.

Sign said, "Would you like me to fetch you a mug from your kitchen? You could pour your tea into the mug. Mugs are so much easier to hold when the nerves are playing havoc. And we don't mind. In our time, Knutsen and I have drunk out of tin cans, bowls, dirty glasses, you name it."

"I have standards." She placed her cup and saucer on a side table. She repeated, "What do you want? Be specific."

It was Knutsen who answered. "We want to know if your husband killed himself or was murdered. If he killed himself, we want to know why."

Mrs. Archer frowned. "But, I've already spoken to Inspector Roberts about this. I told her I'm confused. The police say there is no doubt that it was suicide." Her lip was trembling as she looked away. "But I can't understand why he did this." She looked at the men. "We have no debt. Our children are doing well at university. They have no problems – not that we're aware of. Mark has always been a loyal husband. He wasn't seeing another woman. I know that. Women can tell. He was extremely loyal to MI6. And he was happy. His last job

55

was London-based. In headquarters. He knew it was probably the pinnacle of his seniority, that he wasn't going to go any further, but he didn't mind. He was content. No stress, he told me. Who cares about entering the vipers nest at the top of the tree, he recently joked. I was glad. We were too old to return to the overseas postings merry-go-round. At last, we could enjoy what we had. In England."

Sign asked, "Your children?"

"My son's at the University of East Anglia. My daughter's at Newcastle."

"Have they visited you since the tragic event?"

"Of course! They've returned to their studies, but they'll be back here once the body's released and I can have him buried."

"What are their thoughts about your husband's death?"

She slapped her thigh. "They're distraught! What do you expect?"

"As surprised as you?"

"Yes. They can't understand why this happened. The only reason they've returned to university is they have exams. Goodness knows how they're going to stay focused."

Knutsen leaned forward. "Doctors, and the police for that matter, don't fully understand mental health problems. But we do know that sometimes people are unhappy for no discernible reason. That's the hardest part – dealing with people who are clinically depressed. It's easier to deal with people who are down in the dumps because they're behind on their rent of are going through a rough patch in their marriage."

"*Down in the dumps?*" Mrs. Archer laughed as tears ran down her face. "I haven't heard that phrase for a long time." She withdrew a handkerchief, patted her face, and composed herself. "I must impress upon you both that my husband did not have clinical depression. Nor was he down in the dumps. He was the happiest I've ever seen him."

Sign said, "I need to ask you a hard question."

Mrs. Archer looked nervous, but nodded.

"Despite what the police think, is there any suspicion in your mind – even if just one percent – that your husband was murdered?"

She shook his head. "Forensics were here for hours. They said there was no doubt he killed himself. I found him." Tears were once again freefalling down her face.

"Take your time."

"I... I found him. In the bath. It's funny." Her voice was trembling. "He didn't normally drink to excess. The bath water was bright red with his blood. He'd slit his wrists. But all I could think about was that empty bottle of vodka by his side. I was cross that he'd drunk that much. Stupid me."

"You were in shock."

"Anyway. Why would anyone murder him?"

Sign wondered how far he should push her. "Your husband and I were MI6 officers. There are bad people out there who'd like to see us dead."

Mrs. Archer held her head in her hands. "You'll think bad of me, but I wish it was murder. It would be so much easier to rationalise. Suicide seems so..."

"Selfish?"

"Unexplained."

"And that's why we're here." Sign handed her a business card. "You can contact us anytime if something else occurs to you, no matter how trivial. There are three of us helping you – me, Knutsen, and Roberts. Don't trust MI6. Don't trust anyone in the police aside from Roberts."

"Why?"

"Because organisations don't like problems, particularly when they involve someone with your husband's security clearance and seniority. They find it an embarrassment. They fend off the media and the truth." Sign tapped Knutsen on the arm. It was the signal to leave. The men stood and walked to the hallway. Mrs. Archer followed them. After putting on their overcoats and retrieving their umbrellas, Sign said, "Mrs. Archer – once again, we are so sorry for your loss. I too lost my wife; Knutsen lost a woman who he hoped would give him happiness." He paused by the door. "Did anyone come to see your husband on the day before he died? Possibly a short time before he killed himself?"

She shook her head. "No one."

Sign and Knutsen left.

As they walked down the road, Sign said, "She's lying."

From the opposite side of the street in Weybridge, Karl Hilt watched Katy Roberts leave her house. He knew her husband was still at home. Probably he either worked from home or was unemployed. Hilt didn't care. He waited ten minutes. The street didn't have CCTV, but there was a chance that Roberts' house had security cameras. Given her occupation, there was a slim chance the cameras were hidden on the exterior and interior. Hilt wasn't going to take a risk. Face, ears, and eyes couldn't be exposed, due to modern recognition technology. He jogged across the road, donned a balaclava and sun glasses and ran to the rear garden. He'd brought equipment to force locks if necessary, but they were not required. The rear-facing kitchen door was unlocked. He entered.

The place was modest in size and indicative of a couple who had no children – no clutter, holiday postcards of trips to Thailand and other exotic climes were fixed to the fridge door by magnets, a Post-It note was stuck to the microwave saying *Don't forget – five minutes on full blast, then one minute rest*, and an empty pot of coffee was on the hob.

Hilt moved into the lounge. It contained one sofa, an armchair, a TV, and not much else. Katy Roberts' husband was on the sofa, watching a program about antiques. Hilt moved up behind him, placed his arm around the man's neck, and squeezed. He said nothing as Roberts' husband lost consciousness. For good measure, Hilt punched the man three times in the face.

He stood over him. The man's face was a mess. He was either passed out or dead.

Hilt moved on. He had to make the event look like a random burglary. In reality he was looking for anything that could be of interest to John Smith. He searched the lounge, found nothing of interest, and trashed the room. In the upstairs bedroom, Katy Roberts' wedding ring and other jewellery were in a box on a chest of drawers in the bedroom. Hilt took them all. He rifled through bedside cabinet drawers and found nothing. He opened all of the drawers in the chest and tossed underwear and other clothing onto the floor, to make it look like he was searching for hidden cash, spare car keys, or other valuable items. He ripped down wall framed photos of Katy and her husband, taken in various UK and overseas locations. He stamped on them, shattering glass and sending shards into the photos. He upended the mattress and used a hunting knife to slash it open. Duck feather spilled out.

Reaching behind the heavy chest of drawers, he yanked it forward so that it crashed face down on the floor. The place was a mess.

The other two rooms on the level were a bathroom and an office. The bathroom was of no interest to Hilt. He entered the office. It contained a desk and laptop, table lamp, tray containing papers, and a small metal cabinet next to the desk. Hilt searched the tray. There was nothing of interest – just bills that needed to be paid and other household documentation. He threw the tray against the wall behind him, papers spewing out. Crouching down, he carefully examined each of the four drawers in the filing cabinet. There were a few sheets of paper listing birthdays and marriage anniversaries of relatives and friends of Katy and her husband, mortgage documentation, a will, a list of passwords for Tesco's online shopping, Amazon, LinkedIn, and Skype, a bundle of charger leads, and one business card.

The business card gave the names and address of Ben Sign and Tom Knutsen. The address corresponded to the one Hilt had seen Roberts attend to. He took a photo of the card, then tossed it onto the floor, alongside everything else from the drawers.

He walked back downstairs. Katy's husband was still sitting in the lounge, his eyes scrunched tight, his face covered in blood. He was moaning. Hilt ignored him and left.

Fifteen minutes later and three miles away from the house, Hilt called Smith. "She doesn't take her work home. With one exception. I found a business card."

"Ordinarily that's not unusual," said Smith. "But I'm listening because it's grabbed your interest."

Hilt explained.

Smith replied, "I don't know who Knutsen is. But I most certainly know who Ben Sign is. We may have a major problem. Meet me at four PM."

CHAPTER 9

In Epsom General Hospital, Katy Roberts sat by her husband's bed. He had bandages on his face and was conscious. Roberts had been told that her husband would need to stay in for at least two nights. The doctors weren't worried about the facial injuries; but they did want to monitor his breathing. The crush to his throat worried the medical staff, though they were confident he'd make a full recovery.

Roberts rubbed her husband's hand and said, "I need to step outside for a few minutes."

Her husband coughed and said, "Go home. No... no point you hanging around in this place. Plus, after what the burglar did to our house, the place needs tidying. You better put on your marigolds and get to work."

Roberts laughed. "Be Miss Dolly Domestic?"

"There's a first time for everything."

Roberts' voice trembled as she said, "He took my wedding ring."

"Don't worry about that, my love. It was just a cheap piece of shit I picked up in Dubai. They weren't real diamonds."

Roberts smiled. "You've always been a terrible liar. I know you spent a fortune on the ring. The diamonds were real. I had it analysed by a specialist for house insurance purposes."

Between more coughs, her husband said, "Good. Let's hope the insurance pays out. Then you can nip down to Hatton Garden and pick yourself up another ring."

This was the first time Roberts had seen her husband in a hospital bed. It broke her heart to see him so vulnerable. "Okay. I'll go home and sort the house. I can come back later tonight."

"No point. I'm so damned tired, for some reason. I'll probably be asleep."

She kissed him on the forehead and left the room.

In the corridor was one of her plain clothed detectives. She asked him, "Any updates?"

The detective nodded. "I've just got off the phone to Surrey Police. Because of who you are, forensics went through your place twice. They really pulled out the stops. Only your jewellery's missing. But the burglar made every effort to see if there was anything else of value in the house. We think he must have left on foot. Your laptop and TV weren't taken. No other electrical items he could have flogged. He only took what he could stuff in his pockets."

"He must have left some traces."

"Yes and no. We have size ten boot prints. Forensics is certain they're boots, due to the shape of the soles. But here's the thing – the burglar scraped the treads off, most likely with a knife. Also, most likely he wore plastic shoe covers. There are no finger or palm prints. He wore gloves."

"There should have been fibres from the gloves. And with modern forensics technology, prints can still be partially obtained – not just from the inside of gloves but also from everything they've touched."

The detective nodded. "We got traces of resin."

Roberts frowned. "He coated his hands in a resin compound, let them dry, then put gloves on?"

"Yes. I've never seen that done before. Forensics are both furious and fascinated as to how he came up with that idea."

"What else?"

"He wore a smooth jacket. No fibres were transferred when he grabbed your husband. He was immensely strong – the injuries speak for themselves. And he knew exactly what he was doing. He's been highly trained."

"Ex-military?"

"Could be. But military guys aren't trained to do this kind of stuff. Not that I know of."

"So, most likely a hardened criminal who's learned his trade on the street. A lot of effort just to steal my wedding ring. I wonder if he was hoping to find something more than that." Roberts sighed. "Okay, we're not going to catch this guy through forensics. My husband didn't see his face. The burglar didn't speak, so voice recognition is out. We just have to hope he burgles another place and makes a mistake."

"I'm sorry, Katy."

"So am I." Roberts left. Her priority was to clean her home and get her husband back when he was recovered. She called Sign and told him what had happened. "I'm probably going to be out of circulation for the next twenty four hours. Apparently the house is a mess. Plus, I need to be close to my husband."

Sign replied, "Of course. What's your address?"

Roberts supplied him with details.

"You're heading there now?"

"Yes."

"Do you have anything to eat this evening?"

"I... I doubt it. I don't feel hungry."

"Hang tight, inspector." Sign hung up and shouted to Knutsen. "Put on your scruffiest clothes. Make sure your car has a full tank. In one hour we're leaving. It's meals on wheels time." Sign entered the kitchen.

Two hours later, Sign and Knutsen were in Roberts' house. Knutsen was in jeans and a jumper. Sign was still in his suit.

Roberts was teary as she gestured toward the mess in the lounge. "Look what he's done to my home. I don't know where to begin."

Sign handed her a tray containing two casserole pots. "It's just basic fare that I knocked up in sixty minutes – beef casserole and wild rice. The casserole will need another hour in your oven. I do hope you're not vegetarian."

Roberts shook her head as she placed the dish in the oven. "This is more than I can eat."

"Good, because you've got two hungry labourers at your disposal who are going to need feeding. Mr. Knutsen – this is no longer a crime scene. Let's get it back in order." Sign slung his jacket over the sofa where Roberts' husband had been strangled. He rolled up his sleeves. "Let's look upstairs."

Roberts showed them the bedroom and the office.

Sign said to Roberts, "Could you make us a cup of tea?"

When Roberts was downstairs, Sign said to Knutsen, "You know London better than I do. And you know people. Call in some favours." He wrote on a slip of paper and handed the sheet to Knutsen. "This is what we need. And we need it in the next hour or two. Go."

When Knutsen was gone, Sign set to work. He cleaned up each room, with Roberts' assistance, and hauled the ripped mattress into the garden. He vacuum cleaned the house, head to toe, and used cleaning products to eradicate Roberts' husband's blood from the sofa. Bed sheets, underwear, and every other piece of linen were in the washing machine. Locks on the doors were checked and applied. Ground level garden lights were turned on. So too other exterior lights. But there was still more to be done that was beyond Sign's ability.

When Knutsen returned, he was carrying a bottle of wine and scented candles. Next to him were four men. Two of them were carrying an expensive double mattress. The other two had tool belts and other equipment.

Sign smiled at Knudsen. "Good man. I've taken it as far as I can. Over to you."

The men set to work. The mattress was placed on the bed. The old mattress was placed in their transit van. The tool-carrying artisans replaced picture frames, inserted new glass, and hung the pictures back up. Knutsen placed the bottle of white wine in the fridge, lit candles and shook hands with the four men. They left. Knutsen and Sign remained in the house with Roberts.

Roberts asked Knutsen, "How did you arrange this at such short notice? Who were those men?"

"Cutthroats and thieves." Knutsen laughed. "Something like that. I helped them get on the straight and narrow. They're good people."

"Who owed you a favour?"

"In different locations and time frames, individually they tried to kill me. Obviously it didn't work. They got a bit bruised. I forgave them and marched them off to the Job Centre. I suppose I should have arrested them. What would have been the point? Who else would have repaired your home so well at the drop of a hat?"

"No one else", said Sign. "You made them good men. A superb judgement call. Mrs. Roberts – would you object if I played mum and served up food and wine? Your home is once again beautiful and untarnished. While we eat and drink, I will regale you of an adventure I had in Paris that involved my discovery of a white severed arm clutching a black severed arm." He walked into the kitchen.

Roberts was emotional as she whispered to Knutsen. "Thank you both so much for doing this."

Knutsen smiled. "We had no other plans this evening."

"What did you make of Mrs. Archer?"

"Sign agrees with you that she's holding something back." He gave her details of the meeting.

"What's Sign going to do next?"

Knutsen shrugged. "No idea. But I know what I've got to do next." He checked his watch. "Later tonight I've got to meet a man about a gun."

At eleven PM, Knutsen was in a south London motorcycle shop that was in a converted railway bridge arch. Above the shop, day and night, long and short distance trains passed over the premises, producing noise and vibrations. The noise suited the proprietor. He didn't want complaints when tuning and revving his bikes. But there was another reason that the noise was his friend.

The proprietor – Jerry Logan - was a small, middle age man, bald, who had an aroma of metal and grease. Tonight he was wearing blue overalls that were splattered with oil. His face and calloused hands were dirty. He said, "I'd shake hands, but," he held up his palms, "I've been stripping down and reassembling an old Ducati. I'm hoping to sell it for a song. Haven't seen you in a while, Tom. How are things?"

Knutsen was cautious. Logan was a hardened criminal who'd done stints in prison. Three years ago, for reasons that weren't clear, he'd agreed to work with the police in an undercover sting. The targets were major drug dealers. He enabled Knutsen to meet the dealers. The sting went wrong. At the final meeting with them, Logan pulled out his mobile phone, pretended to read a text message, and shouted, "Shit! This guy's a cop. You're about to be busted!" The dealers fell for Logan's sleight of hand and ran, leaving a stash of drugs behind. Pointing a gun at Knutsen, Logan picked up drugs with a street value of half a million quid, and smiled. "They won't talk. You can't talk because you'll blow your cover. And I don't need to talk. See you sometime, pal." He later sold the drugs and bought the shop and some very rare bikes. His business had been booming ever since. But he wasn't completely legit these days. He still kept one foot in the criminal underworld by supplying discerning customers with weapons. Knutsen knew that.

"I'm out of the police. Doing a bit of private detective work."

Logan picked up a large wrench. "If you've got eyes on me, you're wasting your time." He lied, "I threw the drugs in the Thames. Can't have that crap on our fine streets, can we?"

"I'm not here about that. I need your help."

Logan used the wrench to tighten bolts on the Ducati. He placed the tool down and wiped his hands on a towel. "You want a gun?"

"Yes."

"Loud and proud? Or fuck-them-up small?"

The former meaning a shotgun, machine gun, or rifle. The latter meaning a handgun.

"A pistol, plus at least four spare magazines. Deniable, of course."

Logan said, "Step into my office." He led Knutsen to the back of the shop and into a small shooting range. At the end of the range was a target of a man. The only other items in the range were an eight foot metal cabinet and a desk. Both were flush against the right-hand-side wall. Logan opened the cabinet. There was an array of weapons inside. He withdrew four pistols and laid them on the desk. "Browning 9mm. Bit old school and kicks like a mule. But, one bullet makes a severe mess. A Makarov. Good for rapid firing, plus needs less maintenance compared to the Browning. The bullets sting like fuck, but a leg shot won't kill you unless you're lucky. A Sig Sauer P320-45. This will hit you like a rhino. And it's accurate. But it's loud. And" he prodded a finger on the last weapon, "a Sig Sauer P226. They come in a variety of calibres. This one's 9mm."

Knutsen looked at the weapons. "Where do you get these?"

Logan turned to him, his face filled with aggression. "It'll go bad for both of us if you're wearing a wire!"

Knutsen held up his hands. "Jerry – I'm here to make a purchase. I don't want anyone, least of all the police, to know I've been here."

"You'd better be telling me the fucking truth. What do you need the gun for?"

"At this stage, I don't know."

"Human target?"

"Come on, Jerry."

"Yeah, fair point. Urban or rural?"

"I genuinely don't know. Could be both."

Logan brushed his hand over the guns. "I get a lot of my weapons from soldiers who return from places like Afghanistan, Iraq, Africa, other places. Many of them are on their uppers. I give them a few hundred quid. It pays for their rent in a bedsit for a month or two. Or gives them a night out on the booze and coke. They're trophy weapons taken from their enemies, or they're nicked from their unit's armouries. But I also have other sources. The key thing is I don't buy or sell anything unless I think it's serviceable. I strip down every gun; sometimes I have to reconstruct them with new workings." He gestured toward his shop. "Just like my Ducati motorbike." He slammed his hand on the table. "Best you test all four and see what you think. Prices vary."

Knutsen picked up the Browning. "My father carried one of these." He got into a shooting stance and aimed the gun at the target.

"Wait!" Logan checked his watch. "Anytime now. Anytime now." A train passed overhead; the noise was easily sufficient to drown out gunshots. "You've got five seconds max. Go now!"

Knutsen fired three shots. My goodness, Logan was right. It kicked like a mule. But the target was shredded. "I'll take this."

"You sure? The others are more advanced."

"I know, but this one feels good in my hands."

"That's all that matters. Just remember, your Browning bullets will go through someone and won't stop until they've done with death."

"I'll need at least four spare magazines."

"I'll give you six for a total price of one thousand pounds."

Knutsen nodded. "Deal." He handed over cash and took the gun and magazines, which he secreted in his fleece jacket. He shook hands with Logan, not caring that engine oil made his hands mucky. "You inherited wealth from an obscure relative who lived in Latin America. It enabled you to finance this shop. That's the line. Get rid of the guns. You don't need them anymore. It's time to go legit." Knutsen walked out.

CHAPTER 10

It was eight AM. On the south bank of the Thames, Sign walked behind a man who was smartly dressed and holding a rolled-up umbrella. The man was approximately the same age as Sign. A few tourists were braving the cold air. Everyone else was office workers going to work. Still, the ordinarily bustling pathway was sparse of pedestrians.

Sign walked alongside the man he'd been following and matched his pace. "Thanks for agreeing to talk."

"I agreed to this meeting. But, we have less than a mile to cover whatever it is that's of interest to you. After that I walk into the temple. I understand that you no longer have a security pass to get in."

Colin Parker was referring to the MI6 headquarters in Vauxhall Cross. He worked there as head of counter-espionage. Despite being a senior posting, and a sexy-sounding title, it was a role that required him to sit in London and analyse files. Though Parker had entered the service out of Cambridge as a fast-stream spy, he knew that his current job was a career killer.

Sign knew that as well. "I wanted to talk to you about Mark Archer."

"His death?"

"What led up to his death."

Parker laughed as he carried on walking. "Who knows?"

"Why is the service being uncooperative with the police?"

"We haven't been uncooperative. On the contrary, we invited senior Met detectives to come into HQ to discuss Archer's death. They told us point blank that there was no doubt he committed suicide. What they wanted were two things: first to know if there were any skeletons in the closet; second, to know how to handle the media if it was leaked that Archer was MI6, rather than a diplomat."

"Were there any skeletons in the closet?"

Parker stopped walking. "Come on Ben. You of all people should know how this works. I'm only privy to matters that cross my desk – a Chinese spy tries to blackmail one of our officers, the Russians have set up an eavesdropping station in Pimlico, that kind of thing. What I'm *not* privy to is the machinations of our officers' private lives. You'd have to talk to security about that. And they won't talk to you or me. Their job is so dull that they've developed a them-and-us syndrome. Everyone in security realises they've been marginalised because of their mediocre performance as operators. You won't find a single friend there."

Sign had expected this response. "Were there any rumours about Archer, even if it's just unsubstantiated tittle-tattle?"

Parker continued walking. "If there were rumours, I wasn't privy to them. Service personnel don't gossip to me. They worry what I'd do with that information."

"Who were Archer's friends in The Office?"

"You know us lot, Ben. None of us like each other."

Sign saw the MI6 HQ ahead. "How well did you know Archer?"

"Not that well at all. Different departments; different postings."

"But your paths crossed?"

"Fleetingly."

"Have you been to his house?"

"No. Why would I?"

"Do you know his wife?"

Parker shook his head. "I heard she was a school teacher assistant before Archer swept her off her feet and made her feel like lady of the manor on overseas postings. You know how being a diplomat's spouse goes to some people's heads."

"She came from a humble background?"

Parker laughed. "Nothing wrong with that." He stood opposite the headquarters. "They were kindred spirits. Mark Archer had a brain and good education, though he too came from working class stock. Marrying a working class girl was his two fingers up to the establishment, is my guess." He frowned. "So you're now playing private detective?"

"I'm an advisor, currently to the Metropolitan Police."

"Needs must." Parker looked sympathetic as he said, "Personally, I thought you were the best candidate for chief."

"I thought I was the worst – people like us are bred and trained to run people and make them sacrifice their lives in hostile territories; we're not designed to manage an organisation."

Parker glanced at the temple. "It's turned into a feeding frenzy in there. Sharks turning on sharks. Your departure has created a void that can't be filled."

"That's no longer my problem, Colin."

"Soon, it won't be mine either. In six months, I'm out of here. My partner and I want to retire to our home in Normandy. I've had enough of this game."

Parker was about to leave, but Sign placed a hand on his arm. "Archer's home is way beyond his pay packet. I wondered if he or his wife had inherited the money to buy it. From what you've said about their backgrounds, that seems highly unlikely."

"We all accrue cash expenses on postings."

"A few thousand pounds here and there, yes. But Archer's house is worth at least one or two million."

Parker was motionless. "I did briefly meet his wife once. But not at their home. The Archers had laid on a barge trip down the Thames to celebrate their daughter's acceptance into university. Ten of us from the service were invited. God knows why. Probably just to make up numbers."

"A few people dropped out at the last minute?"

"There's no other explanation. The event was a bit tedious. Aside from Mark Archer, who I didn't really know, the only other people I knew at the event were my colleagues, and I barely knew them. But there was an odd thing."

Sign said nothing.

"It was the champagne. I know you don't have kids. I do. But if you did have kids and your daughter got into uni I'm guessing that, like me, you'd flatter her by laying on a few bottles of Prosecco and a two hundred pound plate of sarnies. Nothing less, nothing more. But here's the thing – Mark Archer had an on board personal chef who cooked lobster with caviar, truffles, and Wagyu beef that had been flown in from Japan. And there must have been a hundred bottles of Veuve Clicqout Brut flowing."

"Where did he get that money from?"

"My colleagues and I thought it must have been down to a soppy dad squirreling his cash away for his daughter's send off."

Sign shook his head. "It was a cry for help. You and others were invited to his daughter's celebration because you needed to be witnesses to his despair. But, you didn't pick up on that or help him."

"Help him?"

"Put him out of his misery." Sign spun around. Over the road was the motorcycle shop that Knutsen had visited last night. It amused him that Logan's gun range was so close to the epicentre of the world's most successful intelligence organisation. "Archer was on the take. The only explanation is that he was being paid good sums by a foreign intelligence organisation that wanted our secrets. He was a double agent. Towards the end, he wanted a way out. He wanted to be caught." Sign turned back to Parker. "This falls bang into the centre of your remit as head of counter-intelligence. Do some snooping for me, will you Colin?"

"So, that's why you approached me, of all people in the service." Parker banged his umbrella on the ground. "You suspected Archer was a double and you decided to use me to get to the truth."

Sign said, "The truth won't bring him back."

"So, what's the point?"

"The point is, there is the slightest possibility that a garbage man is at play."

"A garbage man? What does that mean?"

Sign handed him his business card. "Call me with any developments." He walked off.

CHAPTER 11

Sign stoked the fire in his lounge and poured Knutsen a glass of calvados. "Let me look at your gun."

Knutsen retrieved the weapon from his bedroom.

Sign held it in his hand. "A fine choice. One shot, anywhere in the body, causes massive trauma. It reloads quickly. It rarely malfunctions, providing it's kept clean. And it puts the jeepers into opponents." He laid the gun on a side table. "Drink up. We need to go for a walk. I need to do some late night shopping and could do with company."

They walked across Lambeth Bridge and into the heart of London. Sign explained that he needed to purchase some new brogues. Taking in Regent Street, Oxford Street, the City of London, and Saville Row, they stopped at thirteen shops. In each of them, Sign tried on shoes. It wasn't until they were in the last shop that Sign bought a pair of shoes. They returned on foot to West Square.

Inside, Knutsen rubbed his cold hands and asked, "What was that all about?"

"My previous pair of brogues was getting worn." Sign replenished their glasses. "Plus, I needed to think." He took a swig of the spirit. "We have a limpet."

"What?"

"You and I just walked an anti-surveillance route. The key is to draw any potential followers into a static environment. If they're following, they can't resist entering the static place – in our case shoe shops. Failure to do so could mean they'd lose us out a back door. Key to the technique is convincing the follower that we are oblivious to his presence and have a pattern of behaviour that makes sense. In our case, it was shoe shopping. And even though the route was convoluted, it didn't look suspicious because my pre-planned pattern was to seek out select shoe shops that sold particular brands of shoes. A double sighting of a man or woman is the tell-tale indicator that you're being followed. Tonight we had a limpet – someone who stuck to us. He was good. He changed his jacket three times, put on false glasses, removed false glasses, carried a cigarette, then a vaporiser, twice pretended to be on a mobile phone, different models of course, wore a woollen hat, didn't wear a hat, and never once engaged eye contact with me or you. But he was most certainly following us."

Knutsen was confused. "I've done anti-surveillance. Why didn't I spot him?"

"Because you weren't looking for him or expecting him." He picked up his landline and called Roberts to see if she was okay. She told him that her husband was on the mend and would probably be home later tonight. Sign relayed this update to Knutsen. "The limpet isn't police. I've got no evidence to support that assertion, but I can sniff a spook a mile off. He was western Caucasian, though not Mediterranean or Slavic in appearance, but that says nothing. People's appearances adapt over time. But my hunch is he's British."

"MI5?"

"They have to work in teams because they're so incompetent. And there was no team on our tail. No, this man was MI6."

"Freelance or cadre?"

"Impossible to tell at this stage."

Sign handed Knutsen his gun. "It may be nothing."

"Or something?"

"Yes. MI6 may simply be wishing to keep tabs on us."

"Or maybe Roberts' burglary wasn't random."

"The thought occurred to me." Sign was deep in thought. "Somebody has got wind that we're investigating Archer's death. The route to that is via Roberts' connection to us. Roberts left something compromising at her home, most likely my business card. It wasn't her fault. She didn't want anything that linked her to us being kept in Scotland Yard. I imagine the commissioner instructed her to that effect. The limpet is off the books. That means he's either a deniable agent or he's a retired paramilitary officer. If the former, MI6 has tasked him. If the latter, he's working for someone deeply embedded in MI6."

"Someone who wants to shut mouths?"

"Or someone who wants to open them for their last gasp before the hangman's noose."

"What do you mean?"

Sign didn't answer. "I think we should get a Christmas tree. It is the first of December, after all. Also, I've ordered peacock for the twenty fifth."

"Peacock for Christmas Day?"

"Yes, unless you have anywhere better to go. I wouldn't blame you. But if, like me, you're on your tod then we could have game, celery, plums, roast potatoes, a citrus-cherry sauce, a pud with brandy, and I'd go head to head with you on the Trivial Pursuit board game. I must warn you – I'm superb at geography and history, arts and literature, appalling at science and sport."

Knutsen laughed. "I haven't celebrated Christmas for a long time."

"Nor have I. Too busy being someone else overseas. I have fine vintners in Holborn and elsewhere who can recommend wines to match the peacock."

Knutsen sat and cupped his calvados. "I think we should invite the Roberts."

"Agreed. I'll play host and Santa."

Knutsen chuckled. "You're not like anyone I've ever met."

Sign gave a dismissive gesture with his hand. "One of the first components of being a successful MI6 officer is that we must keep the world off kilter. We must always wrong foot people, usually in a positive way. Secondly, we must believe in the impossible and achieve what others can't. Third, we mustn't give a damn about protocol or what others think." He smiled. "Life's more fun that way. The peacock's from Australia. Inspector Roberts' husband was nearly murdered. You were a highly successful undercover cop. I was tipped to be the next chief of MI6. And yet we are reduced to peacock, a trivial game, and some good plonk. Life doesn't get better than that."

"It doesn't." Knutsen stared at him. "You're lonely."

In a strident voice, Sign replied, "So are you. And the reason we're in this predicament is due to the nature of our jobs. They alienate us from normality. But we crave embracing human norms. Christmas is one of those norms." His voice quietened as he said, "We need to go old school tradecraft when it comes to protecting this flat. Carry your sidearm at all times when leaving the flat. I will rig the door to see if anyone has entered when it's empty. Also, I'll leave misinformation – a draft file containing papers that state that in our opinion there was nothing untoward about Mark Archer's death, another file containing details of a fake new case that we're working on – completely unconnected to MI6 or Archer, and I'll scatter other lies around this room."

"The limpet can't be working alone. He can't watch us 24/7."

"He can't. But my hunch is that he's the only person watching us."

"Why?"

"Because if there was a team on us, he wouldn't have needed to go to all that effort to change his appearance. A team would simply rotate its members, to avoid me getting a double sighting of one of them."

Knutsen weighed his pistol in one hand. "If I kill someone with this I could be sent down for life imprisonment."

"Let's hope it doesn't come down to that." He withdrew a sheet of paper from a stationary cupboard. "However, I have been busy." He handed Knutsen the sheet. "This is from the home secretary. You'll note it is countersigned by the prime minister and the commissioner of the Metropolitan Police. It gives you authority to carry a sidearm. You are able to use the gun only in accordance to the training you received as a cop. Specifically, that means you cannot use the gun unless you are facing someone who has a weapon and is threatening your life or someone else's life. The letter was produced in triplicate." He took the letter off Knutsen, placed it back in the cupboard, and produced one of the copies. "This one I laminated. Whenever you carry your gun, carry this as well. If you're stopped by police or security services who want to know why you're carrying a gun, show them the letter."

"How did you manage to pull this off?!"

Sign smiled. "I may be out of MI6, but I still carry some sway in the corridors of power. Let's leave it at that."

Knutsen folded the letter and placed it in a pocket. "The letter will give me some protection. But, real life situations involving guns can be unpredictable. If I shoot someone who I think is reaching for a gun, but it turns out he's reaching for a knife, I could still face a jury."

"Ah, but that's where I come in. I'm very good at making things seem different to how they are."

"Contaminate a crime scene? Plant evidence?"

Sign's face was mischievous as he said, "Hush now with such crude words. I would protect you from the law. That's all you need to know." He walked to a window and opened the curtain by an inch. "Is the limpet out there? Or has he gone to bed? It's too dark to know. So, there's nothing to be done right now. Tomorrow, I want you to find out when the Archers bought their house in Godalming. It needs a copper's methodology. I don't just want an online land search. I want to know who sold the house, how it was paid for, all details."

"And what will you do?"

"Tomorrow I have a matinee appointment at the Royal Festival Hall to watch the Philharmonic perform Sibelius' Lemminkäinen Suite."

Sarcastically, Knutsen said, "Nice to know you're busy."

"If I have time, I may also take in the Goya exhibition at the National Gallery."

"Jesus! Busy day for you, pal."

Sign smiled. "I'm also hoping to get an answer to something that's been nagging me."

Hilt called Smith at eleven thirty PM. "I'm clocking off. The house is in darkness. I'll be back on it tomorrow."

"Any unusual activity today?"

"No. They went shoe shopping. I followed them."

"Where did they go?"

Hilt gave Smith the details.

"Shit!"

"What's up boss?"

Smith said, "Sign always buys his shoes in one shop in Holborn. He sucked you in to an anti-surveillance route."

"It doesn't matter. He didn't clock me."

Smith exhaled deeply. "You're dealing with one of the finest minds. Not only that, it's a mind that's been superbly trained in our craft. He clocked you."

Hilt asked, "What do you want me to do?"

"Back off Sign and Knutsen. Watch Roberts and wait for my instructions."

CHAPTER 12

Sign was drinking a glass of sparkling water as he sat in the library of his club in St. James's. No one else was in the room. It was lunchtime and a weekend. The few club members who were in the building were dining. Sign tried to read a newspaper, but his eyes were not taking in words. Instead, his mind was racing.

Colin Parker walked into the room and sat in a leather armchair, opposite Sign. The MI6 head of counter-intelligence was wearing a sports jacket, shirt and trousers. The only reason he'd chosen the apparel was so he could conform to the club's dress code. Otherwise, today he'd have been in anything other than the formal attire he needed to wear during the working week. Quietly, he said, "This had better be worth my time. To be here, I had to lie to my wife and tell her that I'd like to take her clothes shopping. I've endured two hours of visiting shop after blasted shop. My frustration and boredom were real, but I made a show of ensuring she could see how agonising the jaunts were. She told me to leave her to browse while I get a drink. We were both relieved. So, I'm here and she's probably buying up half of Oxford Street."

"It's very good of you to come. I know weekends are your precious family time."

Parker checked his mobile phone. "I've got thirty minutes. Then I need to meet my partner in Selfridges."

Sign stood and walked to a trolley that contained tea, coffee, and snacks. He poured Parker a coffee and handed it to him. After sitting back down, Sign asked, "Were you followed here?"

"Impossible to know. It's heaving out there. Not ideal circumstances to run the drills."

"I'm sure. What have you found?"

"I've been through Archer's agent files. All of his reports were cross-checked by security and analysis. There's nothing untoward in any of them."

Sign was still. "You of all people know that files are stories concocted by case officers, to their pleasing. It's the beauty of our job. We go overseas alone, no one is watching over us, we meet our foreign agent, and we write up the contact in a way that makes us look glorious. We lie."

"You never lied, Ben. When things went wrong for you, you told the truth. And when things went unbelievably right for you, you heaped praise on your foreign agents, not you. It's one of the reasons we wanted you to head up the organisation. You were our best operator; but more important, your moral compass was exactly where it should be." Parker bowed his head. "Yes – the files only say what Archer wants us to hear. They're useless. He got intelligence out of his people, no doubt about that, but none of it was remarkable. Low-level shit about troop movements, political posturing, that kind of stuff."

"But there's one thing he couldn't lie about."

Parker frowned, wondering how Sign knew what he had to say. "Yes. Overseas postings. One can't lie about when and where one was deployed. His first posting was under second secretary diplomatic cover to Moscow. Three years later, he returned to London and was put on a year-long Russian language course. He'd told personnel department that he'd got a taste for Russia. Personnel loved that. It was at the time the USSR had imploded and Russia was seen as an unpredictable time bomb. Personnel needed people interested in what happens next with Russia. He was posted back to Moscow as first secretary."

"A prestigious job."

"Yes. Though, a weird thing happened after he'd completed that posting. Archer started messing up. We tried him in a variety of different London-based jobs. He was unremarkable in all of them. So, we thought a change of scenery was required. We gave him the opportunity to be head of station in Pretoria."

"Most people would have snapped up that promotion."

Parker shook his head. "He turned it down and asked to go back to Russia."

"As first secretary?"

"Yes. A sideways move."

Sign nodded. "He needed to be back in the motherland."

"It seems that way." Parker looked at Sign. "I know what you're thinking, but I have no proof that Archer was on the take from the Russians."

"Nor do I, but his suicide speaks volumes." Sign placed his fingertips together. "It's impossible to know for sure when the Russians got their hooks into him. My guess is they used Russian businessmen under the pay of the SVR to get Archer to take money. Probably they told him that he needed an alternate career if ever he decided to leave the diplomatic service. But the money would have been chicken feed. On the second tour, the Russians upped the ante. More money was paid to him. The money would have been for innocuous stuff – consultancy on Norway's position on the latest EU agricultural policy, that kind of thing. Then the businessmen really screwed him. They said they had a major client who wished to deal with him directly. If business came out of that contact, they'd get a ten percent introductory fee and would have no further dealings with Archer. The client wished to do business in the UK but had no idea how to navigate the minefield of our laws and regulations. The client, the businessmen said, was above board and wanted to invest billions in the more impoverished corners of Britain. This would be a huge feather in Archer's cap. But the client turned out to be the SVR. Russian Intelligence had him by the balls and paid him handsomely for the deal. He became their spy."

Parker rubbed his face. "You're speculating and imagining scenarios, but loosely this hangs together. The thing is, Archer was many things, but he wasn't stupid. Over years, he'd have known he was falling into that trap."

"He felt he needed the money." Sign received a call from Knutsen. He listened, thanked him, and hung up. To Parker, he asked, "What were the years of Archer's second posting to Moscow?"

"Two thousand and one to two thousand and four."

Sign ran his finger around the rim of his glass. "I have a bloodhound. He's very good. Today he's ascertained the exact details of the Archers' purchase of their home in Godalming. They bought it for two point four million pounds in two thousand and four."

Blood drained out of Parker's face.

"You should have spotted this, Colin. It's your job."

Parker's hands were sweaty as he said, "I can't spot everyone. We have thousands of staff. And half of them are scattered across the globe. Still," he looked wistful, "yes, it's my job. I should have spotted this."

Sign stood. "Not to worry, dear chap. Archer's dead and the overpriced house is just bricks and mortar that now need constant repairs by a widow who knew exactly what her husband was doing and indeed encouraged him to be a traitor, merely for financial gain."

Sign paused. "Let's keep this between ourselves. Someone else in MI6 knew Archer was on the take. I wonder about that person."

"What do you mean?"

Sign said nothing, left the library, and exited the building via the basement kitchen back door.

Through binoculars, John Smith watched a man walk across heath on the Scottish island of Skye. Beyond him, mountains were being caressed by swirling mist. The air was thick with the scent of grass and other flora. The man was alone; the nearest habitation was five miles away. The man was carrying a shotgun and was oblivious to the fact that he was being observed. He was probably hunting woodcock or grouse. Smith didn't know or care. Smith was wearing a yellow waterproof jacket, with hood on. From one hundred yards away, he waved his hand and shouted at the man.

The man stopped, un-cocked his shotgun, opened the barrel, and cradled his weapon.

Smith ran to him, a smile on his face, rain cascading off his garments. "Sir, can you help me?"

The man was stock still as he eyed him with suspicion.

Smith got closer. "Car's broken down. Where can I get help?" Smith was thirty yards away.

The man gestured to an escarpment. "Get back on the road, walk six miles west, Eddy's got a garage, he'll help you."

Smith walked right up to the man and pulled down his hood.

The man looked shocked. "You! What are you doing here?"

Smith smiled. "Hello Arthur."

Arthur Lake slammed shut his shotgun barrel.

Smith said, "I need to talk to you."

"Can't it wait? I've got another week off before I'm back at The Office." Lake was head of an operational MI6 team in London. It was likely he'd soon be promoted to the organisation's board of directors. His previous overseas postings had been to Paris, Warsaw, Mexico City, and Washington. He was a rising star, considered by most intelligence officers to have an impeccable career.

Smith thought otherwise. "Is there anywhere dry we can go? I'd kill for a coffee."

They walked to the cottage Lake had rented for his hunting holiday. Inside the isolated one-bedroom stone house, Lake put his shotgun on the kitchen table and flicked on the kettle. Out of the slow cook segment of the Aga, the aroma of venison stew permeated the room. Peeled spuds were in a pan on the hob, waiting to be boiled this evening. Carrots and wild mushrooms were in a bowel adjacent to the oven. Lake hanged his sodden jacket on a coat rack that also contained anti-midge mesh smocks, camouflage jackets and trousers, and a six-foot walking stick with a ram's horn.

Smith sat at the kitchen table. "Is it your first time on Skye?"

Lake made no effort to hide the irritation in his voice. "I come here every year. It clears my head."

"How are the wife and kids?"

"What's this about?"

"I was passing by and fancied a chat."

"Bullshit." Lake handed him a mug and sat opposite Smith. The shotgun was between them. "Is there a crisis in HQ?"

Smith smiled. "I'm sorry to have intruded on your solitude. This won't take long." He wrapped his hands around the mug to take the chill out of his fingers. "There is an immediate crisis."

"What?"

"You."

Lake frowned. "You've come a long way if it's just to tell me that I'm no longer being considered for the appointment of director."

"Oh, it's nothing like that. As far as I know, you'll get the appointment next autumn."

"Has something happened to one of my team members, or one of their agents?"

"This is nothing to do with anyone under your control. It's to do with Washington."

Lake was about to drink his coffee. He lowered his mug. "Washington?"

"To be precise, your posting there in two thousand and nine."

"I don't understand."

"Actually, you partially don't". Smith drank his coffee. "You made a deal with the Americans. The CIA to be precise. They and you wanted to bring the so-called special relationship even closer. To do so, the Americans wanted you to plant rose-tinted intelligence into MI6 HQ. They wanted to be seen as a conjoined twin with MI6, thereby giving them complete access to our top agents."

"Now hold on a minute!"

Smith held up his hand. His voice was steady and calm as he added, "In itself, that's not a major sin. You were simply being asked by the Yanks to play spin doctor; be a de facto ambassador for them; promote the cause, and all that. It happens a lot. We've all been there – making judgements on our own when liaising with foreign intelligence organisations. Sometimes we overstep the line by the standards of the rule book, but the rule book is open to interpretation, isn't it?"

"You can drive a bus through the rule book."

"Precisely. So, no high treason there. Just a slap on the wrist. What did the CIA promise you in return?"

"It was just diplomacy."

"What did they promise you?" Smith repeated.

Lake sighed. "You know what it's like at this level. It's not just about support within MI6. As crucial is support from allies."

"If you want to get up the ladder. Yes." Smith ran a finger along the length of the shotgun barrel. "Excellent relations with the Americans, French, Germans, Canadians, Australians, and New Zealanders are crucial when one is being considered for a board level appointment. One person can't have all of that. So the board is put together like a jigsaw, each board member bringing an ally to the table. You'll bring the Americans."

Lake shouted, "And that's a damn good thing!"

"I didn't say it wasn't. But the process of getting there is pertinent."

"Meaning?"

Smith said, "When you were head of Washington Station, you cultivated the Americans, and they cultivated you. It was mutual. You knew what they wanted; they knew what you wanted. Your interests were selfish but they never compromised UK national interest. You trod a fine line, but the end game was sound. Relations with the Americans always ebb and flow. At the time you were in Washington, we were in an ebb. We need their intelligence as much as they need ours. You knew that. You tried to build bridges."

"How do you know all this?"

Smith didn't answer. "The CIA should be delighted when you're appointed to the board. So will MI6. You'll have brought a temperamental mistress back to bed so that you can make love to her."

Lake laughed. "That's one way to look at it."

"But, it's not the only way, because we have a problem."

Lake put his hands flat on the table. "I did nothing wrong. Yes, I bent a few rules. But the endgame was crucial. Still is."

"Ah, but you didn't factor in the possibility that you might be taken for an idiot."

"How dare you. Just because of who you are…"

"Yes, yes, And all that." Smith's tone was blasé. It steeled as he asked, "How are your wife and kids?"

"None of your damn business!"

"Toby and Ella are at the Cotswold School. It's one of the top ten schools in the country. You should be proud."

Lake didn't reply.

"And your loving wife is an entrepreneur, carving a cottage industry living from making bespoke perfumes. She'd be heartbroken if she knew you'd had an affair with a CIA officer called Frédérique Dubois."

"I didn't have an affair!"

"Yes you did!" Smith lowered his voice. "She was your CIA case officer."

"Liaison officer!"

"Call it what you will. You were told by the CIA only to speak to her. The duration of the affair was four days, within which you used her as much as she used you. Both of you understood the game. Frédérique Dubois is an interesting name."

Lake put his head in his hands. "She was from Michigan. Her family were Muskrat French."

Smith nodded. "Descendants of habitants, voyageurs and coureurs des bois in the Pays d'en Haut. It's a good cover for a French DGSE intelligence officer."

"What?!"

Smith swirled his coffee. "See, here's the thing. The woman you fucked moved on to pastures new. She turned up in England. She tried her tricks but we were wise to that and had her arrested. Right now she's in high security detention in Paddington Police Station. Soon, she'll be moved to one our UK black sites where we'll put the thumb screws on her. Frédérique is in fact Marceline Collobert. The French knew Frédérique was due to meet you. Probably they had that information via surveillance. They had Frédérique killed and dumped in a quarry. The Americans have only just discovered her body and put two and two together, with our help. Marceline was deployed against you, pretending to be Frédérique. You fell for it and thought you were talking to the Americans. Instead, you were informing the French about Britain's economic policies towards Europe, our military strategy against Syria, which UK politicians were in the ascendency, and ultimately whether we favoured France over America. Marceline has told us everything about you. She has more to say about the wider picture and we'll work that out of her. She was a Mata Hari, and you couldn't keep your dick in your pants."

Lake was incredulous. "I… I had no idea."

"You were trained to second guess! How could you have let this happen?"

Smith whispered, "If you try to defend your actions, your career will be ruined, you'll face imprisonment, your wife will divorce you, your children will be taken into protective custody, and they and your wife will suffer public humiliation from the press."

Lake started crying. "I had no idea. I had no fucking idea."

"I'm sure. But your actions have put Britain in a pickle with our European partners."

"Why are you here? Why not just send the cops and MI5 to arrest me?"

Smith touched his hand. "You have to think about your wife and children. They're all that matters now. A hearing and court trial – public or behind closed doors – will spew out everything you've done. You'll be a ruined man. I assure you that you'll have not one waking day left on this planet without feeling the weight of a cannon ball in your skull. You'll hate yourself. You'll miss seeing your kids grow up. You'll wonder how they are. They'll be confused at first, then they'll hate you. Your wife will ensure that. And she'll remarry. You will no longer be a father and husband. The world will think you're a traitor. France will think you're a fool. It fucked you. There's nothing Britain can do about that. We like France.

You're a pawn. And a spent one at that. Marceline will die in prison. She never liked you, let alone loved you. She's gone." Smith stood. "There is only one way out. Nip this in the bud before the judiciary gets its hands on you. You have two hours to think it through before I call in the hounds."

Smith left and walked across the moor to his hire car. He needed to be back in London this evening.

Thirty minutes later, Lake placed the barrel of his shotgun into his mouth. His face was blotched, sweaty and covered in tears. His hands were trembling. He didn't want to do it, but Smith's words kept pounding his brain. Smith was right; there was no other way. He wanted to think something profound – anything about his kids, wife, job, youth. Anything. But all he felt was the pressure of massive depression. And it was unstoppable. His life was now useless and pointless. He couldn't bear the thought of his family being dragged through the muck because of him. But more important, he felt like scum. All the good times seemed like a distant memory – chatting up girls when at Trinity, a boozy and fun holiday in Ibiza when he was in his early twenties, being awarded a prize at school for his prowess in chemistry, catching crabs in rock pools with his dad, his mum making a Sunday roast every week because he loved the food and it tempered the feeling of angst about going to school the next morning, playing dragon hunt with his mates in the playground at nursery. None of it felt real now.

He sucked in deeply, the acrid taste of cordite hitting his nostrils.

He pulled the trigger and blew his brains out.

CHAPTER 13

Inspector Roberts pressed the door buzzer in West Square. It was five PM. Light was fading.

Knutsen was at home. Sign wasn't. Knutsen ushered her in to the flat.

"When's Ben home?"

Knutsen looked at a seventeenth century German clock that had been given to Sign by

one of his Iranian agents. Sign had arranged for the agent to escape Iran after his cover was

blown. Sign had put him on a boat in Bandar Abbas and had helped the skipper – a Moroccan

smuggler – sail the boat to Muscat. "He's due back anytime. I'll get the fire going. Blinking

cold out there today."

Roberts sat in one of the armchairs and watched Knutsen assemble and ignite the fire.

"How are you getting on with Sign?"

Knutsen laughed as he rubbed coal dust off his hands. "I've never met anyone like

him before. He comes from a working class background but speaks like royalty. I've heard

him on the phone to people. I'm no good at languages and accents, but I reckon he was

speaking Chinese, Russian, Spanish, French, German, and in one instance English in a

Geordie accent."

"He needs to be who he needs to be on any given occasion. But who is he really?"

Knutsen shook his head. "I reckon it will take me a lifetime to answer that question."

Sign walked into the room. "Mrs. Roberts. An unexpected but lovely surprise. Will

you be staying for supper?" He put a bag on a table. "Sibelius' interpretation of Finnish life

has invigorated me. This evening I stopped off at a trusted fishmonger and butcher and purchased some excellent herring and hare. One will be the starter; the other the main course."

The suggestion sounded intriguing. But Roberts needed to be home for dinner with her husband. She said, "Another time. I'm here for two reasons."

Sign slumped onto his chaise lounge. "One of those reasons will be to enquire about our research into Archer's death. The other will be to do with something bad, though the variables of what that might be are too vast to speculate on a specific."

"Archer."

"He was taking money from the Russians in exchange for supplying Western secrets. His wife supported this arrangement. Guilt overwhelmed him. He ended his life rather than furthering his duplicity. But…"

"But?"

"I suspect a trigger is at play, though have no evidence to support that theory."

"A trigger?"

Sign placed the tips of his fingers together. "When one is in an unhappy marriage, frequently one sticks one's head in the sand and hopes for the best. Things will muddle through - that kind of mentality. Then one day that person goes out for a drink with his or her pals. They have a gallon of booze and pluck up the courage to tell him or her to divorce the bitch or bastard. Usually, the unhappy person ignores the advice, though recognises its truth. It eats at the person. And sometimes the person wakes up and decides that he or she can't ignore the descent into Hell any longer. The person takes action. Foul words, violence, and divorce are common results."

"So, somebody triggered Archer's death?"

"Yes, but not a pal, or a bitch, or a bastard. This is somebody very clever. Somebody went up to the horse's nose and made it think differently."

"But as you say, you have no evidence of that."

"I do have my experience. When I asked Mrs. Archer if someone had visited her home prior to her husband's death, she lied and said no one had visited." Sign leaped off the chair. "I can smell a liar by looking at their face and listening to their voice." He chucked logs onto the fire. "What is the second reason you're here?"

"Do you know Arthur Lake? Our records show that he's a diplomat in the Foreign & Commonwealth Office."

"Why do you enquire about Lake?"

"He killed himself this morning. He was alone in a holiday cottage in Skye. His wife and children remained at home in London. My colleagues informed her of the death. She is devastated and can't give any reason why he would have taken his life."

"What else did she say?"

Roberts said, "She asked if he was killed. She said that her husband had been living a lie for decades. He wasn't a diplomat. He was MI6."

Sign nodded. "Lake was a high flyer in MI6. How did he kill himself?"

"Shotgun in the mouth."

"He was on a hunting holiday?"

"According to the owner of the holiday let, he went there every year to shoot game."

Knutsen asked, "Have forensics been to the scene?"

"Local police were reluctant to deploy forensics. But as soon as I heard Lake was MI6, I called in some favours. They flew over a couple of specialists and a detective from Inverness. The cottage has been thoroughly examined. So too, Lake's corpse and the gun. There's no doubt he killed himself."

Sign said, "Because…"

Knutsen finished what Sign was about to say. "Blood, brain matter, and bone fragments were on the ceiling, meaning the gun was pointing upwards. Cordite residue is in his mouth. The gun could have been forced into his mouth to make it look like a fake suicide, but that would mean he'd have had to have been restrained. Forensics would have looked for rope fibres, bruising from handcuffs, maybe even traces of some kind of head brace that would have locked him still when the gun was put in his mouth. They found nothing, correct?"

"Correct." Roberts looked at Sign. "Why would he take his life?"

"I don't know." Sign sat down and rubbed his eyes. "Our paths crossed a few times, but that's the extent of our contact." To himself, he said, "Come on Sign. Think. Think." He looked at Roberts. "I'm not aware of any chinks in his armour. He liked a beer at lunchtime, but only half a glass. He had an eye for the ladies, but only an eye as far as I'm aware. He was a devout Catholic and regularly attended church when he could. He had no enemies in The Office. He was the perfect example of someone who could make it to the top – a grey man who happened to be a superb operator. But, I'm missing something. Where is his body?"

"In a morgue in Inverness. It will be flown back to London once the inquest is closed in a day or so."

To Knutsen, Sign said, "That's too long. Check out the next available flight to Skye. You and I need to take a trip."

Knutsen used his mobile phone to check flights. "Eight AM tomorrow. Flight to Edinburgh, then we get a small propeller plane to Skye. We land at eleven thirty. I'll arrange for a hire car."

"Excellent. Make the bookings." Sign said to Roberts, "I'm certain that I won't find anything that contradicts your Scottish colleagues' findings. But I want to pursue my theory. This one's tougher. There's no lying wife in play."

"Your theory being the trigger for his suicide?"

"A man. A horse whisperer. Someone who talked to Archer and Lake and persuaded them to kill themselves."

Roberts replied, "It's just a theory. I'm not sure how long my boss will give you slack."

"Mrs. Roberts – in my career, not one senior MI6 officer has committed suicide. Yet, within less than a week, two have. It could be an anomaly. Or they could be connected. Ultimately, we could be dealing with murder."

Roberts was angry. "We know for a fact that Archer and Lake committed suicide!"

Sign's voice was quiet as he said, "Murder can take many guises. An MI6 officer can kill people with words. How is your husband?"

"Can we get back to business? He's fine. Thanks for asking."

"Good. Now, inspector, you are plummeting into a world that is hard to comprehend. But, with your permission, I'm giving you a portal into that landscape. We could be dealing with someone who is killing people by blackmailing them. And he's doing so with merely the power of suggestion."

"A serial killer?"

"Time will tell." Sign stared at nothing. "I wonder, I do wonder, if my theory is right. Is someone getting rid of people? If so, are they in his way? Or is he clearing up a mess? Maybe it's a combination of the two."

"Maybe there is no person. But if there is, maybe it's a woman."

Sign agreed. "I'm not discounting any possibility. If there is a person – a trigger, horse whisperer, garbage man; my labels but slap whatever label you like on the person – the person could be male or female, black, white, Asian, a UK national, or a foreign national. I'm using the gender 'he' as shorthand. But I have a feeling that he's a man and he's British."

"If he exists."

"Indeed." Sign walked to one of the windows and partially opened the curtain. He wondered if the limpet was out there. He closed the curtain. "We must brace ourselves for the possibility of more deaths of MI6 officers."

Roberts checked the time. "I need to head home."

Sign clapped his hands. "Do me a favour. Call your esteemed Scottish friends and ask them to check the UK flight rosters to any port in Scotland during the preceding twenty four hours leading up to Lake's death. Also, ferry tickets to Skye. I need names."

"You think the whisperer will be one of those names?"

Sign picked up Roberts' coat and handed it to her. "I'm most interested to know if he's not on any roster. That would make him invisible and highly trained."

101

The following morning Sign and Knutsen were in Skye. As Knutsen drove, snow was heavy. "Never been here before," he said, "and I'm not sure I want to be stranded."

Sign glanced at the SatNav. "Four miles to go. Can you keep the car on the road until we reach our destination?"

"I've done the advanced driving course."

"I've done a variation of that, refined to be offensive and defensive driving in hot and cold climes. Let me know if you want me to take over driving duties."

"No. You're okay."

Sign smiled. "It's a shame about the snow."

"What were you hoping to do? Trace footprints with a magnifying glass?"

"No. It just changes the image of the place. I wanted to see it how Lake saw it when he died."

"You want to get in his head?"

Sign didn't answer.

Fifteen minutes later, Knutsen drove the hire car off the road and down a track that led to the cottage where Lake had taken his life. A four wheel drive vehicle was parked outside the property. Knutsen stopped his vehicle next to the SUV. A Scottish man got out of the vehicle at the same time Knutsen and Sign disembarked.

The Scot said, "Mr. Knutsen?"

"That'll be me."

The middle aged man shook hands with Knutsen. "Spider McCloud. I'm the estate ghillie. My boss said you're with the police."

Knutsen nodded.

"Come in then, but don't take too long. Weather's closing in. You'll need to get a flight back before they close the airport." McCloud unlocked the front door and led them in.

Sign looked at the kitchen floor and ceiling. "He was sitting at the kitchen table when he pulled the trigger?"

McCloud answered, "Yes. I was the one who found him. We had new guests due to arrive and I needed to check everything was in order in the cottage. He was on his back on the floor, chair underneath him, shotgun still in his mouth. It was a right mess."

"Who owns the shotgun?"

"The estate. We're licensed firearms owners. And we're only allowed to lease shotguns to people who have licenses from the British authorities. Each year we thoroughly checked Mr. Lake's permit to see it was up to date and in order." McCloud sounded hostile as he added, "We're a professional bunch here, mister. It would cost us our livelihood if we bent rules."

"We don't doubt that." Knutsen looked at the large amount of bloodstains. "My goodness. It must have been a horrific sight for you to confront."

McCloud shrugged. "I shoot deer in season, string them up, gut them, and butcher them for sale in Skye. I've seen worse than a man's head blown off. Plus, I was in the Royal Scots Dragoon Guards in the first Gulf War. In '91 I was deployed in the 7th Armoured Brigade. I've witnessed what rockets and grenades can do to the insides of an armoured vehicle containing my pals. Still," McCloud hesitated, "that was a while back. Deer I can handle. They need to be culled to keep numbers to a manageable level. Otherwise, whole herds will die. But human bodies? I thought I'd left that life twenty five years ago."

"Sir, you are a brave man." Sign examined the floor. "You found him. What happened next?"

"I called 999. Two local police officers turned up. I know them well. They're nice lads, but too young to see stuff like this. Robbie threw up; Angus nearly fainted. But they manned-up. They put police tape around the house. Two hours later my boss called me and told me to stay here. Specialist police were coming from Inverness, he told me. When they arrived, they took my finger and boot prints. After that, they asked me to leave. Two hours later, they called me and said that the body had been removed and there were no suspicious circumstances surrounding Mr. Lake's death. I came back to the cottage and cleared up the mess as best I could. But," he pointed at the floor and ceiling, "I can't get rid of the stains. I've got professional cleaners and painters and decorators arriving this afternoon to deal with the rest. The next guests are arriving tomorrow. We can't cancel them. This time of year, the estate needs any cash it can get."

"Of course." Knutsen asked, "Were there any other boot or fingerprints that were unusual?"

McCloud laughed. "We don't take prints of our guests when they arrive. Anyway, you're the police. You should know what was and wasn't found."

Sign snapped, "We're specialist police. We've been asked to look at the suicide with fresh eyes. That requires us not to know details of what forensics found." He looked around the kitchen. "Aside from the mess that you discovered, was there anything that struck you as unusual in the room?"

McCloud rubbed his stubbly face. "Mr. Lake had venison stew on the go. And there were a brace of grouse and one woodcock hanging on the meat hook next to the Aga. They were fresh, caught that morning. I thought it was odd that a man who was going to kill himself would be preparing at least four days' worth of food. I took the birds and gave them to my wife. The stew I put in the bin."

Sign said, "In remote and interconnected parts of the world such as these, trusted men like you are paid to keep an eye on matters. On the day of Lake's death, did you see and vehicles go to the cottage?"

"I can't be in one place all the time. I have my rounds to do. Before coming to the cottage, I had to repair a fence, drive to Portree to get some food and cigarettes, and put turnips and other meal down for the deer. This time of year we don't kill deer; we feed them. They come down from the mountains because there's nothing to eat there in winter. I protect them now; I kill some of them in the warmer months. But they know me. I'm probably the only one around here who can feed them by hand. We're a family. No, I didn't see any visitors to the cottage. But I wasn't watching the cottage."

"Was Lake any different in demeanour compared to his last trips here?" Sign elaborated. "In other words, when you greeted him on arrival, did he seem different?"

"No. He always struck me as a private man who wanted a spot of solitude. He asked me about hunting and where were the best places to bag some game. If you ask me, he looked very happy to be here."

"Thank you very much, Mr. McCloud. You've been a great help."

McCloud checked his watch. "I need to check the upstairs boiler. It's been playing up lately. Is there anything else you need me for?"

"No. Carry on with your chores. We'll be here for five or ten minutes, then we'll take your sage advice and be on our way before the weather closes in." When McCloud was gone, Sign said to Knutsen, "Sit opposite me at the table."

Knutsen did so, wondering what this was about.

Sign grabbed a fire poker that was the length of his arm and placed it on the table. He sat. The poker was between them. "Imagine I'm Lake. Imagine you want me to kill myself. Imagine the poker is the shotgun. What would you say to me to ensure I put a gun in my mouth and blew my brains out?"

"I'd have to know your secrets; ones that you were deeply ashamed about. I'd confront you with those secrets to push you over the edge."

"That's half of the equation. When I was a youngster in MI6 I had a controller who was as wise as they come. And he'd been several times around the block in the Cold War. There was nothing he hadn't seen. He told me that if ever I fucked up and it came to the attention of a hostile foreign intelligence agency who tried to use my fuck up as blackmail against me, tell them 'publish and be damned'. It was sage advice. I'm bullet proof. Archer and Lake were not. But to know they were not requires an in depth understanding of their psyches. The whisperer knew exactly which buttons to press. He knew how to torture them."

"In plain speak, he knew them in person."

"Yes."

Knutsen inhaled deeply. "Ben – you could be so wrong about this. I know it's a massive coincidence that two MI6 officers killed themselves in the space of a week, but coincidences…"

"Are coincidences." Sign picked up the poker and put the tip into his mouth. "Boom." He put the poker back onto the table. "Archer ended his life in a haze of booze and drugs. It was still hard to do, but it's effective because not only does it shut down the body, it also makes the brain no longer care. But suicide by more immediate actions are incredibly exhausting. I've read about samurai who couldn't go through with committing harikari. They were dishonoured as a result, though cared for by the women folk in the tribe. The samurais would sleep for up to three days after sitting cross legged with a blade against their stomachs. It is that debilitating. Lake would have been in mental agony as he held the gun. And yet he still pulled the trigger. And we know that he hadn't planned to blow his head off. Food was prepared by him, he was out on a healthy walk and hunt in the morning, this cottage is his safe place once a year, and he has a loving wife and children."

"As far as we know."

Sign lowered his head. "I know his wife. She adores her husband."

"That could be the trigger."

"Adulation?" Sign replaced the poker next to the fire and gazed at the stunning mountain scenery outside. "The thought had occurred to me. There is nothing more beautiful than a person loving you unconditionally. It is rare, but in some cases it can breed a desire to stray from the path. It is possible that Lake had an affair."

"He felt claustrophobic?"

"No, he sought danger. It's an act of rebellion. He knew how good his wife is; therefore he wanted to taste a woman who was different."

"That sounds messed up."

"It is." Sign washed his hands in the sink. "I have an insider in MI6, but I doubt he'd find the glitch in Lake's history. So, infidelity is but one possibility. But actually the reason doesn't matter. What does is whether someone else knew exactly what would prompt him to put a gun to his head."

"What would you do if you were the whisperer?"

Sign smiled. "You don't want my mind in that space. Nobody does. It wouldn't be pleasant."

"Let me correct my question." Knutsen clasped his fingers on the table. "How would you kill me?"

"I'd tell you things."

"Such as?"

"Such as things I don't want to speak about." Sign's smile was the most glowing example of empathy. "Dear sir: you are the finest man. But to become that, we have to trip along the way."

"Such as executing a man because I fancied a bird who'd been clipped by that man."

"Clever use of language." Sign picked up the pot that had yesterday contained venison. "There are two breeds of man: those that solely care about themselves, and those who don't give a shit about themselves. You and I fall into the latter category. We look outwards, not inwards. We are the *publish and be damned* types. I couldn't kill you with words. Ditto, you couldn't kill me with blackmail. Basically, we don't care about any indiscretions. We just get on with the job in hand."

"And do you have any indiscretions?"

Sign waited five seconds before answering in a quiet voice. "Like you, I've killed people. I've screwed male and female brains. I've played chess on an international stage and at the highest stakes. And I've had to watch friends die. Friends from all over the world. All of that will stay with me for the rest of my life. But it can't be used against me. It is personal business. My business. If anyone tries to throw it against me I'll put a knife to their throat, and it won't be a bluff. Then I'd carry on with my life. My wife is always in my heart. I will never have another woman. She was the best. *Indiscretions* is the wrong word. *Bollocks to it all* is the right response if ever one doubts oneself. If Archer and Lake had fixed that phrase into their heads, they'd still be alive."

McCloud came downstairs rubbing his arms with a rag. "Boiler's sorted. Bloody thing hates the cold. I need to lock up, if you're finished here?"

"We're done." Sign winked at Knutsen. "We have to trade untamed beauty for a metropolitan bee hive. I know where I'd rather be. But work beckons. London it is."

CHAPTER 14

It was dark and rain was pounding the street in Weybridge. Hilt didn't care. He loved being wet. It was one of the many reasons that had got him through the hellish selection into the Special Boat Service and the resultant continuation training. In the course of his career in special forces and MI6, he'd spent nearly as much time in water as on dry land. And some of those waters had been icy oceans in January. He rang Smith. "Roberts is at home with her husband. There's no point me watching her tonight, unless you have specific instructions."

"No. Stay on her tomorrow. Any news on Sign?"

"He's got a guy called Tom Knutsen living with him. Knutsen's ex-Met police. But he's unusual – spent most of his career undercover. He resigned after executing a criminal."

"How do you know this?"

"Don't ask, don't tell. But I will say I have sources and techniques." Hilt walked away from the Roberts' property. "No doubt, Knutsen has gone into business with Sign. They're using their West Square flat as their base of operations."

"And Knutsen is down on his luck with cash, so Sign suggested he move in to the spare room. I'd have done the same, though God knows how Knutsen is putting up with Sign. Ben has so many brilliant facets, but he does tend to carve the world to his choosing." Smith was silent for a few seconds. "Knutsen was chosen by Sign to be his right-hand man. How old is he?"

"I'd estimate mid-thirties."

"Nearly fifteen years younger than Sign. Age is important. Sign wanted a younger business partner in case he needed to deploy him against men like you."

Hilt smiled. "I can deal with an undercover cop, with my right arm tied behind my back."

Smith's tone was icy as he said, "Ordinarily, yes. But consider this: Sign decides to set up business as a security consultant; Sign wants a shooter with a brain to help him run the business; he'd have tapped his contacts from his MI6 days to see who might qualify; he'd have been presented with candidates from MI6, MI5, SAS, and your old bunch. And yet he chose an undercover cop."

"He saw something different in Knutsen?"

"He saw something unconventional; someone who'd look at things differently compared to those who serve in spec ops, and someone..." Smith's mind tried to fill in the gaps. "Perhaps someone who'd lost someone."

"Like Sign and his wife?"

"Yes. Sign never makes mistakes when it comes to the people he works with. There's something unusual about Knutsen. Quite what it is, we don't know. But that doesn't matter. What does is he's proven he can be an executioner."

"Leave that to me. He won't know what hit him if he has a pop." Hilt got into his car. He was hoping to have a beer or two at home, watch *University Challenge* on BBCi catch up, before hitting the sack. Tomorrow he'd be up at six to watch Roberts. "Something else I've got to tell you. Roberts visited West Square yesterday evening. This morning, I watched Sign and Knutsen go to Heathrow airport."

"You were supposed to stay on Roberts!"

"Well, I decided to ignore you. I followed my gut. But what I didn't ignore from you is the certainty that I'd get sucked into an anti-surveillance choke hold if I got too close. So I used binos and a zoom lens camera. Sign and Knutsen got on a plane to Edinburgh."

Smith said nothing.

"Don't know why they went there."

"They went there to get an interconnecting flight to the Isle of Skye." Smith had anticipated this, but still the information was unsettling. In an authoritative voice, he said, "There is a tragedy in Skye that peaks Roberts' interest. She's continuing to liaise with Sign on matters that relate to matters that relate to me."

"Why don't you tell me what's going on?"

"That wasn't part of the deal." Smith added, "I want you to do something for me. It won't be pleasant. But it will be a puzzling message."

"What?"

Smith told him exactly what to do. Hilt had no problems with the instruction, even though he'd miss his favourite TV show.

Sign and Knutsen arrived back in West Square. Sign had barely spoken during the flights back to London. He was preoccupied and deep in thought.

Knutsen made a fire and asked, "What shall we have for dinner tonight?"

Sign was in his armchair. He looked up. "I'm sorry. I've been a tad distracted and hadn't thought about food. That's remiss of me. I'll put my coat on and nip out to the butcher and my vintner and pick us up two partridge and a bottle of Perdrix aux Choux."

Knutsen patted him on the shoulder. "It's time you let your brain rest. I'll order a Chinese takeaway."

Sign's voice was distant as he said, "Chinese food? Yes, I've had that many times – in Hong Kong, Beijing, Chengdu, and Xi'an, among many places in China. But I've not eaten it here."

"It will be different. You can thank the Americans for that. But at least it will allow you to rest."

Fifty minutes later, Knutsen handed Sign a plate containing Peking duck, pancakes, cucumber, and a soy sauce. Both men ate in silence in front of the fire, their plates on their laps.

When he'd finished eating, Sign said, "In 1995, I saw a Mongolian man attempt to ride his camel up a mountain in China. It was for a bet he'd made with four Chinese men. They thought he wouldn't make the summit. They were partially right. The camel dropped from exhaustion halfway up. The Mongolian man felt he had no choice other than to put his beloved beast out of its misery. He shot it dead, then carried on climbing. He reached the summit. We witnessed his achievement through telescopes. He descended and demanded payment for winning the bet. The Chinese men tried to argue with him, saying his camel failed him. But the Mongolian man stood his ground and said the bet was about him, not the camel. The Chinese men pulled out knives. I pulled a gun out and told them to pay up."

Knutsen laughed. "Is there *anything* in your life that is normal?"

"I suppose not." Sign chuckled, clapped his hands and said in a strong tone, "The Peking duck has reinvigorated me. There's a pub within walking distance that serves excellent real ales. What say you to a couple of jars and a game of darts?"

Hilt donned a black wig, glasses that had fake lenses, and a high vis jacket with the logo 'DHL'. He carried a small cardboard box within which were stones he'd picked up from a residential driveway. He walked down the street and rang the Roberts' doorbell. Given it was nine PM, cold, and dark, he expected Mr. Roberts to answer the door. Instead, it was Katy Roberts.

"Yes?" she said.

Hilt put on a Romanian accent. "I have a package for Elliot Roberts. It needs to be signed for."

Katy yawned. "Okay. I'll sign it." She held out her hand.

"No. It can only be Mr. Roberts. I'm under strict instructions and will get in trouble if he doesn't sign." He looked at the box. "It has a government stamp on here. Maybe passport? Bit too heavy for that, though. But it must be something important."

Katy was irritated. "My husband's in bed. He's not feeling well. Leave it at the local post office. He can collect the parcel tomorrow."

Hilt dropped his false accent. "Okay missy." He barged past her, withdrew a silenced pistol, and entered the house.

Katy screamed and tried to grab him. Hilt punched her with sufficient force to break her nose and slam her unconscious against the corridor wall. He walked upstairs. In the

114

bedroom, he saw Elliot Roberts sitting upright in bed, a bedside light on. He was reading a book. Roberts' mouth opened wide as he saw Hilt standing in the entrance, pointing his gun at him.

Hilt said, "Night, night," and pulled the trigger twice. The bullets ended Elliot Roberts' life.

Hilt walked downstairs. He grabbed Katy Roberts' jaw and slapped her on the face. "Time to wake up." He had to repeat the action several times.

Five minutes later, she moaned, opened her eyes, looked horrified when she saw who was in front of her, and lashed out with her legs.

Hilt ignored the blows. "Nah, love. That's not going to do it."

Blood from her nose was drooling down her lower face. She spoke, despite the movement of her mouth causing agonising bolts of pain in her head. "What do you want? Money? Me?" She sucked in air and looked at Hilt with defiance in her expression. "You've been here before, haven't you? Bastard! Your DNA will be all over this house. We'll get you."

"We, Inspector Roberts? You haven't got any pals in your house tonight. And my DNA doesn't exist." Hilt's grip on Roberts' jaw tightened as he put his face close to her face. "Listen carefully, sweetheart. I've just made a delivery. It's upstairs. It might not be your kind of thing, but I don't care. I'm just the messenger. What I do care about is national security. You're interfering in that. Go back to PC Plod work. Zero contact with Sign and Knutsen. It's your choice, darling. But just remember – I can find you anywhere on this planet."

He slammed her head against the wall and left.

It was just after ten PM. The Metropolitan Police Commissioner was in the A&E reception of St. Thomas' Hospital. Britain's most senior police officer was unshaven and wearing jeans, boots, and a Christmas jumper depicting reindeer and snow. The jumper had been given to him by his children as part of their attempts to get him into the festive spirit. When he'd got the call about Katy Roberts, he hadn't thought to change. He just came straight over to the hospital. Given it was a Friday night, most of the people around him were injured drunks. The place stank of booze and disinfectant. Knutsen and Sign strode in and shook hands with the commissioner.

Knutsen asked, "How is she?"

"Mild concussion. Her nose needs realigning. But otherwise she'll live." The commissioner rubbed his eyes. "I've talked to her. She told me exactly what happened. When she came to, she found her husband. The doctors aren't worried about her physical health. But they are worried about depression… grief, call it what you want."

The men sat opposite him. Sign asked, "Was this a message?"

"Yes. To you. Back off or she dies."

Sign and Knutsen glanced at each other.

Sign asked, "What's your recommended course of action?"

The commissioner looked directly at Sign. "Last time I checked, Ben Sign is above the law. Rumour had it that I might be way down the ladder from you. That didn't happen. You resigned from your organisation."

"Rumour is a temperamental mistress." Sign showed the commissioner the palms of his hands. "Sir, I am now simply a humble civilian."

"Technically you are. But I know that you know people and stuff that's way beyond my pay grade." The commissioner sighed. "What happened to Katy?"

Sign pointed to Knutsen while keeping his eyes on the commissioner. "Who was Knutsen to you?"

The commissioner frowned. "A brilliant cop. Excelled in undercover work. The jobs he did would have broken most men. But he survived… until the end."

Sign nodded. "He was the man you sent in to do the laundry. We're dealing with a very similar man. He won't be law enforcement or a criminal. He will be paramilitary – probably ex-special forces, trained by men with my qualifications."

The commissioner glanced around, worried that the conversation might be overheard by the drunks in the room. "Formerly your lot?"

"Could be. But he could also be Mossad, Spetsnaz, SVR, FSB, DGSCE, BND et cetera. The list goes on."

"Katy said he spoke with a London accent."

Knutsen interjected. "I've heard Sign speak with a South African accent."

The commissioner stood. "Let's speak somewhere more privately." He gestured to the back of the waiting room. "I've got two of my best firearms officers in Katy's room. They'll kill anyone who shouldn't be in her room."

Outside the hospital, the commissioner stood in front of a placard saying 'Smoking Is Strictly Prohibited In The Hospital Grounds'. He lit a cigarette. Sign and Knutsen were with

117

him. No one else was nearby. The commissioner said, "I authorized you to investigate the suicide of Archer. Roberts' husband was brutally assaulted and his home trashed. I authorised you to investigate Lake's suicide. Katy was assaulted, her husband is shot dead, and the killer tells her to mind her business because she's messing with national security." He looked at Sign. "What would you do if you were me?"

Sign answered, "If it is a matter of national security, you should go to the foreign secretary and ask him what's going on. If you get no joy from him, demand an audience with the prime minister. And if you get no joy from her, go to the attorney general. You of all people know that on UK soil we don't kill individuals unless there is an immediate threat to life. I don't think this is a UK organisation backing this."

"So, you think this is a foreign agency?"

"It could be. We kill people overseas. Foreign intelligence agencies kill people on our soil."

The commissioner inhaled deeply on his cigarette and blew out a stream of smoke. "If we've got a foreign individual or cell working our patch I need to involve MI5."

"I doubt that will be necessary."

The commissioner flicked his cigarette at the no smoking placard. "You MI6 people always hate MI5."

Sign shook his head. "We're just different breeds of animals."

"And MI6 always thinks it's superior."

"Just different." Sign touched the commissioner on the arm. "Sir: this must be stressful for you. When one of your own gets walloped, it's hard to see the wood for the trees.

But I don't think we're looking at trees. I think we're searching for a solitary oak. That's the person who's doing this. But he has a helper. And the helper is the person who killed Katy's husband."

Knutsen said, "We call him the limpet. He's been following us. Sign spotted him."

The commissioner asked, "Is he watching us now?"

"Almost certainly." Sign looked away. Ambulances were parked nearby, others were delivering casualties to A&E. Aside from the glow from headlights and lamps, most of the surroundings were bathed in darkness. He asked the police chief, "Do you have any armed officers – plain-clothed or uniformed – around the exterior perimeter of the hospital?"

The commissioner replied, "No."

Sign looked at Knutsen. "Walk the perimeter. Kill anyone with a gun."

When Knutsen was gone, Sign said, "Knutsen will tackle the limpet. I will tackle the oak. In the interim, we have a problem."

The commissioner nodded. "Katy." He pulled out another cigarette. "You're thinking two things. First: will she be safe. Second: should I continue to deploy her as liaison with you."

"Correct." Sign sighed. "She won't want to go back to her home. Probably she'll sell the property. You'll be tempted to put her in a safe house, under armed guard. My suggestion to you is to ignore that gut instinct. Does she have relatives?"

"A sister in Northumbria. She's got a cottage in the middle of nowhere."

"Don't put her there. The limpet will find her."

"But the limpet didn't kill her." The commissioner couldn't fathom Sign's logic. "So long as she doesn't communicate with you and Knutsen, she's safe."

"No. She's a move on the chess board. It's too late for her now. She'll be made an example of, even if she never speaks to me or Knutsen again."

"I don't understand."

"Somebody persuaded Archer and Lake to kill themselves. I have a theory as to why, but I need more dead bodies before I can substantiate the theory."

"You want more dead bodies?!"

Sign nodded. "I'm dealing with a serial killer. The most superb one I've ever heard about. I can only beat him if he gives me a pattern. Even then, it's a major problem. How many serial killers are you aware of who've killed men with words?"

The commissioner lit his cigarette. "You're theory might be crazy."

"And yet Katy Archer's husband is dead." Sign pulled out a piece of paper and a pen. He wrote an address on the slip. "No safe houses; no relatives; absolutely nothing official or pertaining to family. The limpet will find them and kill her if I continue with my enquiries. But Katy Roberts is so deeply embedded in what's happening it's impossible to pull her out." He folded the note in half, obscuring the address he'd written on the paper. He waited, looking out into the blackness. The commissioner became impatient. Sign wasn't. He just stared.

Knutsen emerged out of the blackness. Sign walked up to him and asked, "What do you think?"

Knutsen replied, "If the limpet's here, we're dealing with a ghost."

"Then we're dealing with a ghost." Sign spun around and walked back to the police chief. He handed the note to him. "It's the flat below me. Students previously occupied the place. It's now empty. Knutsen and I will sort out the place. Katy will be safe there. Knutsen and I will ensure that."

"I'm going to take her off the Archer and Lake cases."

"Then you're signing her death sentence! And you'd be giving her no chance to obtain revenge against the two persons who killed her husband. What kind of life will it be for her to live in hiding with only SWAT operatives for company? She needs to be very close to Knutsen and I until we identify and destroy the two men who killed Archer, Lake, and Elliot Roberts. There is no alternative."

The commissioner said, "Maybe it's only one man. The limpet."

"You could be right. But I maintain my position that the limpet is hired help. No. We're dealing a far higher power. Almost certainly a senior, uber intelligent, highly trained spook. Knutsen and I call him 'the whisperer'. He's our serial killer."

"So, why's the whisperer doing this?"

"The million dollar question." Sign looked at Knutsen. "I presume Katy will be released from hospital tomorrow. I will make arrangements to secure the flat below ours. Call your pals to sort furnishings. They need to come over in two hours' maximum and set to work. A bed, chairs etcetera. It'll just be the basics. She'll make the flat look pretty in due course. Meanwhile Mr. Knutsen, do you know a trustworthy woman?"

Knutsen nodded.

"Good. Take her late night shopping."

Sign said to the police chief. "Whatever you do, don't take Katy off this case. I believe the whisperer has a kill list. This isn't over. Trust me."

The commissioner would have ridiculed Sign's comment under other circumstances. But Katy's plight was too serious to warrant macho jockeying. "The case remains yours, so long as you understand that you are part of the problem. The whisperer killed Katy's husband to warn you off. He fears you. No one else. That means he knows you."

Sign said, "Can I see Katy?"

The commissioner nodded. "In a couple of hours. She's in treatment right now." He checked his watch. "I need to head off. I'll tell the two SCO19 guys in her room not to kill you when you enter Katy's room."

Knutsen knocked on Wendy's door in the council tenement high rise in Brixton. When she opened the door, Knutsen said, "Hello Wendy. Sorry to turn up unannounced."

She smiled. "That's okay, Mr. Knutsen. Come in. I was just making a pot of tea. Take your shoes off though. I've just had a new carpet fitted."

Knutsen entered the tiny, immaculate apartment. Wendy's son David was sitting on the sofa, playing *Mortal Kombat* on his Xbox.

Wendy called out from the kitchen, "Milk, no sugar? Right?"

"That's right, Wendy." Knutsen sat next to David and watched the TV screen. He said to David, "Your opponent's got a massive uppercut. Go for his legs."

David smiled. "You telling me how to play this game, old man?"

Knutsen leaned forward. "That's it. Hit his shins now!"

David followed Knutsen's instruction. "Got him. KO, brother!" He paused the game.

Sign said, "I need to take your mother out for an hour or so after the cuppa. Are you going to be okay?"

"You mean, am I going to go out and hang round crack dealers?"

"Something like that."

"Nah. You beat them up big time. They think they're tough, until they meet real tough. I don't hang round those guys anymore. Dojo next Wednesday?"

"Bang on." Knutsen held out his fist. "Yes, yes, I know what you're about to say. White boys can't do this. But just man up and get over yourself."

David laughed and pressed his fist against Knutsen's fist. "You on a date with my mum? I'll kick your ass if you are."

Knutsen smiled. "No. Your mother and I are bonded by friendship revolving around our mutual concern about an errant boy."

"Errant? What does that mean?"

"Fuck up. And I'm referring to you."

"Yeah, I got that bit mister." David placed his controller down. "I wanted your advice. I'm thinking about applying for a job with the police. I've checked online and I've just about got the academic grades. But..."

"But you've got a petty crime record that disqualifies you from applying. It's just as well you know me." Knutsen pulled out his mobile phone and called the head of the

Metropolitan Police Service. "Sir, I have a young man – age eighteen – who wishes to join your ranks. He's intelligent, physically very fit, now and again needs a clip round the ear, but is ready to be a man. The problem is, he's grown up around idiot boys. He'll be on your database for stuff he shouldn't have done. I know ordinarily that would mean he can't apply. But he's a great kid. And he knows the streets in south London like the back of his hand. And I reckon, if he's up for it, he could go into my former line of work."

Undercover assignments.

"Would you entertain his application? No other favours. He'll have to pass the physical and mental tests to get in to Henley. And if he doesn't pass those and the Henley training process, then that's as far as it goes. I just want to give the lad a break."

When the call ended, Knutsen said to David, "I'll help you with the application process. The god of police has just said that anything you've done in your past doesn't pertain to your future."

"Pertain?"

"Never mind. I'll also get you a dictionary." Knutsen smiled. "You've got a job interview coming up with one of the finest police forces in the world. You need to get a suit, shirt, tie, and black shoes. No gangster bling for you any more, Mr. Man."

David was overjoyed. He ran into the kitchen shouting, "Mum! Mum!"

Wendy was in tears as she walked into the lounge while holding a tray containing a pot of tea and cups. "I can't thank you enough."

Knutsen stood. In a formal voice he said to David, "Squeaky clean from now on in. You got it?"

David nodded, brimming with enthusiasm.

Knutsen held out his hand. "No fist pumps for you anymore, David. You've just graduated into manhood. That means we shake hands."

David shook hands, smiling as wide as a Cheshire cat.

"Get on your smart phone and research Wyatt Earp. He started out life like you, though in the States. His early life didn't go so well. The law wasn't his friend. But he became one of the best cops in America." Knutsen grinned. "The best cops are always the ones who know the wrong side of the law. Next Monday I'll buy you a suit. I'll be here nine AM sharp. Now, fuck off and download the Met application form."

David laughed. "I owe you one, man."

"You can call me sir. And I'll put you through hell to make sure you graduate top of your class at Henley Police Academy."

When David was in his bedroom, Wendy poured tea. Her hands were shaking. "You've no idea how much this means to me. Did you encourage David to apply to the police?"

"No. In fact, we never spoke about my job. Either it rubbed off, or he just wants to protect his mum."

"Whatever the reason, my goodness me, I couldn't have asked for better." Wendy asked, "Is that why you came over? David? Job applications?"

Knutsen sipped his tea. "Actually, I was as surprised as you at his decision. I need your help. And I'm out of my league on this one. There's a woman who's just suffered a bereavement – her husband. She'll want somewhere to stay but it must be her private space. I've got a flat sorted, but I've no idea what to put in it, aside from a bed and other furniture."

"She'll choose."

"I know, but this is an emergency. I need stuff – cosmetics, bathroom soaps, everything just to tie her over for the next few days."

"Where's the flat?"

Knutsen put down his tea and touched Wendy's hand. "I trust you so much that I can't tell you. It would endanger you and David. It's a police matter."

"She might be hunted?"

"Yes."

Wendy was deep in thought. "What colour is she?"

"White."

Wendy laughed. "Just because I don't have a cock between my legs doesn't mean I know what white girls like."

"Yeah, but you've still got a head start on me."

"When did her husband die?"

"Today. He was murdered."

"Fucking hell." Wendy patted her hand against her braided locks. "What hair colour is she?"

"Blond."

"Real colour or dyed?"

"No idea."

"Age?"

Knutsen shrugged. "Late thirties. Forties. Something like that."

"What scent does she wear?"

"Scent?!"

"Perfume."

"I don't know! I've only met her twice."

"So, you've not had sex with her?"

"No, Wendy!"

Wendy patted him on the hand. "Okay. I know exactly what we need to do. You're absolutely right. We need to create a private place for her. But it must also be a kind place. I'll get what you need to see her through the next forty eight hours. Most of it will be wrong, but that doesn't matter. No one complains that hair products are wrong when they go to their hotel room. There's a pharmacy down the road that's open tonight. We'll start there. What about her clothes?"

"I'm going to her house later. I'll collect them."

"Fold them carefully. It's awkward. You're going to have to get her knickers and bras. I suggest I come with you to her house after shopping and do that. You can tell her that a woman packed her undies. Would that be okay?"

Knutsen kissed Wendy on the cheek. "That would be more than okay. But I must warn you, there's blood in her bedroom."

Wendy shrugged. "Us women are used to far worse than that. Let's get this lady sorted."

Sign entered Katy's hospital room. The two firearms officers were clad in uniform and body armour and were holding Heckler & Koch submachine guns. Using his phone, one of them took a photo of Sign and sent it to the commissioner. Their boss replied and confirmed the man in the room was Sign.

"Could you wait outside the door?" Sign looked at Katy Roberts. "I'd like a moment alone with her."

The cops hesitated.

Sign said, "There's no window in the room. The door is the only way in and out. She's safe."

Reluctantly the officers complied.

Roberts was in a bed, sitting upright. Her nose was covered with a plaster cast. Her eyes were red and her hair dishevelled. She was staring at the wall and didn't seem aware that Sign was in the room.

Sign pulled up a chair, sat next to her, and held her hand. "Katy, it's Ben."

Slowly, Katy moved her head and looked at him. "Ben… Ben Sign."

"Yes, that's right." His tone was quiet and sympathetic. "I'm so very sorry to hear about your loss."

"Loss?" Roberts' voice was distant and weak. "I didn't lose my husband. I found him. In our bedroom"

"Yes you did."

"I... I need to make arrangements. Funeral."

"There's no rush for that." Sign chose his words carefully. "Your husband's in the care of police and specialists who are examining his…"

"Body."

"Yes. His body. Friends and family will help you with the funeral. And if you don't have many of those, Knutsen and I will help."

It was clear that Roberts was in deep shock. "I can't go back there. I can't. My home. How could I? It's not my home anymore. It's a murder scene. My husband… Elliot." She gripped his hand tight. "Is this what your world's like? Men coming into houses and talking about national security while murdering people?"

"Sometimes it can be. Katy, I need to ask you a question – aside from the Archer and Lake suicides, are you working on any other cases at the moment?"

Roberts shook her head. "The commissioner said I had to be ring fenced. Only work with you, he said."

"Have you done any other work recently that could be perceived to be an intrusion on national security?"

Roberts rubbed sweat off her brow. "No." She started weeping. "My husband was killed because of Lake, Archer, and my liaison with you. And I was... Jesus, I did unarmed combat training where I got a few bruises, but I've never been punched as hard as I was this evening. It was like a hammer hitting my face." She touched her nose.

"The doctors say your nose will be fine in a few hours. A day or two at worst. But it will hurt for a while."

"Hurt? I've got worse pain that will last far longer."

"I know." Sign recalled how he felt when his wife was murdered. It took him years before he stopped reaching out in his sleep, hoping to put his arm around her only to wake up in the middle of the night realising he was alone and she was gone. "I'm very sorry that I brought this on to you and your husband."

"You? You didn't do this. The person who killed my husband did this!"

Sign was motionless. "The police bereavement service will help you."

Roberts withdrew her hand from his. "Tea and sympathy brigade? They can't bring him back."

"No, they can't. I have two propositions that may help. I'm on very good terms with the landlord who owns the flats in West Square. The landlord has agreed to let you the flat immediately below mine. You're in danger. Knutsen and I will be on hand to negate that danger. You can have the flat for a few days or far longer if you choose. Right now, Knutsen is getting the place fitted out. And he's collecting your things from your house. A woman is helping him. Only she will handle your more delicate belongings, although Knutsen won't allow her to know where you're being re-housed. Would that be okay?"

Roberts nodded. "I need to clean up the blood and sell the house."

"We have people who can take that burden off your shoulders."

"Yes, yes. I'll move in to the flat." She was shaking. "What is the other proposition?"

"I wonder if you'd like to keep working with us to find the bastards who did this to Elliot?"

Roberts replied, "I'm in no fit state."

In numerous places around the globe, Sign had been in similar situations with his foreign agents. The agents were amateurs, recruited by him to spy on their countries. Sometimes their nerves would crack; other times they would be confronted by severe threats to their lives; and on a few occasions a colleague or family member of theirs had been murdered. One of the hardest parts of being an MI6 case officer was to persuade agents to carry on risking their lives. But judgement was needed. Sometimes the case officer needed to know when to back off and let the agent retire from the secret world. Sign wondered whether his judgement was accurate right now. Should he let Roberts retire? Or should he encourage her to get back to work?

He said, "You can't grieve until you know why this happened. On a battlefield, a soldier can't walk away, even though his mates have been destroyed. He has to continue fighting. Only later do the demons kick in. Before then, he has to kill what's in front of him."

Roberts looked into his eyes. "You send people to their deaths."

"Sometimes yes; sometimes no. Twenty four hours after my wife was murdered in South America, I had to go to Mumbai to meet a chemistry professor who was attempting to sell biological weapons to Yemen. I just wanted to sleep; let the world eat me up. The professor pulled a gun on me. I smiled. Part of me wanted him to pull the trigger. But then I thought about my wife and what she'd want. I knew she'd want me to stop my death and stop potentially thousands of deaths in Yemen. I put a knife in the professor's throat and held it there until he was dead. Blood was all over my arms. It was messy. I washed up and got on a plane to London. When I arrived, I was met by my MI6 boss at the airport. He told me to go to El Salvador and find my wife's killer. It took me three months. And along the way, I had to cut through a number of bandits. But when I found the identity and location of the killer, I spoke to him while holding a gun against his head. He was only twenty seven, but a ruthless gangster. He told me the reason he'd killed my wife was because she worked for an NGO that was funnelling food into his country but not to his criminal gang. I thought, my wife died for that? It felt such a waste. I shot him. I was a different man back then. When I returned to my London home, grief overwhelmed me and I collapsed. But I did at least have closure that the piece of scum who killed my wife was off the planet."

"Your accent has changed."

Sign smiled. "It bends with the wind."

"I didn't know you had a wife. I didn't know she was murdered."

"Why would you? For most of my adult life I've been kept secret. That might sound alluring. Quickly, it becomes otherwise. If you're secret, you don't exist. If you don't exist, you are not alive." Sign's accent returned to that of an aristocrat. "Grief is purgatory. And I died a long time ago. The question is, will you tread a similar path? Or will you give up on everything?"

"I… I…"

"Forget about the next few years. Time and grieving will deal with that. Focus on the next few months."

Roberts winced as she got out of bed. "I want to get out of here. I want to catch my husband's killer."

Sign looked at her while wondering if he'd just made a godawful mistake. "We'll get the doctors in here to make a final assessment. Once you're out of this silly smock and properly dressed, I'll drive you to your new home. It'll have to be a convoluted drive because I'm certain the killer is watching you, me, or Knutsen. But I'll get you there safe and sound. By the way, can you wash men's clothes?"

"What?!"

Sign winked at her. "I didn't say any of this came for free."

"You have to be kidding me!"

"I might be. That's for you to decide." Sign smiled. "I'll wait in the corridor with your burly bodyguards. Let me know when you're ready."

CHAPTER 15

John Smith met Karl Hilt in a grubby pub in north London. Most people would have wondered why someone of Smith's refinement would be in the establishment. But, Hilt understood – it was the last place anyone would expect to find Smith; therefore it made an excellent meeting location.

It was noon. The pub only contained four other customers and a bored-looking bartender. Smith was sitting by a corner table, half a glass of beer in front of him. Hilt sat opposite him and said, "She's out of the hospital. Eleven thirty last night."

"Armed police took her?"

"No. Sign."

Smith's expression was neutral as he said in his icy accent, "He has more skills than the police. He knew you'd be on her. I assume he put her in a car. Where did they arrive?"

"I lost them at Piccadilly Circus. I wouldn't have done if you'd given me a team. The place was heaving, but we could have still put a box around Sign."

Smith chuckled. "Piccadilly Circus? He's taking the mickey. It was theatrical and a finger up to you."

"Yeah, I know." Hilt added, "I went back to her house in Weybridge. She's not there."

"She won't be. I doubt she will ever go back there." Smith took a sip of his beer and winced. "The beer's flat, and this place smells like a fishmongers." He smiled. "But you and I have tasted and smelled worse."

"True. I once had to eat goats' balls in Afghanistan while pretending to be a U.S. Green Beret playing hearts and bleedin' minds with the locals." He leaned across the table. "Where's he taken her?"

Smith looked out of the adjacent window. "If he was dumb, he'd have taken her to a safe house somewhere in the country, or even overseas. But Sign is the opposite of dumb. He'd know you'd track her. And if I gave the command, you'd kill her. I know what Sign has done. He wants Roberts to continue to liaise with him on matters that are important to me."

"Murder? National security? What is this about?"

Smith returned his gaze to Hilt. "If you persist with those questions I *will* get you a team of men. And they'll put bullets in you."

"Alright, pal. I get your point." Hilt could easily kill Smith. But his employer's money was important to him. Plus, Smith's mind was beyond his reach. "Where is she and what's the next move?"

Smith smiled. "I will tell you what has happened since last night. Sign has decided that he only trusts Katy Roberts in the Metropolitan Police Service. He will have used his expertise in human character assessment to reach that judgement. Think of it this way – she's a pawn he's sent out on the chess board. She's too committed to the fight. He knows that. So, the best he can do is put knights around her. And the reason he's done that is not just because of chivalry. He needs her to flush you and me out. He's worked out that whether she's in the game or not, I can crush her. It would be a message to him. Where is she? Extremely close to Sign and this man Knutsen. What's the next move? Forget Roberts for now. She serves no purpose, unless things deteriorate. So, we have a change of plan. Put your energies into Sign and Knutsen. But take some time off first. I want Sign to get frustrated that nothing's happening for a period of time. In one month's time, I will do something that should peak Sign, Knutsen, and Roberts' interest. I will call you before that event and give you details of a specific location. That's when you're back on duty. Watch Sign and Knutsen. But keep your distance. If Roberts, Sign, and Knutsen do nothing it means Roberts is no longer the Met liaison to Sign; no one else in the Met has taken over her job; Sign and Knutsen are no longer advisors to the police. But, if they move after my next event, we have a problem."

"Shouldn't I just solve that problem?"

Smith smiled. "I know exactly what you're referring to. No. Taking Sign out of the equation would put me back to square one. I'd have to work out who has replaced him and is causing me problems. That person won't be as good as Sign, but he or she would be given infinitely more resources. I'd have a highly trained pack of dogs on my back."

Hilt had no idea what Smith was talking about.

Smith knew that. "I keep my own counsel. It's best you don't know what I know. That said, if I give the order, kill Sign, Knutsen, and Roberts."

Four hours later, Knutsen knocked on the door of the flat below Sign's flat. "Katy. It's Tom."

Roberts opened the door. Her face was ashen; eyes lids swollen; and her left arm was shaking.

Gently, Knutsen said, "Sign's cooking some weird Polish dish for dinner. We wondered if you'd like to join us?"

"What… what time?"

"About seven." Knutsen suspected that Roberts had no concept of time. "In three hours. That'll give you time for a nap, if you like; or a walk. When you're ready, just let yourself in."

"Shouldn't you be locking your door, in light of... of..."

"Circumstances? The two flats below you are empty. It's only you, me, and Sign in the block. This afternoon, I've got experts arriving to install higher security on the downstairs communal door. It'll be like Fort Knox. Once all the fittings are done I'll give you details – new security codes, keys, and anything else. We don't need to lock internal doors. But I wouldn't blame you if you bolted your door at night."

"I... I don't know if I'm up for company tonight."

Knutsen expected her to say that. "You need to eat. We don't need to talk. It's just a plate of food."

"I don't feel hungry."

"That'll be due to shock. But, you'll start getting dizzy if you don't get grub inside you. I tell you what – why don't I knock on your door at seven? You can let me know then whether you're up for a bite."

That evening, Sign served up plates of pierogi dumplings, bigos stew, and cabbage rolls. Roberts and Knutsen were sitting at his dining table. Roberts had made an effort with her hair and attire, her nose cast was off, but she still looked like someone had knocked her for six.

Her voice was barely audible as she said, "Thank you. The flat is nice. The food looks nice." She pushed a fork through the stew but didn't eat.

Knutsen looked at Sign and shook his head.

Sign said, "Mrs. Roberts - it would be vulgar for us to eat before you start eating."

She put her fork down and bowed her head. "Just eat."

"No. Tell me about Elliot."

Knutsen wanted to grab Sign and tell him to shut up.

She raised her head. "Elliot?"

"Your husband."

"Dead husband."

"He's still your husband and always will be. Tell me anything."

She was silent for a minute. "I met him at university. He… he wasn't much to look at really. But he was interesting. He used to do magic tricks in front of students in between lectures. Not for money. It was just fun for him. My girlfriends and I tried to work out how he did the tricks. We couldn't. He made me smile. We dated. Got married. No kids because there was a problem with one of us. He took me to Thailand, India in Spring to see the lakes fill up with rainfall in Rajasthan, so many other places. When he got home from work – he was a lawyer – he liked watching Eastenders. God knows why. He used to pat me on the bottom and tell me I was the greatest woman who'd ever existed. He lost his job but never got depressed about that. He had a smile. He only wanted sex when I wanted sex."

Knutsen blurted, "Ben you're intruding on her grief!"

Roberts shook her head. "No he's not. He's helping me. Elliot cuddled me." Tears streamed down her face as she said, "He took me to Mount Snowden once. By then we didn't

138

have the money to fly off here there and everywhere. I didn't care. On the summit he picked me up and kissed me. I was on top of the world." She looked at Sign. "That was my husband." Her voice shook as she said, "Elliot was everything I needed. Now he's gone."

Sign clasped his hands, as if he was praying. "Have you thought about what kind of funeral you want?"

She shook her head. "It never… never occurred to me. Not at this age."

"Would you consider cremation?"

"We… we were never religious. Not that it matters, I guess. I don't know if religion dictates what kind of funeral you should have."

Sign said, "It doesn't matter what religion you do or don't follow. What does matter are memories. Perhaps you could scatter your husband's ashes on Mount Snowden."

"Yes. Yes, that would be perfect. Why did you cook Polish food tonight?"

"Because my wife was Polish. Today is the anniversary of her death." Sign smiled. "But her departure was years ago. I still love every second I spent with her. I too am not religious. It's odd though. I feel she's with me. I'm fascinated by my ignorance. I believe electricity is the key. It drives our bodies. I also hypothesise that it drives our souls, in life and death. If we can understand electricity, we can understand not only life and death, but also why we can feel people's presences when they're not around."

In a stern voice, Knutsen said, "Ben – back off from the intellectual and philosophical shit."

Sign didn't reply. He watched Roberts put a mouthful of food into her mouth.

She said, "Elliot is now a force of electricity. He's here. He transfers electricity to me. I transfer my electricity to him." She nodded. "He gives me his energy. Yes. Yes! He's with me."

"Always." Sign pushed Roberts' plate an inch closer to her. "If it doesn't pain you too much, perhaps you'd care to join Mr. Knutsen and me on a walk around the block after dinner. Christmas lights are in abundance, street lights are illuminated, cars will pass by with their headlights on. My wife is out there. So is your husband. And so is the woman Knutsen wanted to marry for real, outside of his former undercover work." He touched her hand. "Shall we join them and pay our respects?"

They ate in silence.

When Roberts finished her food, Sign asked her, "Why did you join the police?"

Roberts frowned. "I don't really know. It was a whim. I liked watching *Inspector Morse*, *Prime Suspect*, and other cerebral police TV dramas in the '90s. Maybe they rubbed off on me. I was intrigued by detective work."

"And you became the living embodiment of Morse and DCI Jane Tennison. A detective. But you went one step further – you joined Special Branch."

Roberts nodded. "The police's most secret unit. I was intrigued by the unit. They worked behind closed doors. Regular detectives and uniform weren't allowed in SB's offices. But, I never set out to be in SB."

"Perhaps you wanted to hide. More accurately, you wanted anonymity while performing a most noble task."

Knutsen muttered, "She just wanted a fucking job."

Sign ignored the comment. "Knutsen needed the same. He was never happier than when he was working alone; no other cop watching over him. His friends around him were armed robbers and killers. And the thrill of it was that one day he would betray them."

Knutsen looked at Sign. The former MI6 officer was right.

Sign continued. "I was the same. Though it is an organisation, the elegance of British Intelligence is that it gives vent for people like me. Spooks are a bunch of mavericks. Loners. Non-conformists. Rebels. People who spend years in the company of foreign spies who want to put bullets in the back of our skulls when our backs are turned. We'd rather all of that than spending one second in the company of our peers and bureaucracy. The three of us are different breeds of animal compared to normal people. Vive la différence." Sign's eyes widened. "And yet we wish to connect with normal folk. But how difficult is that? Angels or devils walking the Earth trying to make sense of the planet's populous. We try to make friends, but fail because we don't understand what friendship is. We marry. They leave us or die."

"Ben!" Knutsen wanted to guide Roberts out of the room and apologise for Sign's words.

Sign persisted. "But here's the thing: Knutsen successfully mentors a young man called David. The poor lad is from the wrong side of the tracks. Mr. Knutsen is in the process of solving that. You, Mrs. Roberts, take disabled children to a skating rink in Bedfordshire. You make them feel that anything is possible."

Quietly, she said, "I make them feel whole. How did you know that?"

Sign made a dismissive gesture with his hand. "What I know is irrelevant. What I don't know is most relevant."

"And what about you?" she asked.

Sign looked away. It sounded like he was talking to himself when he said, "Most foreign agents I've dealt with have been traitors to their country. Some of them have been double agents. It didn't matter to me. When I looked them in the eyes I saw mirrors to my soul. It sounds melodramatic, but it's the truth. They were like me. They were lost. I didn't care what head office said about the people I ran as a case officer. I knew the beating heart of my flock. HQ didn't. I bought a house for an impoverished Chinese man who earlier tried to garrotte me. He had a wife and four children. MI6 once wanted me to bludgeon a Venezuelan woman, shove her in the boot of a car, and get her to America. She was working for the Russians. British Intelligence and the CIA wanted to interrogate her. But, here's the thing – I liked her because she taught me how to climb the mountain of Pico Bolivar. And she fed me breads and meat at the summit. She knew that I knew she was a traitor to my cause. She had a fiancée and didn't want to die in an American or British black site. I told her she was free. And I also told her to take her beloved to Bolivia and start a family there. I lied to MI6 and said she'd never turned up to our last intended meeting." Sign looked at Roberts. "I could give you a hundred other examples. Nations rage against each other. But it needn't be that way with people. The trick is to know who can stop people slitting each other's throats. That's where we come in, even though it means we lose a little bit of ourselves with every kind deed."

"Because we lose a bit of what we want." Roberts nodded. "Connection with others." She breathed deeply. "You're putting my husband into that melting pot."

"Perhaps I am."

Tears ran down Roberts' face. "So, this is my destiny?"

"I'm afraid it is." Sign held her hand. "My destiny; Knutsen's destiny; your destiny. But, we hold on to hope and feel more than most. Elliot's death is the most agonising pain. Elliot's murder requires the most agonising vengeance. We can do the former; and only people like us can do the latter." Sign looked at Knutsen.

The former undercover cop nodded at him.

They took a walk around South London. Sign pointed at electric lights. Roberts smiled, cried, went stoic, smiled again, and cried again. When she was in bed in her West Square flat, Sign and Knutsen retired to their lounge. Knutsen lit a fire. Sign poured calvados.

Sign asked, "What do you think?"

Knutsen sat in his armchair. "You've made her think about grief differently by explaining to her that she must be cautious about grieving someone very unlike her."

"Yes."

"Not your finest hour."

"No. But necessary." Sign placed another log on the fire. "My finest hours are usually the worst. The moral compass spins in confusion."

"You did the right thing. And it was clever." Knutsen watched Sign and wondered how he'd managed to bear such tremendous ethical complexity throughout his adult life. There was no doubt Sign was an extremely good man who'd devoted his life to saving others. But, unlike soldiers who return from a battlefield, Sign's brain was constantly on the battlefield. He was permanently in war. "We need light relief while we drink. What's light relief for you? Chess?"

Sign sat opposite him, cradling his calvados. "No. Chess puts me back on duty."

"Cards?"

"My father taught me never to play cards. He said it led to drink and debauchery in ports. He was a very clever sailor."

Knutsen picked up a copy of the *Radio Times*. "There's a political debate on TV."

"Boring!"

"On one of the other channels there's a film about cowboys."

Sign narrowed his eyes. "Cowboys or homesteaders?"

"I never know the difference."

Sign smiled. "I do, but that's irrelevant. A cowboy movie it is. Did I tell you about the time I was in Oregon and..."

"Now that is fuckin' irrelevant. Just drink your drink and watch the damn movie."

Sign smiled. "Sage words. But before we switch the TV on, I need to tell you something. Tomorrow I want your help. But I won't blame you if you refuse."

"Refuse?"

Sign looked at the window. "We have to do something that may get both of us killed. What say you?"

Knutsen smiled.

CHAPTER 16

It was early morning as Sign drove his vehicle across Cambridgeshire and into Norfolk. He was alone in the car. The country road he was driving along was deserted. Rain was lashing his vehicle, though it was hard to predict if the inclement weather would persist – interspersed between the black clouds were patches of blue sky sending bolts of sunlight to the flat lands. High winds were moving the clouds at a rate of knots, changing where sunlight fell and darkness prevailed. The strength of the winds was sufficient to smack Sign's car a few inches sideways as he drove onwards. It wasn't a problem. Sign had driven through massive sandstorms in the Middle East, minus forty degrees frozen waste lands in Siberia, and on one occasion had managed to maintain grip of his vehicle after it had been rammed by a rhinoceros in Botswana. On all of those occasions he knew death was likely, but not from the elements or wild animals. There were worse things on his heels – men with guns.

Sign stopped his car and got out of the vehicle. Ignoring the weather, he stood on the empty road and opened an umbrella. He was wearing an immaculate suit. Fields were either side of him. There were no houses, no cars, no sign of life. He pulled out his mobile phone and held it to his ear. He didn't call anyone. No one called him. But he waited, tilting the umbrella slightly back so that his face and phone were visible.

From a distance of seven hundred yards, Hilt watched him through the scope on his high-powered sniper rifle. Hilt was prone, hidden in gorse on a slight rise that gave him perfect views of the road Sign was on. Hilt had followed him here from West Square. Hilt's crosshairs were on Sign's head. It would be so easy. Pull the trigger and put a savage hole in Sign's head. And if he missed, he'd shoot two of the tyres, move closer, and finish Sign off. If Hilt's boss gave the order, Sign was a dead man.

Hilt called Smith. "Sign's in Norfolk. His pal's not with him. I guess it's nothing work-related."

Smith was silent for three seconds. "The chief of my organisation has a country retreat in Norfolk. What is Sign wearing?"

"A suit."

"Stay on him!" Smith ended the call.

Hilt collapsed his customised rifle, placed it in a rucksack and turned, with the intention of sprinting to his car. As he did so, Knutsen punched him in the face. Hilt collapsed to the ground, rolled, and sprang to his feet. He dropped his rucksack and moved close to Knutsen, slamming a boot into Knutsen's ankle and slapping his palm into the ex-cop's face. Knutsen gasped for air as he hit soil and grass. Hilt wanted to thrust his hand against Knutsen's nose and force cartilage into his brain. But Knutsen grabbed his arm and forced him onto his back. Hilt lashed out with his free arm and legs. But, Knutsen held him in a vice-like grip.

"Who are you?!" asked Knutsen. "Who do you work for?"

Hilt used his knee to whack Knutsen in the balls, stood, and stamped on Knutsen's head. "You picked the wrong person, matey." He gripped Knutsen's hand and placed his arm in an excruciating lock.

Knutsen rolled so that his arm was travelling away from the lock, kicked Hilt in the chest, kicked him again in the eyes and throat, and dragged Hilt to the ground. He got an arm around Hilt's windpipe and muttered, "I can do this."

Hilt banged the back of his head against Knutsen's forehead, wrenched his arm free, stood and kicked Knutsen in the ribcage. Knutsen was momentarily giddy as he got to his feet. Hilt smiled and punched him in the stomach and mouth. Knutsen staggered. This is just the dojo, he told himself. Just the dojo. Stay up. Think it through. Find his weakness. Execute. He shook his head and wiped saliva from his mouth. Hilt rushed at him. Knutsen spun around, grabbed Hilt, and used the ex-special forces' momentum to pound him to the ground, a boot on the back of Hilt's neck. Hilt wasted no time, using his fist to repeatedly hit Knutsen on his shin. Knutsen recoiled, in agony.

Both men stood staring at each other, breathing fast, steam coming out of their mouths, sweat dripping down their furrows.

Hilt picked up his rucksack. "Another time, pal. Wrong day. Wrong place." He jogged off.

Knutsen was in a bad state as he limped down the escarpment to Sign's car. Blood was all over his face and arms. He'd been pounded in a way he'd never experienced before. He was gasping as he reached Sign. "The limpet… limpet."

Concern was all over Sign's face as he said, "Dear fellow. Let's get you in the dry." He guided Knutsen into the rear of the car and used bottled water to clean his wounds. "Anything broken?"

"No. No… I don't think so."

"What happened?"

Knutsen explained.

Sign felt immense guilt. "I didn't realise we were up against someone like this. Almost certainly, he's done the paramilitary course."

"Paramilitary?" Knutsen's entire body was in agony.

"MI6. It's our blunt instrument. Blunter than special forces. It's our last resort. Most people fail the course – even our SF." Sign paced outside the vehicle. "I shouldn't have put you up against the limpet."

Knutsen's eyes were screwed shut as he muttered, "You had to. My... my job was easy. You... you had to be the tethered goat. You could have been killed. He had a rifle."

"I suspected he was armed." Sign looked at the escarpment where Hilt had been hiding. When leaving West Square, Sign had told Knutsen to hide in the boot of his car. Sign knew that he was being followed out of London. On a bend in a road in Norfolk, he'd slammed the breaks on and told Knutsen to get out and run. The instructions were specific – Knutsen tries to grab the limpet and make him talk; Sign stands in the road, waiting for death.

Knutsen said, "I've never seen anyone do something as brave as what you did today."

Sign didn't care for the flattery. "We all fall down, one day." He smiled. "Are you up to another job?"

Knutsen rubbed his face. "Damn right."

"Good man." He pointed up the road. "We need to go thirteen miles that way. On the rear seat of the car is your suit, a shirt, tie, and your brogues. Get dressed, because the man we're meeting in thirty minutes won't take kindly to shabby attire."

"Dressed? Where?"

Sign chuckled. "It appears it's too harsh a climate at this time of the day for the Norfolk folk. No one's here. You might as well get on with it."

Ten minutes' later they drove away. Though he was now in formal attire and showed no external signs of the brutal assault he'd suffered, Knutsen was still wincing. Sign leaned across and opened the glove compartment opposite Knutsen. He withdrew a first aid kit and handed it to the ex-cop.

"There are painkillers in there. All you need to do is get through the next thirty or so minutes. After that, I'll drive you back to London. I have a friend who works as a doctor on Harley Street. He can prescribe you stronger pain killers if need be."

Knutsen put two paracetamol in his mouth and swallowed them down with a swig of water. "I'll be alright. I just don't like losing fights."

"You neither lost nor won. The same was true for the limpet." Sign turned into a narrower country lane, while glancing in his rear-view mirror. "Still, we'll have to be more careful next time. I don't like the fact that he has a rifle. And I don't like seeing a master of the dojo sitting in my car holding his seatbelt away from his chest because the strap is aggravating wounds." Sign stopped the car outside an iron double-gate. Beyond it was a gravel driveway that led to a small mansion. "We have arrived at the country retreat of the chief of MI6. He is expecting us. Still, the encounter will be tricky. I will do most of the talking. And I will do my best to counter any mind games he might throw at us. But if you see me faltering, play PC Plod and threaten him with a police investigation. On UK soil he is not above the law."

Two armed bodyguards opened the gates and waved them through. Sign stopped the car outside the front door. He and Knutsen exited the vehicle. The door opened. Two beagles ran out, tails wagging, and ran circles around the guests, sniffing their shoes.

In the doorway was the chief. "They're harmless. I need to walk them later, or they'll be the equivalent of children who've eaten too much sugar. Come in."

The chief guided them through the hallway containing shooting smocks, walking sticks, and a gun cabinet. They entered a large lounge. He told them to sit where they liked. The beagles followed them and rolled onto their backs in front of a log burner. A maid entered the room and asked them what they'd like to drink. Sign asked for tea; Knutsen wanted black coffee. Knutsen looked around the room. It was oak-panelled, crammed with books, paintings, and antiquities. But what grabbed his attention was a glass cabinet containing a samurai sword.

The chief was wearing tweeds, looking every inch a country gentleman. "You are interested in the sword, Mr. Knutsen. Its steel remains as sharp as it was in the Battle of Shiroyama in…"

"Eighteen seventy seven. May I hold the weapon?"

The chief delicately pulled out the sword and handed it to Knutsen. "The last man to have held this in anger is rumoured to have killed thirty six men in the battle. Treat this with respect."

Knutsen moved away from the chief and Sign. He gripped the sword's hilt with two hands and swashed the blade through air. "It's so delicate. I never knew." He handed the sword back to the chief, who replaced it in its cabinet.

The chief said, "All those years studying kendo and yet this is your first time holding a samurai sword."

Knutsen sat near Sign.

The chief sat opposite them. "What do you want?"

Sign replied, "Sir, we…"

"I am not your sir or your chief. You are no longer in MI6." He looked at Knutsen. "And you are no longer with the Metropolitan Police. You are civilians. Anxious ones, I will concede." He looked at Knutsen. "My name is Henry Gable. I am publicly avowed, so I'm the only person in MI6 who can be named. Given it's a weekend, on this occasion you can call me Henry. I answer to the foreign secretary and the prime minister. No one else. Even then, politicians come and go and most of them couldn't organise a piss up in a brewery. I control things. But not for much longer. We have people nipping at my heels, don't we Mr. Sign?"

"I'm not after your job. You know that."

"Yes, I do." Henry smiled at Knutsen. "And there is no route back for you into the police, young man."

"No." Knutsen felt uneasy.

Sign sensed his colleague's unease. "Mr. Knutsen is a highly decorated former undercover cop. He doesn't need to prove himself to anyone, including you and me."

Henry nodded. "Yes, but he did execute a criminal in cold blood." Slowly he turned his head towards Knutsen. "It takes a particular kind of man to do that."

Knutsen was about to reply, but Sign interjected. "Knutsen killed the man who killed the woman Knutsen was in love with. And the criminal was a piece of scum. Knutsen isn't by nature a killer. Let me ask you this, Henry: how many drone strikes have you ordered that sometimes missed their targets but not civilians; how many black ops assassinations have you signed off on; how many foreign agents have you sent to their deaths?"

Henry smiled. "I could ask the same of you."

"You could. So, let's cut the crap. The three of us know what it's like in the real world and what we have to do. We all have blood on our hands."

Henry was silent, though his gaze was penetrating.

Sign clasped his hands and lowered his voice. "I believe we have a situation that is beyond the purview of espionage."

"Elaborate!"

"Mark Archer killed himself because he was corrupt. Arthur Lake killed himself because he couldn't keep his dick in his pants. Detective Inspector Roberts' husband was murdered and Katy Roberts was told to back off consulting with us on the suicides due to *national security*. What can you tell us about that?"

Henry was unfazed. "I can tell you nothing, for two reasons. First, I have no insight on these matters. Second, even if I did it would be none of your business."

Knutsen said, "This is a murder enquiry."

"Conducted by one disgraced cop and one former MI6 officer who refused to tow the party line." Henry shook his head. "You have no authority over me."

"Not so!" Sign looked menacing as he added, "*You* have no authority over us. But we most certainly have authority over you."

Knutsen said, "Mr. Sign and I answer to the police and the judiciary. It wouldn't be difficult for me to arrange for you to be forced to testify in a closed court. Yeah, you'd pull in favours, speak to mates you went to uni with who now work as judges, blah blah. But here's the thing. I'd also pull in MI5 and Special Branch to a court room session. And they hate posh bastards like you who work for MI6. I'd set a ball rolling. They'd drag you through the dirt. I'm sure someone of your intellect would outsmart everyone in the court. But at what cost? You're due to retire shortly. Is this how you want to be remembered? Possibly covering up a murder in the UK?"

"Don't threaten me, Knutsen!"

"He's not threatening you." Sign drummed his fingers on a glass coffee table. "He's laying out the facts. I strongly urge you to cooperate with us. If you don't we will set wheels in motion."

Gable couldn't believe what he was hearing. "You come to my house and…"

"Yes, yes." Sign made no effort to hide his anger. "Elliot Roberts was unemployed. Previously he was a family lawyer. Nothing – *absolutely* nothing – he did in his life brought him anywhere near our world. He wasn't a national security threat. But he was a means to put the frighteners on his wife. And the only case she was working on was the suicides of two senior MI6 officers. So, in the presence of Mr. Knutsen, I'll ask you what you know about those suicides."

Gable looked confused. "Nothing. I was as shocked by their deaths as everyone else. If you have evidence that they took their lives due to past indiscretions, lay that evidence in front of me and the Joint Intelligence Committee. I can assure you that we'll go over the allegations with a fine tooth comb."

"What's the point? Archer and Lake are dead." Sign decided to soften his tone. "It is quite possible that you're not our enemy. On paper, why would you be? You're due to retire. The machinations of MI6 will soon no longer be your concern. But, there is a problem. What links Archer and Lake?"

Gable frowned. "Both senior MI6 men. But they had different career paths. I doubt they knew each other that well."

"Think, Henry! There must be something they have in common."

Gable shook his head. "If you were still in MI6 I could answer you. Given you're not, it's classified."

Knutsen pulled out his mobile phone and asked Sign, "Shall I call the commissioner? He can get a squad car here in minutes."

Gable waved his hand through the air. "That won't be necessary."

"It will be if I decide it is." Sign pointed at Gable. "Here's the thing, Henry. There's a possibility we're dealing with a serial killer. An unusual one at that. But to catch him I need to understand motive. Why did he or she want Archer and Lake dead? Why did he kill Roberts to try to stop the investigation? When we know the reason, we are closer to knowing the killer."

"Roberts' death may be completely unconnected!"

"Come on Henry. Our whole lives have been devoted to connecting the dots. Coincidences never factor."

Gable looked pensive. "Archer and Lake's deaths were by their own hand. How on Earth could they be murders?"

"Someone very skilled could have talked them in to taking their lives."

"It's possible." The chief frowned. "But if that's the case, who? Lake and Roberts never shared the same geographical targets. The Russians might have targeted Roberts to shut him up, but they'd have no bug bear with Lake."

"So, maybe we're dealing with someone closer to home." Sign leaned forward. "The motive might be personal, not professional."

"Your ideas are supposition."

"Yes, they are. But in the right hands, supposition is instinct that out-speeds deductive reasoning. A woman looks at a man and knows he's a wrong 'un. Only later may she be able to work out why she reached that conclusion. I'm thinking there's a wrong 'un out there. Why, who, and how, are eluding me, though I do have a thought. Who's on the shortlist to become the next chief of MI6?"

Gable looked mortified. "I can't give you that information!"

"You will give me that information. Or I hand you over to Mr. Knutsen. Trust me – he'll move faster than your bodyguards."

"You are both looking at a prison sentence!"

"That's alright. We'll share a cell with you. We can pass the time by playing board games and wondering how we all got locked up."

The chief smiled. "How is life out in the cold suiting you, Ben?"

"Just fine. Let me know how it goes for you after you retire in a few months' time. No more bodyguards; no chauffeur-driven limousines; no hotline to the prime minister; no invitations to banquets at the palace; no private jets to Washington DC; just you and your beagles. But the beagles are looking a bit old. They won't be around for much longer. I understand your daughters are married, with kids, and are living overseas. They won't see you that much. We all know your wife moved out a while ago. Rumour has it she's got a fella." Sign's tone of voice was cold as he added, "If I were you I wouldn't sit there all smug and gloating, asking me how it feels to be out of the fold. You'll know soon enough what it's like to have no power."

"Ah, Ben." Gable's eyes were twinkling. "You'd have made such an excellent chief. But you backed out of the game and decided to play private detective." He looked away, deep in thought. "I can tell you this for free. Alongside you, Archer and Lake were on the shortlist of candidates to be my successor. You know how it works – the candidates are chosen by me and the cross-party JIC. Each person is picked due to varying capabilities so that the final choice can reflect the current mood in Westminster and the mood of our closest allies. Archer was deemed unremarkable, but a safe pair of hands. That could have been useful. Lake was deemed a good operator, but perhaps too much of spy to be a manager. And you, Ben, were our best spy. But you did have a negative against your name. You were deemed by all to be cavalier. That negative could have worked exceptionally well in the current climate – keep our allies and detractors on their toes by having an unpredictable spy chief." Gable pointed at the samurai sword. "Knutsen will know that Shiroyama was the last battle of the samurai. They'd reached the end of the line. Technology was outstripping them. Guns and canons were the new way of things. I keep the sword to remind me of who I was and who I cannot be. It's soon going to be my end of the line. But you, Ben, were young enough and mentally adroit to adapt to the times. But you fucked it all up."

"I resigned." Sign pulled out a sheet of paper and a fountain pen. He placed both on the table in front of Gable. "Give me the shortlist names."

"I've already given you my response to that request."

"And I haven't accepted your response. How many are on the list?"

Gable shrugged. "I can tell you that. Seven in total. Thanks to you, Archer, and Lake, we're now down to four."

"Who's your favourite candidate?"

"Don't insult my intelligence, Sign!"

Sign stood, walked to the beagles and rubbed their bellies. "Okay, Henry. Let's do it this way. You call the foreign secretary or prime minister and get their permission to release the names to me. I call the home secretary and tell her that the chief of MI6 is obstructing a murder enquiry. She'd love that. You know how much she's hankering for a domestic scandal that will put her in the shining light as the woman holding the scales of justice."

Slowly and with a deep authoritative tone, Gable said, "Be *very* careful, Mr. Sign. I am adhering to security protocols. *You* have no proof that the suicides are linked, nor that Roberts' murder is linked to the suicides. You have everything to lose and nothing to gain by meddling in matters that don't concern you."

Sign faced him and smiled. "That's the beauty of my current position. I have nothing to lose and everything to gain. Make the call. The names may turn out to mean nothing. But I don't want it on your conscience if they turn out to be something."

"You are making a big mistake!"

The noise of Sign's voice made the beagles scarper as he said, "I am an official emissary of not only the Metropolitan Police but also our government. Make the call!"

Gable stood. "God help you, Sign." He walked to the adjacent conservatory and picked up the landline phone. He spoke for ninety three seconds, listened, and hung up. He returned to the lounge, sat, picked up the pen, hesitated, then wrote seven names on the sheet. "The prime minister has assured me that I will be immune from prosecution by revealing these names to you and Knutsen. Every phone call in and out of here is recorded by me. It's my insurance. If the PM denies the conversation I've just had with her, I'll publish and be damned."

Sign took the sheet. "Thank you, Henry."

Gable pointed at the sheet while looking at Knutsen. "I've just given you the names of our top seven spies. You and Sign have authority to read their names. But, if you want to share their names with anyone in the course of your investigation, you will need me, the foreign secretary, and the home secretary – all three of us, not just one – to vet that person and give you authority or otherwise. Am I clear?"

Knutsen nodded.

Sign folded the paper in half and placed it in the inner pocket of his jacket. "We fully understand."

"That includes the commissioner of the Metropolitan Police. He's security cleared, but not to the level of the UK intelligence agencies. You understand?"

"Yes."

Gable pulled Sign to one side and said in a quiet voice, "Ben – you could be making a huge mistake. Maybe your train of thought is skewed. This may all be nothing."

Sign nodded. "I'm aware of that. But since when did men like you and I believe in the impossible?"

That evening, Sign and Knutsen were back in West Square. Sign cooked guinea fowl encrusted with a marmalade glaze, butter mash potato, and vegetables drizzled with lemon juice. After dinner, Sign sat opposite Knutsen in the lounge. He stared at the sheet of paper.

"What does it tell you?" asked Knutsen.

Sign didn't answer his question. "When are you next on the dojo?"

Knutsen frowned. "Wednesday."

"Take Katy with you. Pair her up with David. They both have broken wings. Exercise and focus will help repair their ailments. Have you checked on Katy this evening?"

"Yes. She's ordered an Indian takeaway and is making funeral plans."

"Good. She's eating and is busy." Sign stared at the paper before placing it in front of Knutsen. "What do you see?"

The list read:

Ben Sign

Mark Archer

Arthur Lake

Edward Messenger

Nicholas Pendry

James Logan

Terry File

"I see a list of men."

Sign looked resigned. "One day we'll have a female chief." He took the sheet off Knutsen. "I see a kill list." He turned the sheet over and withdrew a pen. On the back he wrote:

MURDER VICTIMS

Mark Archer

Arthur Lake

Elliot Roberts

POTENTIAL MURDER VICTIMS

Ben Sign

Tom Knutsen

Katy Roberts

Henry Gable

Edward Messenger

Nicholas Pendry

James Logan

Terry File

Beneath that, he wrote:

Who is the limpet?

And:

Who is the whisperer?

He handed the sheet back to Knutsen. "Messenger, Pendry, Logan, and File. They may all be dead men walking. Or maybe one of them is the killer. The whisperer."

"Why?"

"Remember – he's cleaning out the garbage. I think he wants to be chief. He is eliminating the competition and ensuring that he does not inherit any bad apples. It is pure self-fulfilment. He wants the top job."

"Ben, this is a…"

"Stab in the dark? Yes, I know. But I was hired to investigate this case because I know the mind-set of a spy. This is what I'm doing. I'm ascertaining motive and methodology. But if I'm right, we have very dark waters to navigate. Right now, we have a number of low IQ sociopaths who are presidents around the world. That's one thing. But imagine if a supremely intelligent serial killer becomes head of MI6. He'd have at his disposal huge power and resources. I can imagine what he'd do with that power. He'd corrupt others and send our men and women to kill."

"Spies would become his army?"

"Yes. But it would be more complicated than that. He'd do what spies do best – he'd manipulate foreign powers; change landscapes; start wars; and he'd do it all purely for the thrill." Sign's voice quietened. "In my time, I've dealt with many, many, sociopaths and psychopaths. I've outwitted them all. But, a psychotic MI6 officer? That would be a whole new challenge for me."

"No one else is better suited to that task than you."

"If indeed it is a task. I could be so wrong." Sign frowned. "Do you think it would be a good idea to erect a cross on Mount Snowdon for Katy's husband? I have sway with the MP of that district. She'd give me permission for the construction."

"It would be inappropriate. Let Katy make her own plans."

"Yes, you're right." Sign touched the paper. "This is all I have to go on."

"But, your instinct tells you that all that's needed?"

"Yes."

Knutsen lifted the paper. "Tell me about the others."

"You could put a cigarette paper between their intellects. All of them are overachievers. Messenger is currently head of all European operations; Pendry is on the board of directors as head of communications; Logan runs Asia; File heads up the paramilitary wing."

"File runs people like the limpet?"

"Yes."

"Then, he could be our man."

"Maybe. The problem is, all operational MI6 officers use limpets from time to time."

"We could meet File and get his opinion."

Sign shook his head. "And tell him what? That a highly trained killer with an English accent has been following us and has killed a detective inspector's husband, allegedly for the sake of national interest. File would laugh us out of his home. He'd remind me that he has dozens of UK killers under his control; that he also has hundreds of foreign paramilitary assets overseas; that the killer may not be intelligence, but rather a regular criminal; and that this could be a foreign intelligence operative posing as a Brit. Plus he'd remind me that special forces types come and go. If the limpet is retired and reactivated, we can treble or quadruple the number of suspects. File would tell me I'm looking for a needle in a giant haystack. He'd be right."

"We should warn Messenger, Pendry, Logan, and File that their lives are in danger."

Sign looked weary as he rubbed his face. "Were it that easy." He sighed. "If we talk to all four of them, and one of them turns out to be the whisperer, we'd be signposting our knowledge of the kill list to the whisperer. No. We have to let things play out."

"Play out?"

"We need three of them to die; and one to stay alive. Whoever stays alive is the whisperer."

Knutsen was incredulous. "You want more murders to identify the killer?!"

"Logically, can you see an alternative?"

"Yes! Forget the investigation. Protect all four. Maybe some other evidence will come out in due course."

Sign looked wistful. "It won't. I believe we're dealing with a highly capable thinker and operator. The only way to flush him out is to leave him isolated. If he kills the others, he is the killer. If we warn him off he'll go to ground."

Knutsen desperately wanted to find a flaw in Sign's logic. He couldn't. "You might be sending your former colleagues to their deaths!"

"I know." Sign wrung his hands. "I hate this. But what else is there to do?"

Knutsen's mind raced. "Has it occurred to you that Gable might think you're the whisperer?"

"Yes. What do you think?"

Knutsen was silent for a moment. "I don't think you are. But it's hard to tell with you spooks. You're such thoroughbred liars."

Sign laughed. "Indeed we are. But I have no vested interest in the deaths of the men on the list, one of whom is sitting in this room. And both men sitting in this room are on the back of the paper as likely targets for assassination." He touched Knutsen's hand. "My agenda is to catch a killer, even if the killer is someone I know. It deeply saddens me that I have to await more killings. I am not the whisperer. Do you understand?"

Knutsen nodded. "I understand and trust you implicitly. So, what do we do now?"

"We wait."

CHAPTER 17

Four weeks later, Katy Roberts entered Sign's flat. She'd just returned from her husband's funeral and scattering of his ashes on the mountain. The funeral had been delayed because her husband's corpse was subject to a murder enquiry. She was wearing a light pink jumper and sky blue trousers.

Knutsen asked, "You didn't wear black at the funeral?"

"Should I have done?"

"No. You were celebrating Elliot's life, not his death. Your colours are perfect. Fancy a brew?"

Roberts nodded. "Where's Ben?"

"Tearing up half of London, I imagine." Knutsen grinned. "He's been going out of his mind with boredom during the last few weeks. The commissioner has threatened him that he might cancel the investigation and not renew his contract. Sign and I have been working on chicken feed – divorce cases, infidelities, financial fraud, basically anything to pay the bills. Sign is not in the best temper."

Roberts laughed. "I can imagine." A tear ran down her face, brought on by the fact this was the first time she'd laughed since Elliot's death. "Do you think I'll ever remarry?" She had no idea why she'd blurted out that question. Men, companionship, relationships of any kind were the last thing on her mind. Mind you, she cherished the contact she had with Knutsen and Sign. They helped her in the same way she'd help them if they'd gone through her ordeal.

Knutsen replied, "Don't ask me. I killed a man who killed the last woman I fancied. I'm not exactly a balanced example of wise relationship counselling." He smiled sympathetically. "Emotions run high at times like these. It's like hitting puberty again. The body and mind have no idea what the fuck's going on." He handed Roberts her cup of tea. "You're a good-looking woman, successful, and kind. Who knows what waits for you out there?" He felt he needed to change the subject. "Let's do some kendo practice with David this evening. I'll get Sign on the case for dinner after. The bloody guy needs a distraction."

"Yes to both ideas." She sat in Sign's armchair. "I'm selling my house. I'll find somewhere else soon, but if it's okay with you both I'd like to stay on in the flat while I'm in… transition."

"Of course it's okay. Look at it this way: when you're not around I'm cooped up with the fractious bastard. I welcome your company; so does Sign."

Roberts smiled. "You are the oddest couple. Chalk and cheese." She took a deep breath. "I'm going back to work. Do you think I'll be watched by the limpet?"

"Hard to say. If the whisperer's work is done, it may be that we're all out of danger."

"What does Sign think?"

Knutsen hesitated. "Katy, we're in possession of a list of names. Ben calls it a 'kill list'. He wonders if one of the names on the list is the whisperer. On the back of the list are the names of the people the whisperer has killed. Also, there is a list of the people he may kill. Me and Sign are on that list. So…"

"Am I." Roberts looked calm. "What is the kill list?"

"Seven names of predominantly current MI6 officers, one of whom was tipped to be the next chief. Two of them are the suicides, so they're out of the game. Sign is also on the list, because he was in the running before he resigned. So, he's also out of the game. That leaves four names – all men. One of the four could be a psychopath."

"That's if the whisperer even exists."

"Yes." Knutsen wondered if he should reveal more about what he knew. He made a decision. "Sign's idea going forward is... unusual. He wants to see if anyone else on the list is killed. That way he narrows down the list of suspects."

Roberts digested the information. "It makes sense, to a point. But surely there is a more humane route forward. If we can grab the limpet, we can get to his master."

"Make him talk?"

"Arrest him. Interview him. Throw the book at him. Offer him twenty years in prison with the chance of parole, if he cooperates, or life imprisonment with no chance of parole if he doesn't."

Knutsen admired the fact that Roberts would be willing to offer her husband's murderer a degree of clemency. Most people wouldn't have the balls to think that way. "It won't work. Sign thinks we're dealing with a highly trained black ops guy. The limpet will sit in your interview room, say nothing, and suck up a lifetime of jail. And when he's in jail, he'll be a massive problem. He'll end up running the place."

"So, you're suggesting we capture the limpet and torture him to get the name of the whisperer?"

"Yes."

Roberts nodded. "Just make sure I'm in the room when it happens. Come and visit me in prison if I get caught and you don't." She rubbed her eyes. "I'm going back to work because I want to keep the investigation into my husband's death open. If needs be, I'll put my bitch hat on. I'll tell the commissioner that if he doesn't renew your contract to continue the investigation then I'll cause him trouble. He'll capitulate." She looked Knutsen directly in the eye. "My husband's free. But so are the limpet and the whisperer. Where's the yin and yang in that?"

"We get the bastards."

"Yes. Only Sign can access the whisperer's mind. But we can get the limpet."

"Agreed."

Roberts looked around. "Where did he get all this stuff? All these antiques, paintings, books and other things?"

"He travelled the world. I think of him as a magpie – scavenging things in the same way he scavenged and collected souls." Knutsen laughed at the absurdity of his analogy.

Roberts didn't laugh. "You're right. Everything in this room is all he has. The souls never stuck by him. He's alone." She picked up a diary. On the inner cover were Sign's handwritten words 'My great, great grandfather's love letter to a woman he lost while he was at sea'. It wasn't per se a love letter, rather Sign's ancestor's diary while at sea on board a clipper navigating the waters around the Americas. But the diary was most certainly written for a woman. Roberts gently replaced the leather-bound journal back on the bookshelf. "Sign still seeks love."

Sign entered the flat while holding bags of groceries. "God damn, fucking shits out there have clogged up traffic. Just because there's a bit of rain it seemingly means they all have to jump in their cars and bring London streets to a damn standstill."

Knutsen winked at Roberts and whispered, "There is a reason why he has no woman in his life."

Sign placed his grocery bags on a table, and hugged Roberts. "Today was the day. My sincerest condolences." He stepped back. "Tonight I'm cooking Mexican food. Given it's a Wednesday, I'm guessing that you two are shortly off to bash each other over the heads with bamboo sticks. Does a late dinner at nine PM sharp suit?"

They nodded.

"Good, because I've got nothing else to worry about and do aside from solving why Mrs. Parson's husband was caught in flagrante with a gay Lithuanian man, why a rebel Tory MP adhered to the whip and voted against his fellow rebels, and whether an escaped London Zoo golden eagle, that's been terrorising small dogs in Hyde Park, legally constitutes a redefinition of assault versus natural predatory behaviour. I am bored."

Knutsen went up to him. "Katy's going back to work. She will ensure we're still on the whisperer case."

Sign looked at her. His demeanour and tone of voice changed - less strident; more thoughtful. "You wish to catch your husband's killer. You've enrolled Knutsen to help you snatch the limpet. Together, you'll aim to get the truth out of him. Who is the whisperer?"

. "Yes."

"We tried that already. Knutsen came out of the encounter battered and bruised. And For nearly a month I've seen no evidence that the limpet's been following us. We need another development. If that happens, we spring into action; he springs into action. At that point, you have my blessing to try to get him. But you'll have to be very careful. He'll try to kill you both. And he'll only talk if he's under extreme duress. Hurt him to the point he thinks he's going to die. Offer him medical assistance on the condition he tells you the name we need." He looked at Knutsen. "A leg shot might suffice. Be accurate. The limpet will know about battle injuries. He has to be convinced he'll bleed to death unless you apply tourniquets, give him morphine, extract the bullet, stitch him up, and place paddings on the wound. Search him thoroughly. He must have zero means to communicate with the whisperer. What you do with the limpet after that is of no concern to me."

Roberts asked, "And if we get the whisperer's name, what will you do?"

Sign slumped into a chair and placed the tips of his fingers together. "I'll put the whisperer out of his misery."

Hilt met John Smith in *Pizza Express* in Hertford. He ordered a mineral water but no food, sat opposite the senior spy and said, "I've been watching them."

"All three?"

"Yep."

"Good. You have a pattern of behaviour?"

"Tonight, two of them are going out. The other will stay in and cook. Least ways, that's how it's worked every Wednesday evening so far."

"Okay. Tomorrow morning I want you to do something very unpleasant. But it won't be unpleasant for you." Smith smiled, though his expression was cold. He handed Hilt a small rucksack. "In there are things you'll need. Did you get the rifle?"

"Yeah. Lee Enfield .303. Bit old school, but it will do the job."

"Old school is necessary. And you've put a message on the gun?"

Hilt smiled. "An engraved message on a brass plate on the rifle's butt."

"Good. Tomorrow, wear a face mask that covers your mouth and nose. I can't have one drop of your saliva or any other involuntary excretions on the weapon. Obviously wear gloves. And wear a coat that has a hood and won't release fibres — a rain mac or similar. Bottom line, there must be no DNA, fingerprints, or other suspicious traces on the rifle." He told Hilt exactly what he had to do in the morning.

CHAPTER 18

Snowflakes the size of saucers sank slowly downward as Hilt lay prone and trained his rifle on his targets. Two people were walking slowly along a street; houses and commercial buildings were either side of them. They were only fifty yards away. If they moved out of sight, Hilt would simply reposition and get them once again in his sight. Either way, they were dead if he wanted them to be. On top of the World War 2 rifle, Hilt had gaffer-taped a modern scope. He had no idea why Smith wanted him to do this job. He didn't care. This was target practice. Out of the rucksack Smith had given him, he withdrew a laptop and tiny camera. He attached the camera to his right eye and plugged a cable between it and a laptop. Into the laptop he wired a mobile phone that gave him Internet connection. The laptop was good to go; the camera was good to go. He Skyped Smith, looked at the targets through the camera and sniper scope, and asked, "Are you getting this?"

Smith replied, "Yes. Visual is good. Whatever happens, keep them in your sight." Smith walked along a street within a housing estate. It was early morning; people were leaving their houses to attend to their daily chores. He reached a detached house – modest in size and identical to all of the other houses surrounding the property. He was wearing a suit and overcoat, because he was due to be in work soon. He rang the doorbell and waited.

A man opened the door, chewing the last mouthful of a bacon sandwich that he'd prepared for breakfast. He looked shocked. "What are you doing here?"

"Hello Terry. We have an emergency."

"At the office?"

"Yes."

"You'd better come in." Like Smith, Terry File was smartly dressed, though he wasn't yet wearing his jacket. As they walked to the lounge, the head of MI6's paramilitary unit said, "I've got a meeting with the chief at ten o'clock. That means I have to catch the…"

"0817 from Hertford North to King's Cross."

File's eyes narrowed. "How did you know that?"

Smith shrugged as he waved a hand through the air. "You live in Hertford. It's the next available train into London. I need to be on that train because I too have meetings this morning in head office."

"What's this about?"

"It's about an assassination. Actually, potentially three assassinations. It falls right into your remit."

"You wish me to deploy some of my team to stop it happening?"

"It might be too late for that, but I do need your advice. I have data I need to show you. I'd value your opinion. I must warn you – it makes for uncomfortable viewing."

File sat in a chair. "In my time in this job, I've seen things you wouldn't believe – videos of beheadings, rape, genocide, and so much more. I doubt what you're going to show me will be more upsetting."

"This might be." From his briefcase, Sign took an IPad and its stand and placed both on a coffee table, facing File.

"Should I ring the chief and cancel our meeting?"

"That won't be necessary. This won't take long. You'll have enough time to get your train." Smith sat next to the coffee table. "The assassination attempts pertain to an MI6 officer and his affiliates. We need to move very fast on this."

File frowned. "Why didn't you just call me on the secure line, rather than come all the way up here? It would have been so much quicker."

"We have a breach of security. It's most relevant to the assassinations. Even secure communications might be compromised. This had to be dealt with face to face."

"Breach of security? What, exactly?"

"Someone is corrupting MI6. The Office doesn't yet know who. It may never know. But we do know lives are at stake." Smith held up his hand. "Don't worry. You're not a suspect. We know you're loyal to the cause. Plus, you're a devout Catholic. It would be inconceivable for you to betray your country and your ethics. The only thing that matters more to you than patriotism and your religion, is your family. You have a wife and a five year old boy, I believe."

File bristled. "I do. Why's that relevant?"

Smith turned on the Ipad and activated Skype. "There they are. Your wife; your son. How sweet – they're holding hands. As usual, your wife is walking your son to pre-school nursery. She'll drop him off, do some shopping, and return most likely around mid-morning."

File was incredulous. "What's going on?!"

"I told you – we're dealing with one or possibly three assassinations. The numbers will be down to you. What you're seeing is a video taken by my sniper. It's in live time. My sniper will kill your wife and child if needs be."

"You fucking…!"

Smith smiled. "You're a big man. You could probably overpower me and call the police. The problem you have is that my sniper is listening to our conversation. My orders to him are that if he has the slightest indication that I'm in danger, he must pull the trigger. First it will be your wife. The son will be utterly confused. Most likely he'll stay with his mother's body. But, if he runs, he'll make five yards or so before his head is blown off. And cops will be of no use to you. Their response time is three minutes at best. You of all people know that a bullet is considerably faster than that."

File looked at the screen and saw his wife and son walking down one of the streets they always took in the outskirts of Hertford, en route to school. "This could be a pre-recording from yesterday or any other school day."

"It could be but it's not. And you know that. Look at your wife's garments. Did she wear them yesterday, the day before, or anytime this week? And if she did, were they the same combination as she's wearing today."

File walked up to Smith and grabbed him by the chin. "Why are you doing this, you bastard?!"

Smith was unperturbed. "Because I want to remove you from the shortlist of candidates to be the next chief of MI6. Take your hand off me or they die."

File backed away, breathing rapidly. "You won't get away with this!"

"Well, we'll see. But your wife and son can certainly come away from this situation alive if you do the honourable thing."

"Honourable thing?"

Smith took a length of rope from his briefcase. He expertly tied a hangman's noose at one end, screwed a hook into the skirting board, attached the other end of the rope to the screw, and slung the rope over another screw-hook that he'd inserted into the wooden beam traversing the ceiling. He pulled up a dining chair directly under the noose. "You must choose - your life versus your wife and son's life."

File was shaking. "You... you can't."

Smith placed a finger on the screen. "My sniper has repositioned to get a clean line of sight of the final leg of your wife and son's journey. Ordinarily they'd reach school in about five minutes. That can still happen, but only if you comply. If you don't they'll be shot dead before they complete their journey. Get on the chair!"

File whipped out his mobile phone.

"By all means call your wife. She'll be dead before you utter a word to her."

Tears were running down File's sweaty face.

"Time is running out. What does your conscience tell you? How will you live with yourself if you let your family die to save your skin? In what direction is your moral compass pointing? What would God say about your decision?"

"You're... you're bluffing."

"I never bluff." Smith spoke to Hilt. "Shoot her in the ankle, then train your rifle on the boy's head."

File shouted, "No!" as he saw his wife collapse to the ground.

The boy was bent over her, clutching his mum.

Smith laughed. "She'll need reconstructive surgery. But she'll live. There might be some concerned civilians who come to her assistance. But," he looked at the screen, "That's not happening yet. Your wife's pulled out her phone. She'll be calling emergency services. After that she might call you. If so, I give you permission to speak to her providing you are on the chair with the noose around your neck. If you tell her to tell your son to run, he'll be killed first, your wife second."

File was gripping his head so hard that blood was oozing out of his skull. He screamed again. "You bastard. Bastard!" He stood on the chair. "May God have mercy on your soul, you piece of scum."

"The clock is ticking, Mr. File." Smith turned to the Ipad and said to Hilt, "Prepare to kill the child. We are moments away."

File's mobile rang. It was his wife. He answered the call. His voice was trembling as he said, "I love you, Debby. I love you and Thomas so very, very much. This is not what it seems."

Smith wagged a finger.

File ended the call and dropped the phone onto the floor.

Smith checked the phone to ensure the phone wasn't still transmitting. He replaced it back on the floor.

File stared at Smith. "You... you might kill them anyway."

"Tut, tut, Mr. File. I am not a monster. Once you're dead I have no interest in your wife and son. They'll be left alone."

"You are a monster!"

"Maybe. You have ten seconds to kick the chair away. If you don't, the fireworks begin in earnest."

File closed his eyes and started muttering a prayer.

"Your god isn't going to save your wife and child. Right now, I'm God. Move fast."

File was hyperventilating. He looked at the ceiling. "Forgive me, Lord." He kicked the chair away and dangled while choking and writhing. It took a minute before he went limp, dead.

Smith shut his IPad and called Smith on his mobile. "It's done. Get to the house asap. The woman and boy are of no use to us now. Leave them alone. Remember what we spoke about – sorting the house is vital. We'll only have a few minutes to get it done. I'll make a start now while you're heading here. Your gun is vital; so too eradicating all traces of our presence. Meanwhile, I'll plant the evidence." Smith smiled and set to work.

Roberts hammered Sign and Knutsen's door, her heart beating fast, face pasty and oily after a sleepless night. She was in her pyjamas and didn't give a hoot about her appearance. Sign and Knutsen were like brothers to her. They'd seen her in worse states.

Sign opened the door. He was unshaven and wearing a dressing gown. "Everything okay?"

Roberts was breathless as she said, "I've just had a call from the commissioner. There's been another suicide. In Hertford. Terry File. MI6 confirmed to the commissioner that he's one of yours."

Sign bellowed, "Action stations!" He grabbed Roberts arm. "Call for a Met car and driver. The car must not be unmarked. The driver must be expert. His number plate must be flagged as unstoppable by other squad cars. We'll need to break speed limits." He turned. "Mr. Knutsen – we have ten minutes to get shaved, showered, and dressed!"

Fifteen minutes later, Roberts, Knutsen and Sign were hurtling through London, heading north. The driver was a traffic cop. His vehicle's blue lights and sirens were on permanently.

Sign cupped a hand around Roberts' ear. "We can't speak openly here. The driver isn't security cleared. I'll tell you what you need to know when we're at our destination."

Normally the route at this time of morning would have taken at least seventy five minutes. But with the help of driving that entailed cars swerving left and right when they heard the vehicle's sirens, the cop driver utilising not only road but also pavements, and a driving speed that constantly produced an adrenalin rush for the car's passengers, they made it to Terry File's house in forty minutes flat.

All of them got out of the police car. The driver lit a cigarette and wandered over to the only other police officers who were leaning against their vehicle while drinking coffee. Next to their response car was a white van belonging to forensics. Alongside that was a black BMW. Colin Parker, the MI6 head of counter intelligence, was in the vehicle. He got out when he saw Sign.

Sign walked up to him while glancing at the house that was surrounded by blue and white tape with the words, POLICE LINE. DO NOT CROSS. "What happened, Colin?"

The senior MI6 officer replied, "File shot his wife while she was taking her kid to nursery. Then he hanged himself. Forensics is in there now. They've been here for an hour."

"The body?"

"Taken to Watford General Hospital. The media haven't been notified. But if some of them get wind of this I'll ruin their day."

Sign nodded. "What's your take?"

"Face value or instinct honed over decades? Face value is as follows: we found bank statements in a filing cabinet belonging to his wife. The wife had been running up credit card debts way beyond File's paygrade. They were financially crippled. She also had photos of her husband with another woman – nothing lewd; just street shots of them together in daylight. And her husband's prints and DNA are all over the Lee Enfield rifle he allegedly used to shoot his wife. He missed and hit her in the ankle. She's in the same hospital as her dead husband. She'll be alright."

"But what about your instinct?"

Parker rubbed his face. "Actually, *instinct* is the wrong word. *Intellect* and *covert experience* would be the right phrase." He nodded at the house. "Go in there and see what you think. Forensics will require you to wear head to toe white garments and gloves. See what you make of the suicide scene."

Sign asked, "Who do the police think you are?"

Quietly, Parker replied, "MI5. They know File was MI6, but I can't have them knowing that I'm also MI6. I suggest you adopt a similar cover story."

Sign agreed. MI5 was one step away from being a police agency. MI6 was nothing like that. It was a top secret spy agency and its members – past and present – had to remain in the shadows. Five minutes later, he, Knutsen and Roberts were in the house. Two forensics officers were also in there. They'd finished their job and were preparing to leave. On a dining room table were clear plastic bags containing the evidence they'd collected – the bank statements, rifle, rope that File had hanged himself with, File's mobile phone, his wallet, train tickets to London, shoes, and photos of him with the woman. Sign examined them all.

The forensics officers were removing their white overalls. Sign asked one of them, "What do you think?"

The female forensics officer shrugged. "Detectives will interview Mrs. File when she's out of surgery. Everything points to a domestic dispute. He may have been having an affair; Mrs. File found out; she got emotional and wanted revenge; she binged on her credit card, just to spite him; she confronted him and told him that she knew he was seeing a woman and that she's created one hell of a financial debt; he cracked and shot her with his rifle; then he killed himself." She frowned. "How would he be allowed to have a rifle?"

"He worked in MI6 special projects. The inscription to him on the gun suggests it was a gift – most likely from a foreign ally. Technically he shouldn't have kept the gun at his house. Sometimes guys like File break rules."

The forensics officer smiled. "These MI6 people make up the rules as they go along. Unlike you MI5 guys, they don't follow procedures and laws."

"Quite." Sign looked around. "Did anything strike you as odd in the house?"

"No."

"Fingerprints?"

"All normal. Fingerprints of the Files and their son – upstairs and downstairs. No other prints."

"And File's prints were on the gun?"

"Yes. Also his saliva was on the side of the weapon. He also had cordite on his forearms. It's not visible to the naked eye. But we have specialist equipment. Most shooters don't know they leave traces of their presence when they shoot guns."

"It was File's job to know such matters." Sign swung around and pointed. "The chair was here." To himself, he muttered, "Where, where?" He knew the answer and sat on a chair facing the place where File killed himself. He knew this was where the whisperer sat, because it was the exact spot Sign would have chosen under the same circumstances. He addressed the forensics officer. "You must have examined hundreds of domestic homes in your career. All of them contain tell-tale signs of the inhabitants. Also, they contain signs of visitors. Did the chair have File's prints on it?"

"Yes. Also Mrs. File's prints. It was a dining table chair, identical to the chair you're sitting on."

"So, it was well used." File drummed his fingers on the adjacent dining table. "Did you check for prints of any kind on the table and other chairs around me?"

The forensics officer checked her notes. "Yes. There were no prints whatsoever – not the Files' or anyone else. The table and chairs must have been cleaned recently, or not used for a long time."

"Yes, that makes sense." Sign stood. "Thank you, officer. As you say, this looks like a tragic falling out between husband and wife. There's no role for me and my colleagues in this matter." He left the house with his colleagues. To Knutsen, he said, "Wait here with Katy for a moment." He walked to Parker and said to him, "It was murder. Meet me at my flat at seven PM this evening."

Hilt watched Sign through high-powered binoculars. He cursed and called Smith. "The pain in the ass is on your back again. He's been to the house. Roberts and Knutsen are with him. They're all leaving now."

Smith replied, "Sign will know the scene was stage-managed. But he'll have no proof." He laughed. "That will considerably annoy him. He's digging a hole for himself. In the end, he'll be a laughing stock and his credibility will be shattered. Stay on him though. And watch out for Knutsen and Roberts. They'll try to grab you while you're watching Sign. They'll try to use you to get to me."

"Understood boss. If that happens, what are my protocols?"

"Kill them."

"No problem."

That evening in West Square, Sign paced back and forth in front of Roberts and Knutsen. He checked his watch. "We don't have long. In five minutes' time, the man you saw me speaking to outside File's house will arrive here. He won't be late or early. He's a very senior MI6 officer and is the only person at that grade that I trust. I won't introduce him to you as MI6. I'll leave it to him to decide how he couches his credentials. I'd be put in prison for blowing someone's cover without authority. But when he arrives, I am going to break other rules that are equally detrimental to my freedom. Win him over; charm him; show him you mean business." The downstairs communal intercom buzzed. Sign looked at Knutsen. "Do your usual security checks first. If all is good, let him in."

Two minutes' later, Colin Parker was in the room.

Sign gestured to the others. "This is detective inspector Katy Roberts of the Metropolitan Police Special Branch. You saw her this morning. She has been working with me for several weeks and is my sole link to the commissioner of her service. The gentleman sat next to her is Tom Knutsen. He has recently retired from the Metropolitan Police. When in service, he was a detective and an undercover operative. Their credentials are impeccable."

Parker nodded at them and slung his overcoat onto a chair. "You're all working on File's suicide?"

Sign pulled out a chair. "Take a seat dear chap. We're working on a pattern of behaviour. Archer, Lake, and now File. In a matter of weeks they took their lives."

Parker was impatient. "I know!" He sat.

"Would you like to tell Mrs. Roberts and Mr. Knutsen who you are?"

"I work in government service."

"They'll need specifics if they're to trust you."

Parker looked horrified. "Ben, what the..?"

Sign smiled. "They know I'm formerly MI6."

"Good for you. I didn't realise you were so loose lipped."

"Three deaths. But it's not just three deaths." He pointed at Roberts. "Katy's husband was murdered by a killer who I strongly suspect is working for the man who's orchestrating the suicides."

Parker looked at Roberts. "I'm sorry… I heard, but didn't know it was your husband."

"Why would you?" Roberts pointed at Sign. "Knutsen describes Sign as a magpie. He collects things. But only things of extreme value to him. He's collected Knutsen and me. Maybe he wants to collect you." She gestured to the antiquities, other artefacts, and books in the lounge. "As far as I can ascertain, there are four things that are vital to his life and work: trust, kindness, authenticity, and expertise. You won't find one item in this room that doesn't match all four criteria."

The accurate observation startled Sign. He decided to lighten the tone and opened a drawer in his wooden writing desk. "Thank you for being so flattering, Mrs. Roberts. But, I do have some things in here that don't quite match those criteria. An eighteenth century cutthroat razor used by a man who wanted to cut off my head," he rummaged through the contents of the drawer, "a leather sheaf containing a pin dipped in poison – I would have died in two seconds if the woman had succeeded in sticking it in me, a defused bomb inside one of my old mobile phones, a revolver that nearly blew my head off, and so many other things. He slammed the drawer shut. My Pandora's Box. But Mrs. Roberts is right – everything else, organic or inorganic, in my flat matches her criteria." He looked at Parker. "We're dealing with matters of national interest. That bothers me of course, though I'm no longer in that game. So, all a humble civilian like me can do is deal with the immediate problem. We're dealing with a serial killer. If we capture or kill him we…"

"Nip the bud before it grows into an oak." Parker looked at Knutsen and Roberts. He was silent. All were silent. Then he said, "I am head of counter intelligence at MI6. I am due to retire in six months' time. By declaring my status to you, the only things I have to lose are my pension and my dignity."

Knutsen replied, "We don't breathe a word to anyone outside of this room. That's how we're wired."

"It had better be." Parker addressed Sign. "You've spoken to the chief?"

"Yes."

"As cantankerous as ever?"

"Correct. But he did help." Sign pulled out an old school chalkboard that he'd rescued during a Pakistani bombardment of an empty Indian school. "I'm not supposed to do this." He winked at Knutsen. "But I'm going to." He started writing on the board, using chalk. "The outgoing chief gave me the list of candidates for the top job in MI6." He wrote the list. "One of them could be the whisperer."

Parker frowned. "The whisperer?"

"The person who whispers people to death." Sign drew two lines down the board, thereby dividing it into three columns. At the top of column one he wrote the title, *List of Candidates to be Chief of MI6*. He drew a line through Archer, Lake, and File. "That leaves me, Messenger, Pendry, and Logan on the list. I'm no longer in MI6, but could I be playing a canny game, hoping to get back into the organisation at the very top?"

Knutsen said, "No."

Roberts and Parker agreed.

Knutsen added, "You weren't anywhere near the death scenes when the suicides happened. I bear witness to that."

Sign put a line though his name. "So that leaves Messenger, Pendry, and Logan. All potential victims? Or, is one of them the killer? In the middle column he wrote the title, *Tangential Victims*. Beneath that he wrote the names Elliot Roberts and Debby File. "Any of us could join this middle list." On the right column he wrote the title, *The Murderers*.

Beneath that he wrote the words 'whisperer' and 'limpet'. He looked at Parker. "The limpet, I am sure, is former paramilitary MI6."

"Shit!"

"Yes. But he's not the brains. He's an employee. An extremely ruthless one at that." Sign patted Roberts, Knutsen, and Parker on their shoulders. "Everything – absolutely *everything* – is kept within this room. Mr. Parker – would you care to help us with our investigation?"

Parker glanced at Knutsen and Roberts. "I have a day job."

"Which is vital to us. What does MI6 think about the suicides?"

"It thinks there's a conspiracy between Archer, Lake, and File. They got caught out by a foreign intelligence agency. They killed themselves rather than face the music."

"Idiots!" Sign started pacing again. "MI6 knows that's not the case. But it wants this to be swept under the carpet."

Parker bowed his head. "Ben – you know these are troubling times. We have an idiot savant U.S. president, problems in Germany, major problems with Russia, the possibility of nuclear war with North Korea, China breathing down our necks, Brexit, terrorism at the drop of a loony tunes hat, UK politics all over the show, and UK workers overseas looking at our shores as if they're stranded troops on the sands of Dunkirk. We need a new head of MI6. No one outside of the list is qualified for the role."

"MI6 could recruit someone outside of The Office; perhaps from the Diplomatic Service. It's happened before."

Parker shook his head. "Not in this climate. Right now we need an expert spy; a combatant. These are not times for diplomacy."

"And what about you, Colin? You could postpone your retirement. You are both senior and experienced. The only reason you're not on the list is because you're soon leaving the service."

Parker shook his head. "I've told you before – My partner and I have plans. We've bought a restaurant in France."

Sign stared at the board. "So, it's down to Pendry, Messenger, and Logan."

Parker said, "We could put protection around them."

"We could. But in doing so, we could be protecting the whisperer from himself. We'd never find out his identity." Sign walked up to Parker. "Are you prepared to help us?"

"Doing what?"

"Work from the inside. How do you get on with the head of security?"

Parker shrugged. "He's a bumptious plodder who has ideas above his station. But he does the job right. I can work with him."

"You'll need Gable's permission for this, but why don't you and the head of security interview and brief Messenger, Pendry, and Logan. Ostensibly it will be to flesh out their understanding of operational security and counter-intelligence. The meetings would be couched as part of the selection process for the next chief."

"The chief interviews are not scheduled until two months before Gable retires. You know how it works. There's a ring of steel put around the process to ascertain the next chief.

Only a handful of people in MI6 are privy to that process. To interview candidates now would be premature and unprecedented."

"I know." Sign sat in his armchair. "But these interviews would be data sharing, not the real deal. Look at it this way: when an election is about to take place, MI6 always briefs potential foreign secretaries from all major parties, on the basis that elections can be unpredictable and whoever wins must hit the ground running. This could be a similar dynamic."

"It could." Parker was deep in thought. "I'll speak to the chief. I'm sure I can set this up. Presumably what you want me to do is get the measure of Messenger, Pendry, and Logan."

"Yes. See if one of them is a psychopath."

Parker laughed. "I'm good at my job, but a highly intelligent serial killer is hardly going to reveal himself to me."

"Ask them, 'What would you do?' questions. What would you do if you met an agent in Islamabad, and your agent was compromised? Would you save the agent or get out of there on the basis that you carry a treasure trove of secrets in your head? Work the angles; keep probing. Eventually the answers to your questions may paint a picture. We're looking for a narcissist; someone who only prioritises himself. The whisperer is ruthless and single minded. He doesn't care about others."

"Logan, Pendry, and Messenger are too bright to fall for that."

"Then set them up for a fall. Tell them these are troubling times. We need clear thinkers. People who are not afraid to make tough decisions. Lure the whisperer out with the backdrop of a world that's turned to madness. See if the whisperer bites and answers your questions truthfully."

Parker sighed. "I'll try. But let me put it this way: if I interviewed you under similar circumstances, you'd run circles around me, the head of security, the chief, the prime minister, in fact anyone in power."

"But, you're not interviewing me."

"Have you considered the possibility that the whisperer is as clever as you?"

"I've considered the possibility that his intellect outstrips mine." Sign said, "Give it a shot. Sometimes it's not about the answers, but rather the demeanour of the interviewees. Use your antennae. Who, sitting in front of you, could be a murderer?"

Parker stood and put on his coat. "I'd be going out on a massive limb for you all." He hesitated. "But I'll do it. Oh, and if I took your question literally, I can see two male murderers in this room." He left.

Sign said to Knutsen and Roberts, "Good. We have Parker on our task force. Now – I need to cook a stir fry. It's my own recipe, adapted from a recipe I received from a Chinese prostitute I rescued from a slave trade program. Mrs. Roberts – I suggest you stay for supper. There are no aromas of food coming from your kitchen and one can only eat takeaways now and again. Mr. Knutsen – shall we all eat our Chinese food while playing a board game? Trivial Pursuit?"

"No! You always win."

"Monopoly?"

"You cheat."

Sign considered the options. "Texas Hold'em poker. Five quid in loose change maximum per player. Winner takes all." Sign paused before entering the kitchen. His face and tone of voice were serious as he said, "Parker will not be able to achieve much beyond character assessments. Even that will be flawed because Logan, Messenger, and Pendry are chameleons. Parker's use to me is not to flush out the whisperer; rather, to tell him the net is closing around him. The whisperer will see through Parker and know he's working for me. We must pray nothing bad happens to Parker."

CHAPTER 19

Roberts entered the commissioner's office in New Scotland Yard. Wearing a smart black trouser suit with her ID badge pinned to her collar, and with her hair pinned up, she looked every inch the top detective the Met had to offer. Much to the consternation of the commissioner, she sat on the edge of his desk and addressed him. "Let's cut to the chase. I'm still grieving, but am rational. Knutsen's a power house. Sign's IQ is off the charts. And we have a fourth member of our team – an MI6 officer – who may be able to help. We also have a list of three people who may be potential victims or suspects. I can't tell you who's on that list – it's classified – but I can tell you we're making progress. Keep Sign and Knutsen on the payroll. If you don't, you may be compromising national security. I want your assurance that you'll keep us all on the case."

The commissioner partly wanted to bollock Roberts for being so impertinent. But secretly he loved the fact that she was back in the saddle. "I presume the three people on the list are MI6."

"Yes, but it's more complicated than that. There are other potential victims in play. Plus, we have a hitman in the mix – my husband's murderer."

The commissioner looked away. "I will renew Sign's contract from my slush fund. Stay on the case and stay focused. MI5 is breathing down my neck. They're gunning for an MI6 scandal."

"Just tell MI5 to fuck off. They're reasonably good at catching terrorists on UK soil. They're bugger all use for anything more cerebral." Roberts stood. "I want to interview Debby File."

"She's been interviewed already."

"But not by me. Where is she?"

The commissioner replied, "In the same hospital." He sighed. "You can see her. I'll notify the appropriate authorities." His eyes narrowed. "You have your war-paint on, and I'm thankful, but what's the devil in the detail?"

Roberts wondered if she should tell her boss the truth. She decided she should. "My husband put a flower in my hair on the summit of Mount Snowden and kissed me; I burned his body and tossed the remains onto the rocks. We bought a house that was to be ours forever; I've just sold it to an anonymous cash buyer. My stomach cramps at night. I smell him, even though it should be impossible to do so. So, the devil in the detail has a new face.- a murderer. I've put my affairs to bed. I need to catch the killer."

The commissioner stood, walked round his desk, and touched Roberts' elbow. Ordinarily it would have been an inappropriate action for such a senior officer to make. But, the commissioner was happily married and viewed Roberts as a daughter. "Time heals. Work helps."

"I hope so."

"Go interview Debby File and find out if something's amiss." The commissioner smiled sympathetically. "The anonymous cash buyer for your house was Ben Sign. He wanted the place off your hands as soon as possible. He paid more than the asking price. When the transaction's complete, he'll hopefully sell the place. He took a mortgage out against his pension."

Roberts was startled. "His pension? That could cripple him. I don't need his charity!"

"You don't. But you do need friends. Sign wasn't giving you charity; he was giving you closure, despite the cost to himself."

Hilt watched Roberts enter Watford General Hospital. The limpet was in a car, holding a zoom lens camera to his face. His handgun was tucked under his belt at the nape of his spine. He called Smith and told him what he was seeing.

Smith replied, "Let Roberts proceed. I've geared this to make it look like Debby File is integral to her husband's death. Lack of evidence to the contrary is all that matters to us. But stay on Roberts. I want to know where she goes next."

Roberts entered Debby File's hospital room. Aside, from File and Roberts, the room was empty. File was on a bed, her left leg elevated and held in place by straps. A plaster cast and bandages were on her ankle; a drip was by her arm, its liquid intravenously entering her forearm via tubes. Her auburn hair was matted, eyes bloodshot, face blotchy.

Roberts pulled up a chair and sat next to her. "I'm Detective Inspector Katy Roberts of the Metropolitan Police Service. I know you've been interviewed before, but I'm working a different angle. I'd like to talk to you."

"Detective Roberts – I have nothing to add to that which I've already said to your colleagues. I was shot in the ankle. My husband committed suicide. I never spent the things the bank said I spent on my credit card. If my husband had that rifle in our house, he must have kept it well hidden from me. My husband loved me and our son. He showed no signs of instability. He was a clever man. He'd have worked us out of debt. Why did he kill himself? It makes no sense."

Roberts pulled out copies of File's credit card statements. "These say you spent nearly twenty three thousand pounds in two days. None of the purchases were blocked by your bank, because the things you bought were typical of the kind of items you'd bought in the past – food at Tesco's, online shopping at Amazon, ditto M&S and Next, utility bills, and petrol. Plus, you paid a rather hefty bill for your car to be repaired at your local mechanics, on top of which you booked a holiday at your local travel agent for you and your family to spend four weeks in a series of luxury resorts in Asia. That holiday alone cost seven thousand pounds, factoring in business-class flights."

File shook her head. "I didn't buy any of those things. The last time I used my credit card was about three weeks ago. And that was to buy lunch at a pub. This must be a mistake."

"Your credit card statements are delivered to you once a month. It looks like you requested these copies in advance of your regular statements."

File looked confused. "I didn't request them. I'd never seen them before one of your colleagues showed them to me."

"And yet they were found in your filing cabinet. Could your husband have requested them?"

"No. We have separate bank accounts. He doesn't have authority to access mine."

"Are you sure your husband didn't see these statements?"

"No, I'm not sure! I don't hide things from my husband. My filing cabinet is unlocked. I didn't know the statements were in there! But he never snoops. Least ways, not at home." She started sobbing. "Anyway, why would he shoot me and hang himself over twenty three thousand pounds? It doesn't make sense."

"No, it doesn't. But it makes enough sense for a coroner's report to conclude that you and your husband were under marital stress. It will conclude that violence led to these outcomes." Roberts showed her the photo of Terry File and the woman. "Have you seen this before? It too was in your filing cabinet."

"No! No, no. no!"

"Do you know who she is?"

"I've never seen her before. My husband was faithful."

Roberts put the photo back in her pocket. "I believe you. The woman was one of his colleagues. They were working. I've no idea who took the photo."

File breathed deeply. "What's happening?"

"I'm trying to find out. Who's looking after your son?"

"My brother and his wife. They live nearby."

"Has your husband ever expressed suicidal thoughts before?"

"Never. He was happy."

Roberts nodded. "You are security cleared to know exactly the nature of his work?"

File replied, "He's been MI6 all of his adult life. His last job was head of the paramilitary unit. He didn't go out and do the 'guns and glory' stuff, as he used to call the work of his department. He merely managed his units from his office in HQ."

"Did he know how to use a gun?"

"Of course."

"How good?"

"If he wanted to kill me, he'd have done so." File winced as she adjusted position in her bed."

Roberts stood. "Nothing you've told me or my colleagues is admissible in a court of law. You're on morphine painkillers. Anything you say until you're off morphine cannot be deemed as evidence. But, for what it's worth, I believe you. Something's not right. There is a team working on your case. I'm part of that team. We have access to places that other police and investigators can't access." She paused before leaving. "I've recently gone through the loss of my husband. I suppose it varies per person, but if you're like me it starts bad, then becomes hell, but finally gets into the realm of being a new chapter in your life."

"Do you have children?"

Roberts shook her head.

"Imagine explaining to a child that their daddy isn't coming home. That new chapter you speak of may never come to me, let alone my son."

That evening, Parker was in Sign's lounge. Sign, Knutsen, and Roberts were also present. Sign had made mince pies and mulled wine. He handed out the food and drink to the team before taking his seat.

Parker said, "The head of security and I interviewed and briefed Messenger, Pendry, and Logan."

"All three of them together, or individually?" asked Knutsen.

"Individually. But we didn't have much time, given it was arranged at short notice. We had thirty minutes with each officer." Parker took a sip of his mulled wine. "Ooh, this is good. You've put something different in here."

"Ginger." Sign tapped his finger against Logan, Messenger, and Pendry's names on the chalkboard. "How did you couch the interviews?"

"As we agreed. I told them that the interviews were not part of the upcoming formal application process to become chief. I added that, if anything, today's meetings were designed to bolster their knowledge of security matters and thereby enhance their chances of success within the application process. I said matters were becoming urgent. All three of them were aware of the suicides of Archer, Lake, and File. We told them that MI6 is cooperating with the police but MI6 is also conducting its own investigation. I said that it was probable that the suicides were linked; that all three may have taken their lives because they were in some kind of conspiracy that compromised the integrity of MI6. Most likely they were blackmailed by a foreign intelligence agency. They cracked and took the easy way out."

"Good." Sign brushed chalk dust off his fingers. "Do you think they bought that falsehood?"

"Of course not. But not one of them indicated they knew I was lying."

"To be expected." Sign closed his eyes. "Logan, Pendry and File. Two of them may be potential victims. One of them may be the whisperer." He opened his eyes and stared at Parker. "Which one is the whisperer?"

Parker sighed. "I couldn't tell. Messenger has fourteen aliases. That means he's fourteen different people. Pendry has adopted the mantle of spin doctor. Anything that comes out of his mouth is utter shite. Logan is ruthless and arrogant. He prides himself on speaking five Asian languages with fluency. He keeps his cards close to his chest."

Sign repeated, "Which one of them is a killer?"

"Come on Ben! We're all in that ballgame! It's like gathering a bunch of lunatics and asking them 'Which one of you has been a naughty boy?'"

Sign ignored the astute comment. "Messenger is head of MI6's European Controllerate. Fourteen aliases is a heavy burden. At peak, I did sixteen. Managing that for years induces schizophrenia. Pendry is Head of Communications. That means he needs to speak to every component of UK government, together with the media and foreign governments. He's a political animal. Power has rubbed off on him. He knows how to manipulate the world. Logan is the dark horse. He thinks like an Asian. Family is essential; the lives of others are not. He'd happily cut out your eyes if it meant he could save his wife and kids." Sign wrote three words next to the suspects on the board. "Schizophrenic, megalomaniac, psychopath." He looked uneasy as he spoke quietly to the board. "Which one of you is the whisperer?"

CHAPTER 20

John Smith entered the chief's office in MI6 headquarters. The large room contained framed photos of every chief who'd served in the organisation since it was created in 1909. Typically, each chief served five years before being told to retire. The current chief was no exception. He had three months left in MI6 before he'd swap his cloak and dagger for something more benign. Smith was counting down the days for that to happen.

He sat opposite Henry Gable. "You wished to see me, sir. I have to say it's inconvenient. I'm running a misinformation exercise in parliament. MPs are nibbling at the false intelligence I've fed them. It should sway them on their vote on Syria."

Gable sighed. "Games, games. You were always very good at them. But yes – we need parliament to vote the right way." He ran a finger around his tea cup. "That's not why you're here. Archer's dead; Lake's dead; File's dead. That leaves you and two others in the running for my job."

"Who are the others?"

"You know full well who they are." Gable wondered how MI6 would fare if Smith was made chief. Still, Smith was exceptionally bright and ruthless. Maybe that's what the service needed right now. "I've been advised by an external agency not to protect you and the other two candidates. As contrarian as it sounds, the rationale behind that advice is that we must weed out the bad apples. Are you a bad apple?"

"Yes."

"Don't be flippant with me. Do you have any links to Archer, Lake, and File?"

"Of course. We've all gained seniority in MI6."

"And they're dead."

"And I'm not." Smith looked at the pictures of the chiefs. Soon, he'd be up there. "You'll be going out having hit the zenith of a remarkable stint of service. But you won't matter when you're gone. The service will put a picture of you on a wall. It's the equivalent of getting a gold pen at the end of a career where you've sacrificed everything and received little in return."

"So, why do you want the job?"

"I want to change things. Get rid of the pomp and bullshit in The Office."

"Do you now?" Gable chuckled. "You have ambitions above your station."

Smith shook his head. "You're in charge of a bunch of free thinkers who don't give a shit about what you say. Name me one other government organisation – Crown Service, military, Civil Service – that contains people like that."

Gable was silent.

"Free thinking is crucial. But I want us to adopt a U.S. model – more militaristic in chain of command; and I want UK special forces to report to the chief of MI6, not the director of UKSF. In fact I want the post of director scrapped."

Gable frowned. "You want control of the SAS, SBS, and SRR?"

"And MI5. It's about time those knuckle heads were merged with MI6. I'll sack most of them and get people with brains to replace them."

Gable said, "You'd be building a fiefdom."

"I'd be building a streamlined and efficient structure. Come on Henry. We both know this has been under consideration for a decade or so."

"And rejected. UKSF is very different from MI5, which in turn is very different from MI6."

Smith breathed in deeply. "MI6 sets the bar. It's gold standard. The others are not. With good selection and training, we can change that. I'll redefine the benchmark of excellence."

"Save your speech for the interview process." Gable sipped his tea while keeping his eyes fixed on Smith. "Why do you think Archer, Lake, and File killed themselves?"

Smith shrugged. "Logically, there's only one explanation – they did something wrong. A foreign intelligence agency knew that and decided to try to blackmail them. They'd have been wracked with guilt. They did the honourable thing and took their lives, rather than risk shame and prison. Which foreign agency did this is unknown. But, it will have been one of the usual suspects – Russia, China, maybe Iran. You know all this. My views are shared by you and other senior MI6 management."

Gable nodded. "Why this has happened is not the priority. What matters is that we get a new chief. Are you sure you don't have any skeletons in your closet?"

"I'm a career spy. If you raked over my past in the field, you'd discover actions of mine that might be morally ambiguous. That's true for all MI6 operatives. But, I've never passed secrets to foreign agencies without strict authority to do so from our service; I've never slept with a foreign spy; never taken cash; never misappropriated funds; never done anything that would compromise my application for your job. If I was approached by a hostile agency who thought it had dirt on me, I'd laugh and tell them to do their worst. They've got nothing on me. I'm armour plated. Clearly, Archer, Lake, and File were not."

"Yes." Gable addressed Smith by his real name and said, "As you've described, I think you would be a force for change if you were appointed. We shall see. You're up against two other highly qualified candidates. They're different from you, but they also have huge strengths. When you're interviewed for the job, I'll be there – alongside the prime minister, foreign secretary, members of the Joint Intelligence Committee, psychologists, police chiefs, and plus as you know we always throw in a wild card such as a senior former KGB defector. But know this: my voice will be heard. If I smell a rat, I'll exert my influence."

Smith smiled. "Of course, sir. You have nothing to worry about."

Two hours' later, Hilt sent Smith a text message with a photo.

This guy turned up at Sign's place last night. Knutsen met him at the door. Know who he is?"

The photo very clearly showed the man's face.

Colin Parker.

Smith texted back.

We have an insider helping Sign. Meet me in one hour at the safe house in Chelsea.

In West Square, Knutsen stood in front of the chalkboard. "You, me, and Roberts could individually follow Logan, Messenger, and Pendry."

Sign replied, "We'd be spotted by them."

"You wouldn't."

"Maybe; maybe not. Regardless, the risk of scaring them off is too great."

"What about their mobile phones? If we could get hold of them, I know a hacker in Peckham who could work wonders. I could insert tracking devices. Possibly even intercept devices to monitor their calls, texts, and emails."

Sign chuckled. "How very *Jason Bourne* of you. Alas, the real world of espionage doesn't work that way. When Pendry, Logan, and Messenger go to head office, they are required to hand over their mobile phones to security. The phones are examined with state of the art equipment designed by GCHQ. Any tracking or intercept devices will be discovered. We would have blown our game and made future steps considerably harder."

Knutsen paced. "There must be something we can do!"

Sign interlaced his fingers while deep in thought. "Let's presuppose that the whisperer is either Logan, Messenger, or Pendry. The end game is that one of them becomes chief. The whisperer has two chess moves that are difficult to defeat: first, he's killing the competition for the post; second, it's hard to resist the assumption that the shortlist is being murdered by a hostile foreign agency. But the third chess move plays to his strength but also his Achilles heel. Whichever man on the shortlist is left standing will know that he's the suspected whisperer. MI6 will wonder why he wasn't killed."

Knutsen disagreed. "MI6 is desperate for a new chief. Once that person takes office, he'll be protected day and night. The whisperer has done his work. He doesn't need to kill again."

"You think MI6 will turn a blind eye and move on?"

"Yes."

"I fear you may be right. However, there is something you're missing."

"What?"

Sign smiled. "You and I won't turn a blind eye."

At nine twelve PM, Smith and Hilt moved silently into the rear garden of a detached rural property in Oxfordshire. It was dark; they were wearing clear, thick, plastic black overalls. Underneath Smith's external garment, his suit, shirt and tie were visible. Beneath Hilt's overall, he was wearing a jumper and jeans. Both had shoes that were too big for their foot size, but had toilet paper stuffed inside them to compensate for the size-differential between foot and shoe. Over them were blue disposable covers of the type that doctors wear when performing surgery. They had Sellotape wrapped around their fingers, gloves on their hands, face masks covering their mouths and nose, and gaffer-tape wrapped around every thread of their hair.

A dog was barking nearby, but not at them. There were two other houses that were one hundred yards away. No other properties were within miles of the tiny hamlet. Bats were flying overhead, chasing midges in a star-encrusted sky. A fox screeched close to them, sounding like a woman or child screaming. It was probably just calling to its mate or cubs, or it was warning the barking dog to back off from its aggressive tone.

Hilt was the first to reach the rear kitchen door of the two bedroom property. Through the gap between the hallway and two doors, the lounge was partially visible. A middle age man was sitting on a sofa, watching a natural history program. There were no other signs of life. This was to be expected. Smith had told Hilt that the man lived alone and had a boyfriend who resided six miles away at the end of a country lane. Hilt tried the door. Locked. He used lock picks to open it. He entered, holding a silenced pistol. Smith was close behind him. Hilt wasted no time. He punched the man on the head, though not hard enough to render him unconscious, wrapped his arms around the man's arms, yanked him out of his seat, maintained his vice-like grip as they crashed against a wall and slumped to the floor, and wrapped his legs around the man's legs. The victim couldn't move an inch as Hilt held him in place.

"Hello, Colin," said Smith as he stood over the man.

Colin Parker looked shocked. Though most of Smith's features were covered, his eyes were exposed. There was no doubt it was Smith. "You!"

Smith sounded bored as he replied, "Yes, it's me."

"You're the whisperer!"

Smith laughed, though the sound was muted by his face mask. "The whisperer? Is that was Sign calls me?" He angled his head while thinking. "Actually, I like the name. It makes sense." He looked at Parker. "I've bought you a gift." From the small holdall he was carrying, he pulled out a one and a half litre magnum of Johnnie Black Label. "It's twelve years old. I believe it's your favourite tipple, though you're very cautious with booze – only a dram once or twice a week. You don't drink beer, wine, or any other alcoholic beverages. I always think that middle age is when men make steadfast decisions about what they like and dislike. It brings clarity to the mind, after years of putting up with shit we don't like. Regardless, your alcohol tolerance will be very low."

"What do you want?"

Hilt gripped harder. Parker gasped.

"What I want is for you to have a drink, in a slightly different way than normal. It's always good to try out new things, even at our age." He unscrewed the bottle's cap and crouched in front of Smith. Out of his bag he withdrew a plastic funnel that was attached to three foot length of rubber tubing. "You may be aware of this technique of supplying food and drink into someone. The Russians used it on prisoners in the Cold War. I must warn you, it will hurt."

Hilt adjusted position so that his hands were around Parker's head, while retaining the lock on his arms and legs.

"Open wide." Smith forced the tube into Parker's mouth.

Parker writhed, sweat pouring down his face, his eyes screwed tight.

But Smith's hand was steady. He pushed the heavy tube down Smith's gullet, and kept pressing until the tip of the tube was in his stomach. "There we go. That wasn't so bad."

Parker was in agony.

"So, here's the tricky bit. You're going to polish off this magnum in stages. What I need you to do is take a deep breath through your nose. Then I'm going to briefly block your nasal airway. Ready, steady, go."

Parker inhaled air.

Smith clamped his nose shut with forefinger and thumb and poured whisky into the funnel. He waited a few seconds before releasing his grip on Parker's nose. "Breathe now. We'll continue in a moment."

Smith repeated the process twelve times, before the magnum was empty bar a few drops. He pulled out the tube. "That should do the trick."

Parker was moaning but still conscious, though he was paralytic. Hilt released his grip on him and stood.

Smith said to Hilt, "Check his breathing." Smith put the tube back into his bag.

Hilt said, "Breathing's fine, for now. But he's blacked out."

"Good." Smith moved fast. He put Parker's finger prints all over the bottle and screw top, grabbed a tumbler from the kitchen and put Parker's finger tips around the exterior and his saliva on the rim, poured the tiny amount of whisky left into the glass, swilled it around, and placed the glass and empty bottle on a coffee table next to the sofa. He picked up Parker's mobile phone. "Key code protected. But here's the thing – Parker was never good with numbers. He's right handed." He grabbed Parker's right hand and placed his thumb against the unlock function. "There we go – thumbprint recognition. I'm in." He scrolled through the list of contacts. "Got you." He examined texts previously sent by Parker to his boyfriend. He wanted to see his style of language. He typed a text to Parker's boyfriend.

Feeling a bit down this evening. Got any whiskey? Am coming over. Don't say no. x

He sent the message. Within seconds the boyfriend was ringing. Smith ignored the call. "Car keys, car keys! Where would they be?" Smith found Parker's keys in a tray in the hallway. "Time for some heavy lifting." He placed the phone in Parker's pocket. "I'll bring his car to the rear of the house. Make sure you lock the kitchen door behind you." From the locked front door, Smith took out keys that were on the interior side of the door. He put them in Parker's other pocket. He smiled as he looked at Parker. "There we go – house all locked up, and you're about to make a journey to see your lover. Cops will take a dim view of that, given how much you've had to drink."

Smith left to get Parker's car.

Hilt hauled Parker onto his shoulder and walked out of the house. Previously, the former special forces operative had carried men twice Parker's weight over miles. This was child's play. Without dropping Parker, he stopped outside the kitchen door and used the lock picks to secure the entrance. He carried Parker to his car. The engine was running. Smith was standing by the car.

Smith said, "This is where I vanish. Over to you." He walked off into the darkness.

Hilt put Parker into the front passenger seat and placed a seat belt around his limp body. He got into the driver's seat and motored down the deserted country lane leading to Parker's boyfriend. It was dark, no street lamps. Hilt stopped the car two miles away from Parker's boyfriend's house.. He looked at Parker's comatose body. "Time for us to go loud, my friend." He put Parker in the driver's seat, no seat belt attached, sat in the front passenger seat, placed his foot on the accelerator, steered the vehicle until it got to sixty miles an hour, swung the steering wheel left, and leaped out of the car. Parker's vehicle smashed into a tree. Parker careered out of the car, via the windscreen, and smacked the ground. Hilt grimaced as he staggered to his feet. The landing on grass had cushioned his escape. But at that speed he still felt raw. Parker was motionless on the ground. The car was a wreck. Hilt ripped off a dangling piece of metal from the car and beat Parker around the head and body. Police forensics would never know what had really happened. The violence of Parker's ejection from his car would account for any bruises, broken bones, lacerations, and brain damage.

Hilt wiggled Parker's neck. It was broken. Parker's face was a bloody mess and swollen. One of his eyes was closed. The other was dangling by a thread and nestled on his face. His arms and legs were all at the wrong angles. Clothes were lacerated. Shards of glass were in his head and clothes. There was no breathing.

Parker was dead.

CHAPTER 21

The following morning, Sign was growing impatient as he kept glancing at his lounge wall clock. "Where is he? Parker was supposed to be here at eight o'clock." It was now eight forty five.

"Something must have come up," said Knutsen.

"Most likely. But he could have texted me."

Roberts asked, "Was it important for him to be at this meeting?"

"Yes!" Sign regretted snapping. "Sorry, Katy. I had an idea. Parker is integral to that idea. He could assemble a team of MI6 surveillance experts and get them to follow Messenger, Pendry, and Logan for a week."

"Would the chief allow that?"

"He wouldn't have to know. Parker could tell his team that it was simply a training exercise. All of the team members are cleared to know the identities of other MI6 officers, so technically Parker wouldn't be breaking rules. It's unlikely, though possible, that our three targets would spot the team. What's crucial is that the limpet *does* spot them. That way we take his eye off the ball. His focus will be on the MI6 team. Meanwhile we search for the limpet." He started pacing. "But I need Parker! No one else in MI6 would do this for me – they'd ask too many questions."

Roberts said, "Parker might say no. Technically he might not be breaking rules, but he's still deploying MI6 officers against high ranking officers. Parker's retiring soon. The last thing he needs is a disciplinary charge and a potential threat to his pension."

Sign waved his hand dismissively. "Parker will do it; and his pension is ring fenced, even if he steals the crown jewels." He checked his mobile. "Still nothing."

Knutsen said, "He must have needed to go to head office early."

"Yes." Sign rang Parker's mobile. It went straight to voicemail. He called the switchboard number of the Foreign & Commonwealth office. He asked for Parker. The call was transferred to Parker's office in MI6. His phone rang four times and went to voicemail. Sign hung up. "This is most unlike Parker. Things would be different if he was overseas – situations then are more fluid – but he runs a prestigious department in London. Every morning he gets the same train to London; every evening he returns home at the same time. It's his reward to himself after spending years in the field where there's no structure to daily life." Sign looked at Roberts. "Call the Met. Ask them to check their police national computer and incident logs to see if there's any reference to a Colin Parker of Oxfordshire." He gave her Parker's address. "I don't know his date of birth."

"I don't need it." Roberts was on the case. After she got off the call, she waited. "They're checking." Ten minutes later her phone rang. She expected it to be from the woman in Scotland Yard who was doing the checks. It wasn't.

A man asked, "Inspector Roberts?"

"Yes."

"I'm Superintendent Moore of Thames Valley Police." He was about to continue.

But Roberts interrupted. "I need to verify you are who you say you are. I'm calling your switchboard and will tell them to transfer me to you." She hung up, made the call, and listened as the call was transferred. "Superintendent – now we can talk freely. What do you have?"

Moore replied, "Colin Parker is flagged on our system as a senior government official whose wellbeing is vital. Last night he got drunk; *really* drunk. He drove a few miles and lost control of his car. He's dead."

Roberts looked at Sign.

Sign immediately knew something was wrong.

"Anything suspicious?" she asked.

"No. Traffic police and forensics have been all over the road traffic accident, plus detectives have examined his home. He got sozzled, got in a car, and drove. He wasn't wearing a seatbelt. Death was probably instantaneous. He was a mess when we found him."

"Where was he driving to?"

"We don't know. Toxicology reports show that he was at least twenty times over the limit. It's an open and shut case."

"Thank you, sir." Roberts ended the call and told Sign and Knutsen what she knew.

Sign was silent for a moment. He picked up his tea cup and smashed it against a wall. "Parker wasn't a heavy drinker!"

"Why was he driving at such a late hour?"

Sign rubbed his face, exasperated. "Because on one level it makes sense to MI6 and the police, if the latter were privy to what made him do something so stupid. Parker's been openly gay for years. He has a boyfriend in Oxfordshire. They've been steady for fifteen years and love each other faithfully, though now and again they throw their toys out of the pram and have a tiff. Passion is key. MI6 will think it was out of character for Parker to go on a binge and drive, but it will also conclude that passion corrupts every soul. However, what we're dealing with is murder."

Knutsen said, "You heard what Katy said. The police examined his house, car, and body. Nothing! This is not linked to our case."

"It has everything to do with our case. No doubt Parker was photographed by the limpet coming to our digs. The whisperer realised that Parker was my insider in MI6; my informant and pawn. This had to stop. Parker was force-fed booze. Either the limpet did it or the whisperer did it. My money is on the whisperer, while the limpet held Parker down. They'd have been wearing specialist clothing and other accoutrements to protect their presence in Parker's home. One or both of them would have driven him a few miles while Parker was passed out – I suspect the limpet drove and the whisperer wasn't present for the journey. Close to the death scene, the limpet put Parker in the driving seat while he was still blacked out. The limpet reached across from the passenger seat and drove at high speed. Parker wasn't wearing a seat belt. The limpet jumped. The car crashed. Parker flew through the windscreen." Sign shook his head. "If there were any indications of life, the limpet would have quashed them with a piece of metal from the car. Paint or splinters from that piece of metal would be attributed to the accident. There are no traffic cameras on the country lane he died on. No one would know the limpet was the driver. It's a perfect murder."

Knutsen walked up to Sign and placed a hand on his shoulder. "You've no evidence of this."

Sign shrugged off his hand. "Evidence?! I once caught a traitor because I'd noticed that he was wearing a green tie rather than his usual blue; I put a bullet in the head of a man who usually smoked Marlboro Lights but on the last day I met him was smoking the full strength brand – his cigarette contained a toxin aimed at me; I stripped a Russian woman and found an FSB wire, merely because she had an uncharacteristic twitch in her eye. She'd been forced to work for the FSB, under threat of death if she failed to comply. I got her out of Russia. She'd have been dead had I not noticed the tiniest minutiae. She's now happily married in France and is safe. I could go on and on with other anecdotes. Evidence is for cops. Don't put me in that category!"

Knutsen briefly glanced at Roberts. He said in a gentle voice, "Ben – Katy and I trust your instincts, we really do, and we'll back you up, but what you're suggesting sounds fanciful. I know he was your friend, but don't let that cloud your judgment."

"He wasn't a friend; he was a trusted associate. There is a difference. And I'm not being fanciful. This reeks of an assassination. I should know. I've conducted similar acts overseas." Sign walked to the window. Calmly, he said, "I thought I'd permanently given up violence. But it seems violence is coming for me. When bad men wish ill of you, you want it to happen when you're in your twenties or thirties, when you can still run half marathons and play rugger at the weekends. But at forty nine, those things become harder. My mind's agile and I can walk a fair lick, but I couldn't defend myself against the limpet."

"That's why I'm here."

"I know, dear chap." Sign smiled. "I'm sorry."

"For what?"

"Your first case in our business has thrown you straight in at the deep end. We're probably dealing with a serial killer who wants to be chief of MI6, together with a lethal assassin." Sign laughed. "You could have got a job with a local security firm."

"Where's the fun in that?" Knutsen saw the weight of the world on Sign's shoulders. "You once told me that anything is possible. At first, I thought you were spouting some mumbo jumbo positive thinking shit, like those alleged gurus do in California. Then I thought you were referring to negative stuff – how to kill someone; how to manipulate the Establishment; how to cover your tracks. Finally I realised your assertion was simply a statement of fact. Anything is possible. But, unless a person understands that, they won't even aspire to the near-impossible, let alone achieve it."

Sign nodded. "It is a mantra of sorts, but very few men and women have that gift. The problem is, you have men like me and the whisperer who strive to dally with the art of challenging the impossible. But that doesn't mean we're all good."

"You and the whisperer are very different. He's a psychopath; you're not."

"I'll let higher powers decide whether that assessment is accurate." Sign sat in his chair and interlocked his fingers. "Seven years ago I ordered a drone strike on fifty armed rebels. They probably had wives and kids. I've planted information on traitors, leading to their incarceration and probable execution; and I've shot people point blank. I may not like death, but it seems to stand by my side in life."

Knutsen repeated, "You're not a psychopath. You care. You're a good man."

Sign looked at Knutsen. "How's David and his mother?"

"The mother's clean. David has his first interview with the Metropolitan Police on Monday. I'm helping him."

"Will he get in to the force?"

"We call it police service these days."

"Regardless of terminology..?"

Knutsen hesitated. "Hard to know. Standards required of new applicants have risen dramatically during the last few years."

"Bring them here before Monday. We'll do a mock interview."

"Them?"

"Yes. Mother and son." Sign seemed distracted. "I need to go to Oxfordshire. Not to the crime scene. That won't tell me anything that I haven't already deduced. But, I'd like to have a chin wag with Parker's boyfriend. You both need to come with me, though your role will be to see if you can spot the limpet. Bring a long range camera. See if you can get a shot of him. We'll leave West Square by the front door. Hopefully the limpet will follow us."

Two hours later, Sign rang the doorbell of a converted barn, eight miles south of Oxford. The property was in countryside. Flat heathland, fields, and a few trees were all that surrounded the house. A low mist hovered above the moorland, staying fixed in place because there was no wind. Frost covered the ground. There was no noise, aside from a couple of pheasants calling in the distance.

Sign waited. There was a possibility that Parker's boyfriend was out, though Sign had earlier called his employer – Oxford University – and had been told that today he was working from home. The boyfriend was a professor of English Language and Literature at Corpus Christi college. Today he had no lectures or seminars to conduct.

The professor answered the door. He was a lanky fifty seven year old, with a full head of medium length grey hair that looked messy, though had been fashioned that way to make him look contrarian. In all other respects he had the image of a country gentleman – tweed jacket, hunting shirt, corduroy trousers, and stout boots. He frowned as he looked at Sign, who was wearing a formal suit. "Do you work at the university? I vaguely recognise you."

"Not the university. We met once at a drinks function in the British Embassy in Jakarta."

The penny dropped. "You work with Colin. What do you want?"

"Can I come in?"

The professor looked annoyed. "I was just about to go on a walk. There's been a Richard's Pipit spotted near here. I was hoping to take my binoculars and see if I could spot him."

"Richard's Pipit – native to Asia, but sometimes strays west. That would be an extremely rare sighting."

The professor's face lit up. "Ah, you too study ornithology."

"Actually, no. But I do have a good memory. At some stage in my life I must have read about the bird."

The professor was enthused. "Come in, come in." He ushered Sign into his home.

Five hundred yards away, Knutsen and Roberts were in a car on the lane leading to the professor's house. Knutsen grabbed his camera and said to Roberts, "Time for me to leave. Lock the doors when I'm out. Keep the engine running. Any problems, get the hell out of here. Don't wait for me or Sign."

With sarcasm, Roberts replied, "How very chivalrous. Ladies first."

"Nah mate. I'm going to hide in the trees over there. You're exposed. As far as I'm concerned, that's good. If anyone's going to take a bullet in the back of the head today, it will be you. You're bait." He winked at her and left.

Sign sat in a leather armchair in a lounge that was crammed with books on shelves, academic papers in piles on the floor, art, and indoor plants. Logs were burning in the fireplace, a metal guard the only protection against a spark setting the barn and all its contents into ash. A lamp with a green shield was on a wooden writing desk. There was no computer on there; just more papers, pens, and other stationary. The only electronic item in the room was the professor's mobile phone, being charged.

The professor sat close to the fire. "You know my name?"

"Eduard Delacroix."

Delacroix nodded. "Because of my association with Colin, I've been assessed by your organisation for security clearance every five years. The last assessment was four months ago."

"It's not about that. Has anyone official phoned or visited you since last night?"

Delacroix looked shocked. "No! What's happened?"

Sign breathed in deeply. "Then, I have to be the bearer of very bad news. Last night Colin was in a car accident. He died."

"What?!" Delacroix stood and rubbed his face. "Dead? Dead?"

"He's dead. Is there anyone I can call on your behalf? Family, friends, colleagues?"

Delacroix was in utter shock. "How..? How did it happen?"

"He got blind drunk and drove over here from his home five miles away. It was a miracle he didn't crash his car within one mile of his house. He was coming to see you. His mobile phone was smashed in the impact, but the sim card was intact. Security services have analysed it. He texted you before he drove, saying he was coming over to see you."

"I know! I know!" Delacroix picked up his phone. "I got the message and tried calling him. Last night wasn't a good time for me. I had papers to mark."

"Colin's parents are deceased. He has no brothers or sisters. He has…"

"No next of kin! And I don't fucking exist. We weren't married. I'm just his gay lover." Delacroix punched a table.

Sign crossed his legs, his composure calm. "Legally, that's correct. You don't exist. But, I know the attorney general. I will impress upon him in the most forthright terms that all decisions about Colin's funeral and personal administration must be given to you. There will be no dispute on this matter. You were in a loving relationship for fifteen years. You know Colin better than anyone. It is your right to be sole guardian of his affairs."

Delacroix was breathing fast. "Tell me everything! Colin was an expert driver. You guys taught him all sorts of stuff. What happened?"

Sign told him what he knew.

Delacroix shook his head. "He wouldn't have got drunk. Not even in a fit of depression. I've seen him down – assets he'd lost in China; that kind of stuff. Whenever he was sad, he stayed sober. It was his way of coping."

"Sometimes people get drunk when they're elated."

"Not Colin. He was always in control." Delacroix ran fingers through his hair. "If anything, I was the emotional one. Colin was my rock."

"Has he ever come over to your place at short notice before?"

"Never! He was a creature of habit. Even though we only lived five miles apart, we had rules. He does his spy stuff in the week; I do my academic stuff; he drives up Friday night with a weekend bag; we go for a meal; Sunday evening he drives home." Delacroix had tears running down his face. "Did he..? Did he..?"

"He felt no pain. Death was instantaneous." Sign leaned forward. "My colleagues will ensure that a Thames Valley Police bereavement officer comes over to help you."

"Bereavement officer?! Will that person bring Colin back to life?!"

"No. You'll carry the burden of Colin's death for the rest of your life. Maybe one day you'll find love again, but I doubt it given your age and circumstances. You'll move into the top quartile of probable suicides. You won't notice anything around you. Your work will suffer. You might be sacked. You won't eat properly. Drugs or alcohol will temporarily numb the pain. Anything anyone says to you will be judged by you to be wrong. Your stomach will gnaw on itself. Ultimately, you will no longer be in charge of yourself. Hence the need for support."

"Fucking MI6 mind games!"

"My wife was murdered. Colin was murdered."

"What?!"

Sign remained calm, his tone measured and soft. "On the former point, my wife was raped and shot in Latin America. She was Polish. Rebels thought she was a Russian spy.

They crucified her and put a bullet in her brain six hours later while she was still on the cross. It was a warning to others. They left her there. Vultures fed on her. I managed to get her bones and give them a burial. On the latter point, Colin's death isn't suspicious to the cops or MI6. He won't be afforded a full police investigation or post-mortem. And even if his body was sliced open, it would be near impossible to discern foul play. He was mashed up by the crash. However, I think a tube was pushed down his throat and into his stomach. He was force fed strong alcohol, probably his favourite whiskey. He never drove the car but it was made to look that way. He stood no chance."

Delacroix couldn't believe what he was hearing. "A tube down his throat will leave traces. Blood, maybe rubber, whatever."

"The potential traces will only be discerned by a top police forensics expert. Even then, there will be no evidence to prove murder. If I were the killer, I'd have made the tube out of the same material as the tyres on the car. The tyres were burnt out in the crash. A coroner would conclude that Colin inhaled their burning fumes in the last moments. Blood and rubber would be explained away."

"You're not a cop! How do you know these things?"

"It is precisely because I'm not a cop, and have conducted matters that would blow the minds of police officers, that I know these things." Sign's eyes didn't blink as he said in an authoritative tone, "You need a police bereavement officer here to help you get through your loss and to help you with all administrative matters. Do I have your permission to organise that visit?"

"Yes, yes." Delacroix's voice was distant. "Murder? Who would have done this?"

"There are a number of possibilities. The most likely possibility is one that I'm pursuing. I believe that Colin was the victim of a serial killer. A very unusual killer."

"Get the bastard!"

Sign nodded.

From his hidden position in the copse, Knutsen focused his camera on Delacroix's front door. His mobile phone had an ear piece and throat mic attached; the phone was dialled in to Roberts' phone. He said, "Sign's leaving. He'll be with you in a few minutes."

Roberts replied, "Okay."

Knutsen panned his camera to the right. He froze. "There's a man walking down the lane towards you. Opposite direction from Sign, but same distance."

Sign and the man were five hundred yards away from Roberts' car. Sign was walking from the north; the man was walking from the south.

"He's wearing jeans, boots and a jacket. Hood's up. I can't see his face."

Roberts sounded tense as she said, "Could just be a rambler. There's a country footpath off the lane, close to Delacroix's house. The man could be headed that way."

"Probably. But I don't like this. I'm moving position." Knutsen got to his feet and sprinted two hundred yards across heathland. He threw himself to the ground and trained his camera on the lane. Here he was more exposed. He muttered, "Come on you bastard – show your face."

Roberts said, "This doesn't feel like the limpet. He wouldn't do something like this."

"I know!" Knutsen was breathing fast. He swung his camera left. Sign was three hundred yards away from the car. Knutsen focused his camera back on the man approaching the car from the rear. "Get out of there, Katy! Pick Sign up. Don't worry about me. I'll make my own way back to London."

"No. I'm bait, remember. I'm staying put until you get that photo."

Knutsen cursed and moved to another location.

The man was a hundred yards from Roberts' car.

Knutsen made adjustments to the camera's lens. Given the angle he was now viewing the road, he was confident the man's hood would no longer expose his face.

The man was fifty yards from the car.

Roberts said, "I see him. He's in my rear view mirror. He's walking slowly. But his head's down. Can't see his face."

Nor could Knutsen.

The man was twenty yards from the car.

"Katy – get out of there. Now!" Knutsen dropped the camera, withdrew his pistol and ran across open ground towards the lane. He stopped in his tracks as the man turned to face him. They were one hundred yards apart. The man was wearing a ski mask. He put his hand inside his jacket, pulled it out – holding nothing – two of his fingers and his thumb positioned in a way to mimic a handgun. He was stock still as he turned towards the car and pretended to shoot Roberts. He turned toward Knutsen and repeated the action at him. If he'd had a real gun, both would have been dead. He turned and ran.

Knutsen pursued, firing warning shots in the air and shouting, "Police! Stop!"

Sign ran to Roberts when he heard the shots.

Knutsen raced past him while saying, "Limpet. Get Katy safe!" Knutsen continued his pursuit.

Roberts was in the driver's seat. Sign pushed her to one side, took control of the car, reversed it at full speed up the lane, performed a hand break turn, drove for another hundred yards, then stopped, the engine still running. He'd performed the manoeuvre in five seconds. He waited, staring into the rear mirror.

Roberts said, "I can drive, you know?"

Sign ignored the comment. He muttered, "Come on Tom." In a louder voice he said to Roberts, "Call Delacroix." He gave her his mobile number. "Tell him who you are and that there is a threat. Tell him to lock every single entry point in the house and then stay away from windows. Tell him there's no threat to him per se, but we have a prowler in the vicinity."

When Roberts ended the call she said, "He's calling 999."

"It will be of no use."

Knutsen was breathing fast as he jumped over ditches and small bushes, his gun held at eye level, sweat pouring down his face despite the chilly air, muscles aching, and lungs feeling like they'd ingested battery acid. All of his senses were operating at optimum level. He swivelled left and right, searching for the limpet. He ran onward into an open field, rotated three hundred and sixty degrees, and stamped his foot on the ground.

The limpet had vanished.

Four hours later, Sign, Knutsen, and Roberts convened in the West Square lounge. They'd arrived ninety minutes earlier, had showered, changed, and made some calls. Sign lit a fire and poured three glasses of calvados, which he served with espresso black coffee and muffins. He sat in his armchair. Knutsen and Roberts took their drinks and sat near him by the fire. Sign was no longer in formal attire, though was smartly dressed in a shirt and trousers that had an immaculate crease down the centre. Knutsen and Roberts were in jeans and T-shirts. They didn't want to look like they were sitting in an officers' mess.

Sign sipped his calvados. "I've just spoken to Delacroix. Thames Valley Police are with him. He's in no danger."

"How do you know that?" asked Knutsen.

"Because he serves no purpose." Sign looked angry. "Katy's husband was killed in order to stop her snooping. It didn't work but it was a chess move. Delacroix isn't on the board. His death serves no purpose. The whisperer and the limpet will know that executing him won't stop us. No purpose," he repeated.

"What happened today?" asked Knutsen.

Sign placed his glass down. "It was a shot across the bow. It was another warning. The limpet deliberately showed himself on the lane. Normally, if he was going in for a kill, we wouldn't have seen him. Instead, he sauntered up the route, not a care in the world, and pretended to put bullets in your brains." Sign lowered his head. "If he'd pulled out his gun, you'd be dead."

Roberts said, "Why did you push me out of the driver's seat. I could have got us out of there!"

Sign lifted his head. His voice was loud and aggressive when he said, "Because I've done escape and evasion in Tehran, Moscow, Beijing, Kabul, Nairobi, New York, Melbourne, and a hundred other places! You haven't! I was saving your life! If you want to get all girl-power on me, go ahead, but try a few years at the real sharp end before you earn my respect."

"Ben?" Knutsen was worried about the outburst.

Sign maintained his aggressive tone. "Let me make this simple for you both. We're dealing with two people who want us out the way. I don't care if you like me or hate me. I don't care if you think I should drive or you should drive. I don't care who carries a gun and who doesn't. But let me tell you this: I damn well care if one of you gets hurt." He stood and chucked a log onto the fire. "We're dealing with highly trained psychopaths. It would be remiss of me to allow your egos to get in the way of your lives." He watched the wood burn. In a quieter voice he said, "Mrs. Roberts – you have skills and contacts that I do not have. Plus, you have a police badge. It opens doors. You are crucial to this investigation."

"Don't patronise me!"

"I'm not." Sign smiled. "I'm putting you in your place."

The comment was met with stunned silence by Roberts and Knutsen. Then both couldn't help laughing. It was as if a pin had burst a balloon.

Sign didn't laugh. "Parker's death has set us back. Henry Gable won't further help me – I can assure you of that. Ergo, I might be of use to you because I think like an MI6 officer; but I no longer have access to MI6." He stared at Roberts. "You see? I have limitations." He asked the Special Branch inspector, "What am I missing in this case? Don't mimic my style of thinking. Instead, think like a police detective who's investigating a series of murders."

Roberts considered the question. "In murder cases, detectives want to ascertain motive. It brings us closer to narrowing down a list of suspects. But, in this case it's weird. You've ascertained that the suspects are Messenger, Pendry, and Logan. One of them might be the whisperer. The other two could be dead men walking. The suspects might be the murderer's kill list. I've never worked a case like that. I don't know any detective who has."

"What do we do next? Parker's of no use to us, God rest his soul."

"You could separately meet Messenger, Pendry, and Logan. It would be easy for you to get their DNA. Just a handshake would suffice. If there are any more murders, we could see if DNA links the crime to the murderer."

Sign shook his head. "There's been no DNA at any of the previous crime scenes. The whisperer and the limpet have been meticulous about that."

Roberts' voice trembled with emotion as she said, "Interview them anyway! Use your brilliance to ascertain who's the killer."

"That won't work. Remember – we're dealing with a schizophrenic, a megalomaniac, and a psychopath – respectively, Messenger, Pendry, and Logan. They will all appear to me to be the killer. Alas, I won't be able to discern one brute from the others."

"Then we maintain our focus on the limpet. We grab him and make him talk."

"Therein is the problem." Sign prodded a finger on a coffee table. "If I was faced with a similar problem in Ankara or Casablanca, I could torture the limpet to within an inch of his life. I'd get the whisperer's identity. Then, I'd kill the limpet. But both of you are schooled in the art of following United Kingdom rules. You're police officers. You don't have what it takes to be unconventional."

Knutsen wasn't having any of this. "I'm *ex*-police. And Katy is Special Branch. We don't follow rules."

Sign smiled. "I hoped you'd say that." He stood and stoked the fire. "But, I must warn you that it's an unpleasant business seeing a man gasp for air as water is poured down his throat, or screaming for his mother as his fingers are cut off and seared with a car cigarette lighter. It's not like the movies. Most tough guys are not defiant at that moment. They just want the pain to stop." He turned to his colleagues. "The limpet, however, will be defiant until the very end. It will be a matter of pride, as well as training. We would have to do things to him that would make a billy goat puke. My question to you is whether you could endure that experience."

Knutsen and Roberts glanced at each other.

"Also, it would be highly illegal." Sign re-took his seat. "Don't worry. I need to explain something that will resonate with your exemplary service to our country. The torture methods I've described are not for us. Not for me anymore, at least. I've had the opportunity to conduct extreme surgery on people in order to extract secrets from them. In all cases, there was a ticking time bomb to be discovered, so to speak. But in recent years I chose not to take that route."

"You chose the high ground."

"I chose the moral compass. If a state or its associates torture someone, we define our country by that action. We must do unto others what we wish to be done to ourselves. In the case of Great Britain, we must be gentle men and women, and humanely kill people who aim to hurt us."

Knutsen said, "Other cultures and states would disagree with you – Native American Indians, Russians, Germans, Japanese, Chinese, parts of Africa, et cetera."

Sign nodded. "Correct. But, for the most part, that was in the past, though I concede that those countries and territories' DNA permeates through to the current generations of your examples. But savagery, driven by survival or unnecessary aggression is not us. Agreed?"

"Yes."

"Of course."

Sign's brain was thinking on multiple levels. "We must find the limpet's most sensitive nerve ending and press it hard. The limpet is being paid by the whisperer. We could pay him more and try to get him to turn on his master. It won't work. The limpet's reputation would be in tatters. He'd never get another job. Speak or be damned in prison for thirty years or more, is another option. That won't work either. The limpet would keep his mouth shut and escape or become a hero inside the penitentiary's walls. But, there is one thing we could take away from him – his pride. He won't like that one bit, particularly if he's facing life in prison."

Roberts was following his logic. "If he goes to prison a hero, he breezes through jail time. If he goes in a loser, welcome to hell."

"Correct. I have an idea, but it's a useless idea unless I have the limpet's name." Sign rubbed his face. "This would all be so much easier if I was wrong about the whisperer. All I'd have to do is get the three MI6 officers twenty-four-seven armed protection."

Knutsen said, "That still might be an option. We'd be protecting a shortlist of candidates for chief. If the whisperer is one of them, there's no guarantee he'd be selected for the post."

"Are you willing to take one-in-three odds?" Sign stared at the names on the board. "Let's say Logan is the whisperer and he isn't appointed chief. Messenger gets the job. What would Logan do? He'd use the limpet to circumvent or neutralise Messenger's bodyguards and he'd kill him. MI6 would be forced to then replace Messenger with either Pendry or Logan. Logan would kill Pendry. He'd then fake an attack on his life to make it seem that the whisperer is an external force. He'd play the victim. Logan would be heralded a hero by his peers for surviving an assault from a hostile foreign agency. No – none of this will end until the whisperer gets what he wants."

"Power over MI6."

"I would think more than that. Power over the whole UK special operations community." Sign said with authority, "I've thought through multiple options – bugging the shortlist's homes; examining their mobiles; the three of us following them; grabbing one of them and making him contact the others with false information; producing to them a fake doctor's analysis of Henry Gable's health, showing he has stage four cancer and will be leaving his post in a matter of days, thereby accelerating matters and perhaps getting the whisperer to make a wrong move; and many other chess moves. Mrs. Roberts – pretend you didn't hear what I'm about to say next. I've even thought about killing Messenger, Pendry, and Logan. Two innocents die. One killer dies. But, I can't bring myself to do the latter option. And the other options won't work. Pendry, Logan, and Messenger are too clever and attuned to the nuances of tradecraft. They won't make mistakes. They'll see through any bluffs and intrusions on their privacy."

Knutsen said, "I've had to sacrifice people for the sake of the bigger picture."

"So have I," said Roberts. "Maybe killing the shortlist is our only option."

Sign sipped some more of his calvados. "Remember – we are defined by our actions." He looked at Roberts. "If we kill the shortlist, we will never find out the limpet's identity; the man who killed your husband."

Roberts bowed her head.

Sign smiled sympathetically. "Katy, we must find the limpet. I must give you peace."

She raised her head. "I… I just want to know what's going on. And when I know what's going on, I'll pull out my police ID and throw the law at the people responsible for Elliot's death."

Sign clapped his hands. "That's my girl."

"Woman."

"Detective." Sign was being mischievous, but for the right reasons. He wanted fight back in Roberts. "I guarantee you – you'll be the one to arrest the limpet." His voice trailed as he said, "But we must get a photo of the limpet's face."

Roberts said, "Knutsen and I have both seen the limpet's face. We could try a sketch artist."

Sign was dismissive. "You only saw the limpet briefly and under duress. Sketch artists are notoriously inaccurate because the victims describing the perpetrator are inaccurate. Compound that with the fact that we're dealing with a special operative who won't be on the police radar. He's not a common criminal. But, that doesn't matter. If I get his face, I get his name." Sign's voice rose as he said, "Tomorrow I'm going to meet

Messenger, Pendry and Logan. At least I hope I will. I will call them this evening and tell them it's an emergency. Mrs. Roberts – the meeting location has good cameras." He gave her details. "But tonight I want you to check they are all operable, and recording devices are intact." His voice turned grave as he said, "The MI6 officers are of no use to me tomorrow. All that matters is that we spot the limpet. But that is very high-stakes territory. One or all of us could die."

Hilt finished his shift watching West Square. He drove in early evening London traffic. It was dark, though the city was bathed in the glow of artificial light from car headlights, street lamps, shops, homes, and office buildings. He felt tired, having been surviving on four hours sleep per night during the last few days. He ignored the sensation. In his view, a full night's sleep was overrated. Many times, in MI6 and the SBS, he'd spent months on deployment, operating with far less sleep than he was getting now.

He parked his car and entered the one-bedroom flat he'd been renting in south London since he'd been commissioned by Smith. His real home was eighty three miles north of here. He locked the door and placed two wedges under its base. After withdrawing his handgun and placing it on a table, he had a shower, put on a clean T-shirt and boxer shorts, shoved his worn clothes in the washing machine, and grabbed a beer from the fridge. He slowly supped his drink as he checked the workings of his pistol and sniper rifle. Adjacent to them were three mobiles phones, all being charged via a socket with an adaptor. One of the phones was his hotline to Smith. He finished his beer and rang the MI6 officer. "Nothing's happened since they visited Delacroix. They tried to get a photo of me. I made sure that didn't work. They're back in West Square and it doesn't look like they're going anywhere. I've called it a day."

"They've got nowhere to go to tonight. Nowhere that bothers me, at least. Tomorrow is a different matter. Sign has just called me. He wants to meet me and two of my colleagues at ten AM tomorrow. If I go, there is a possibility I will be arrested or killed."

"Then don't go."

"Were it so simple. Sign has constructed a double-spring trap. I'm damned if I go one way and damned if I take the other route."

Hilt frowned. "I don't understand."

"Sign is trying to identify me. There are only three possibilities, and I'm one of them. He's summoned his list of suspects to tomorrow's meeting. I've made you aware of the consequences. If I don't go and the other two attend his meeting, I have a red flag draped over me. So, I will go. Take precautions. Don't go in unless you see Knutsen or Roberts enter the building. But don't take a gun or knife. There is a security scanner at the entrance. Rely on your training and ingenuity. If Roberts or Knutsen approach the meeting, this is what I want you to do." He explained what he had in mind. "Protection and extraction are key." He ended the call.

Hilt lay on the single bed. No duvet was required – he liked feeling cold when sleeping. He closed his eyes and did what he always did when trying to get to sleep – imagining people he wanted to kill. It was his version of counting sheep jumping over a fence. Most people who'd crossed his path had ended up dead; but, there were some who'd escaped his wrath. He knew who they were. As he was blissfully drifting off to sleep, he imagined shooting a Taliban leader who'd executed one of his colleagues, a Russian mafia gang lord who'd set twenty of his armed henchmen on Hilt in Murmansk, a barmaid in Berlin who'd slept with him and tried to stab him, a highly dangerous American computer hacker who'd escaped death by creating a confusing maze of false identities and addresses, a few pricks in MI6 who thought he was too unhinged to maintain his security clearance, and many others. Ultimately, he was at peace as he imagined killing Sign. He had no personal grudge against the man. Their paths hadn't crossed in MI6. But, he knew Sign was coming to kill him.

Right now, that made Sign Enemy Number One.

CHAPTER 22

At seven AM, Sign, Knutsen, and Roberts were in Sign's apartment. As instructed, Knutsen and Roberts were wearing robust clothing that would enable them to move fast. Sign was wearing a suit. He'd prepared coffee and croissants for breakfast. It was nearly daylight, though the sky was moody and rain was lashing windows. Roberts couldn't help yawning. Knutsen was bleary-eyed and unshaven.

Sign said to them, "Grief and anxiety are bad bedfellows. But we must be alert now. Strong coffee will help. You can sleep later."

"If we're alive." Knutsen rubbed his stubble and looked out of the windows. "It's a piss poor day to die."

Sign was full of energy, despite having had no sleep. And he'd taken care over his morning ablutions. "It's my job to ensure that I might die today and you won't." He handed Roberts a sealed envelope. "In the event of my death, open that. It contains specific instructions, the contact details of a man, a letter of introduction, and my signature. Don't take the envelope with you today. If the limpet grabs you he will strip search you. Hide the envelope somewhere outside of West Square. Don't tell me the location." He turned his attention on Knutsen. "Sir – today is about a sleight of hand. I want the people meeting me to see one thing, wherein what's actually happening is a wholly different matter. Katy's job is to act like an arresting officer. Your job is to focus on the limpet. No guns can be taken into the building. But you're a dab hand at unarmed combat. If you have to tackle the limpet, hurt him but don't kill him. Dead people can't give us answers. And most important – let him escape."

Roberts asked, "Shouldn't we swamp the building with plain clothes Met officers?"

Sign shook his head. "The whisperer will spot them in a jot; so too the limpet and the other two MI6 officers. Logan, Pendry, and Messenger will tell me they had to abort the meeting due to the hostile nature of the meeting location. And they will be right to say that. The whole exercise will have been a waste of time." He looked at Roberts. "But, I do want them to see you. And I want the whisperer to feel smug because you're all that I've got."

Hilt sat in front of a mirror in his flat. He applied makeup to his face, making his complexion look paler than normal, and a fake moustache and grey wig. He dressed in cheap clothes that looked like they were bought in the 1970s and sprinkled sugar on his jacket's lapels to make it look like he suffered dandruff. He took a swig of Special Brew lager, gargled and spat the mouth-full out, ensuring that some of the spit dropped onto his clothes. He picked up a wooden walking stick and left the flat, limping as he proceeded to central London.

At 0955hrs, Pendry walked through the huge pillars that fronted the entrance to the British Museum in Covent Garden. Hilt watched him. From a different location, so did Roberts. Knutsen was nowhere to be seen. At 0956hrs hours, Messenger arrived at the location and entered London's largest museum. Hilt remained static; so too Roberts. Logan was the last to arrive. Once he was in, Roberts ran to the entrance. Hilt hobbled there, pretending he was disabled.

Hilt approached the ticket counter and purchased an entrance ticket to the establishment. He handed the ticket to an official who was standing next to the museum's metal detector.

The official asked him, "Is there any metal in your walking stick?"

Hilt shook his head. "Just wood and rubber. I can't manage without it."

The official could smell the alcohol on Hilt. "We have disabled ramps and wheelchairs if that would help?"

"Nah thanks. Fell over outside the boozer last week. It's just temporary. The stick will be fine." He emptied his pockets of all metal items, winced as he took off his belt and watch, and placed all items into a tray. He hobbled through the X-ray machine, collected his belongings, and continued onwards. He knew Sign was already in here.

He spotted Roberts, but couldn't see Knutsen. Most likely Knutsen had entered the museum earlier. That didn't matter. Only Roberts could throw the law at Hilt's paymaster. He followed her. She was walking at a leisurely pace, pretending to read a museum brochure. The building was at half capacity, but that still meant there were hundreds of tourists in the venue. Hilt moved closer to Roberts, fearful he'd lose sight of her. He passed displays of Greek artefacts, Buddhist art, French ceramics, and Roman sculptures. Roberts entered the huge reading room in the centre of the museum. Hilt followed.

In the north end of the circular reading room, Sign stood in front of Messenger, Pendry, and Logan. All of the men were in suits. Sign's guests looked pissed off.

"What's so urgent that we had to be summoned here?" asked Messenger.

"And who are you to summon us?" asked Logan. "You're no longer one of us."

Pendry was silent, though looked hostile.

Sign looked around before he returned his gaze to the men. "It is possible you're being targeted for assassination."

All three laughed.

Pendry said, "We take precautions."

"Of course." Sign scrutinized each man.

Messenger, the schizophrenic. A medium-height man who today was playacting the façade of being a well-groomed gentleman, but tomorrow could transform himself into a Russian bar brawler, if the need arose.

Pendry the megalomaniac. A tall spin doctor who schmoozed which ever government was in power, and all because he wanted to run the country via the power of suggestion.

Logan the psychopath. A short man whose muscularity was that of an Olympian weight lifter and whose spine was reinforced by steel after an accident in a rugby match. He'd had problems getting through the museum's metal detector, just as he always had problems at airports. Logan didn't care. He always got to where he needed to be and he always got what he wanted.

Sign said, "I am authorised by the commissioner of the Metropolitan Police to investigate the deaths of Mark Archer, Arthur Lake, Terry File, and Colin Parker. There is a fifth death of a man who has no connection to our service. It is most likely related to the other deaths."

"*Our* service?" Messenger chuckled. "You are a private detective. You're no longer one of us."

Sign was unperturbed. "Be that as it may, I retain authority." He lowered his voice. "I am not here to antagonise you. I'm here to say that there's a killer on the loose. Most likely it's a foreign operative. He or she is killing the shortlist to be chief; also, anyone who gets in the way of the objective. I asked you here because I felt duty bound to warn you that your lives are in danger."

In a sarcastic tone, Logan said, "How very *noble* of you. Are you close to identifying the identity of the assassin?"

"No. And that's why I'm here."

Messenger's eyes narrowed. "You're not here for that. Something else is going on."

"Yes. I'm getting a whiff of bullshit." Pendry crossed his legs, clasped his hands, and said calmly, "Mr. Sign is attempting to play games with us."

"Poor Mr. Sign," Logan said in fluent Chinese. "The only treason I'm here today is because Pendry and Messenger called me to say you'd summoned them as well. We're busy people. We do the games, not you."

In impeccable Mandarin, Sign replied, "You decide if your death is a game." He switched to English, his voice cold and clipped. "There is the possibility that one of you is the killer and there is no hostile foreign agent in play. Somebody in front of me wants to kill off the competition for the post of chief."

Logan slapped his hands. "Bravo, Mr. Sign. I hope the commissioner is paying you handsomely for that absurd analysis."

Messenger looked less cavalier as he glanced at his colleagues. He returned his gaze to Sign. "It's preposterous, but feasible."

"It is." Sign saw Roberts approaching the group. He frowned, knowing the expression would be noticed by his guests. Roberts walked right up to him. "Katy – what are you doing here?"

Roberts showed him her police ID. "I'm here on official police business. The commissioner sent me."

Sign said to Messenger, Pendry, and Logan, "Gentlemen – leave now. I don't know what's going on."

"Stay where you are!" barked Roberts.

Hilt wasted no time. He dropped his cane, ran, knocked over Roberts, and grabbed Pendry. "Time to get out of here," he muttered to the MI6 officer. With his vice-like grip, he frogmarched Pendry away from the others.

Like Hilt, Knutsen was wearing a disguise. He'd been in the reading room for ninety minutes, waiting for the limpet to show up. He dashed toward the limpet and Pendry, ripped off Hilt's wig and fake moustache, and yanked his head back.

Hilt released Pendry and punched Knutsen in the face. Tourists were screaming. The room was turning into chaos as people ran like headless chickens. Knutsen struck Hilt in the chest and shin. Hilt staggered, regained his footing, and flicked his heel behind Knutsen's ankle while at the same time slamming his palm into Knutsen's jaw. Knutsen flipped onto his back. He gasped for air, rolled as Hilt attempted to smash his foot into his skull, and got back to his feet. Hilt and Knutsen stood before each other breathing fast.

Sign called out, "Knutsen – forget him! Protect Pendry!"

Knutsen grabbed Pendry and backed away from Hilt, toward Sign, Roberts, Logan, and Messenger. Roberts had withdrawn an extendable nightstick. She stared at Hilt, silently daring him to come close.

Hilt turned and ran, easily knocking unconscious two museum security men who'd entered the room. He kept running until he was out of the museum. Then he vanished.

Sign acted furious with Roberts. "What just happened?"

"I'm here to question Pendry, Messenger, and Logan."

"Are you now?!" Sign strode right up to her. "To do that, you'd need to have written authority from the foreign secretary or the prime minister. Let me see your paperwork."

Roberts hesitated.

"You don't have such paperwork, do you?"

Pendry brushed his hands over his jacket, but looked calm. He said to Messenger and Logan, "We leave separately, but we most certainly leave now." To Roberts he said, "Detective – your actions will cost you your career, if I have anything to do with it. Look on the bright side. You can sit at home and cry into your vino as you recall the death of your husband. Goodbye."

Pendry left first.

Then Logan.

Messenger was about to leave. He walked up to Sign and whispered, "If you're right and the killer's one of us, I don't think you'll have any chance of identifying that person. But, if I can help, call me." He left.

When Messenger was out of the room, Sign said to Roberts, "Set to work. When you're done, meet us in West Square."

Roberts walked away.

Sign approached Knutsen. "Are you okay, dear fellow?"

Knutsen rubbed his jaw while feeling pain all over his body. He stamped his foot on the floor. "The dojo has a bit of spring in it. And when I'm there I'm covered in armour. Not the same here. But I'll live." He winced as he placed his hand on his back. "I hope there's enough hot water in the flat's tank. I'll be using all of it because I need a very long bath."

Hilt was ten miles away from the museum when he called Smith from a payphone. "They've got my face!"

"I know. You have only two uses to me now. I want you to vanish and keep your mouth shut. I presume you no longer have any alias passports?"

"No. All confiscated when I left The Office."

"Okay. Lay low."

"I can deal with them if they come for me, though Knutsen's a handful. And Roberts might bring in SWAT, in which case I'm screwed."

"Roberts and Knutsen are not your problem. It's Sign who you should be worried about. He'll find your weakness and make you talk."

Hilt shook his head. "I've been through worse before and kept my mouth shut. Plus, I'll take them down before it gets to that."

"Make sure that happens. Just don't let Sign get close to you. I'll give you an extra payment when this is done. For now, don't speak to me until I call you." Smith ended the call. He cursed and called his deputy in MI6. "I won't be in today. Something's come up. Make sure you nail that problem in Cambodia." He took the tube and a taxi to his house in

Richmond. His wife was at home and was surprised to see him. He muttered to her that there was a crisis at work and all essential staff had been told to vacate HQ for a few hours. He went into his living room. It contained framed maps of parts of the world, photos of him shaking the hands of three world leaders, decanters of fine brandy and single malt whiskey, and furniture that had been procured from an antiques dealer in Berlin. He sat on a sofa and clasped his hands, deep in thought. Hilt had done the right thing in the museum. But, in doing so it had compromised him. There were two others on the list who needed to be killed. Smith smiled and breathed in deeply. He had no need to worry. He'd outplayed Sign.

Sign tossed logs onto his living room fire and looked sympathetically at Knutsen and Roberts. "You did well today."

Knutsen looked exhausted. "What will you do now?"

Sign looked at the photos Roberts had obtained from the museum's cameras. The limpet's face was visible from several angles. "Inspector Roberts has run these photos through UK national police databases. It's taken her six hours to be ninety percent sure that the limpet has no criminal record and isn't on a list of criminal suspects with no formal police record. That comes as no surprise." He stared at the limpets face before sliding the photos into a beige A4 envelope. "The police can be of no use to us on this. But I have an idea. I need to meet someone who might know who this man is. But that can't be done until tomorrow morning."

"Why the delay?" asked Roberts.

"Because the man I need to meet is currently travelling back from India and he doesn't touch down in Heathrow until seven AM." Sign's demeanour changed. He smiled, clapped his hands and said, "Our local pub is trialling a new ale. Why don't we brave the weather and see what we think of the beer?"

At seven AM the following morning, Sign waited in the Arrivals section of one of Heathrow's terminals. Despite the hour, the airport was bustling. Around him were chauffeurs holding placards with names written on them. Announcements about flights were regularly made over speakers. People were staring at monitors. Others were waiting alongside Sign and the chauffeurs at the metal fence, scrutinising each face that was emerging from the British Airways flight from Mumbai. None of them looked happy. They were saving their smiles for when they spotted the person they were here to meet.

Sign saw the individual he was waiting for. He was a tall, middle-aged man, immaculately dressed in a suit, and was clean shaven. He must have shaved on the flight just before the plane entered UK airspace. He was pulling a trolley bag and seemingly had no escorts. Sign looked at other passengers. Yes – one younger men and one woman worked for him but they were keeping their distance and were wearing less formal attire. The woman was carrying a diplomatic bag. Almost certainly, guns were in there.

As the middle-aged man exited the barrier and traversed the concourse, Sign casually walked behind him, then alongside him. "Hello Freddy. There's nothing to worry about. I just want to talk."

Freddy Vine glanced over his shoulder, gave the slightest shake of his head at his colleagues, and looked at Sign. "I heard you were out of the community. What do you want with me?"

"I need your help. This will only be a quick conversation."

General Vine was the Director of United Kingdom Special Forces. He said, "In two hours' time I have to brief the prime minister. *Quick* is good. We can talk in my car."

Ten minutes later they were in the rear seats of a black BMW, stationary in one of the airport's log-stay carparks. The special forces woman and man were in the front of the car. Sign handed Vine the envelope containing pictures of the limpet. "This person has access to a target of significant interest to me. I believe the man in the photos is a British former special forces soldier. It's possible he was latterly MI6 or MI5 paramilitary. I don't know him. But I want his name."

Vine looked at the photos. "Are you acting freelance now, or do you have official authority?"

"I have the authority of the prime minister, the foreign secretary, and the commissioner of the Metropolitan Police."

Vine's expression was neutral. "I'm responsible for the SAS, SBS, SRR, 18 Signals Regiment, Special Forces Support Group, and the Joint Special Forces Aviation Wing. Combine them and you have thousands of men and women. Multiply that with former operatives of this man's apparent age," he tossed a photo onto his lap, "and you have ten times that number. Plus, I have no access to MI6 and its paramilitary work. This man could be a ghost."

Sign placed a hand on the general's arm, not caring that the act made Vine bristle. "A photo gives me a name. You'll have records. I'm not getting any help from MI6."

"The prime minister could order that assistance!"

Sign removed his hand. "She could. But in doing so she wouldn't know who was paying the man in the photos. He'd go to ground. National security is at stake. It is possible that the next head of MI6 is a serial killer who's contracted the man in the photo."

"Where did you get these photos and when?"

Sign told him what had happened at the British Museum.

"I don't know who he is, but then again I've only been in this job for two years." Vine leafed through all of the photos. "Caucasian; adept at disguise; presumably adept at surveillance; and unarmed combat given he managed to get away – he could be one of ours. But he could equally be American, French, German, or Russian."

"I know." Sign wondered if Vine was going to cooperate. "But, I think he's British."

"Why?"

"A hunch."

Vine laughed. "A hunch?" He placed the photos into the envelope and sighed. "I'll do what I can to help identify him, *if* he is or was one of my boys. But I can't tell you how long that will take. It could be a matter of hours; or it could be days if we need to talk to former operatives to see if one of them knows who the man is. And if one former operative does recognise him, there's every chance he won't tell me his name and may call the man to warn him off."

"I concede it's a risk. If I were you I'd pre-empt any conversation with a statement."

"A statement?"

"Tell your former colleagues that the man in the photo has betrayed the special forces community." Sign opened the door. "I'm not exaggerating, Vine. Do what I tell you to do.

This *is* a matter of national security. If you don't cooperate, I'll ensure you're out of a job by tomorrow." Sign exited the car.

Mid-morning, Sign was back in West Square. He told Knutsen and Roberts about his encounter with Vine. "The general will do what he can. He has no alternative. But we must now wait."

"Wait?!." Knutsen paced the room. "The limpet is probably now long gone. And the whisperer will be laughing at us.!"

In a calm tone, Sign responded, "You are right, dear fellow on both counts. But we have something on our side that the whisperer doesn't – time. The clock is ticking before the appointment of the next Chief of MI6 is announced. The whisperer must attempt to kill the last two on the three-person shortlist. But we have muddied the waters. He's going to find murder a far harder task now that I've confronted them."

Roberts said, "The whisperer must be Pendry. He was the one who was grabbed by the limpet."

"Most likely." Sign didn't say what he was thinking. The intercom buzzed. Sign smiled and said to Knutsen, "That will be your young lad David. Show him in. And show no mercy."

When David was in the room, Sign slid a desk into the rear of the lounge, placed three chairs behind it, and put a chair in the centre of the room, facing the desk.

Sign looked at the nineteen year old black man. "Sit."

David sat in the solitary chair. He was wearing a suit that Knutsen had bought him. Sign, Roberts, and Knutsen sat behind the desk.

Knutsen said, "You have your first interview with the Metropolitan Police in two days' time. You have to pass that interview if your application to become a police officer is to progress. We're here to help you prepare for the interview. For the next hour, I am not Tom Knutsen. I am not your friend or mentor. Understood?"

David nodded.

"Yes or no?!"

"Yes." David was perspiring.

Roberts asked, "Why do you want to become a police officer."

David's voice was trembling as he answered, "I want to help my friends. Well, at least I thought they were my friends. I want to set them an example. Get them off drugs and crime."

"Wrong answer!" Knutsen slapped the table. "As a police officer you'll be helping a whole community, the vast majority of who you won't know."

"I… I hadn't thought of it that way."

"Think of it that way." Knutsen nodded at Roberts.

She said, "A police officer enters homes she or he has never entered before. They meet people they don't know. Some of them are liars. Some of them are criminals. Some will want to put a knife in your gut. But some of them will be good people. How are you going to spot the differences?"

David replied, "I... I know my neighbourhood. I know which bros are on the take, their mums and dads, their friends, and I know the streets."

Roberts shook her head. "If you join the Metropolitan Police you may be stationed in a part of London you don't know. You'll have to start from scratch. You'll need to use your brain, knowledge of the law, and your ability to read people."

David was lost for words.

Sign interjected. "Don't be nervous, David."

David frowned. "You a cop as well, mister?"

Sign gave him a half truth. "I work for the Metropolitan Police commissioner. No one else." He placed his hands on the desk. "Nerves are good. It means you respect this forum and it means you're not cocky and arrogant. But you need to get a grip of your nerves. We can't have nervous cops on our streets, can we?"

"No... no sir."

Sign stared at him. "Remember Mr. Knutsen's kendo training. Breathe properly. Always remain in control. Stay poised. Do not let your mind tell you that you've lost before you even raise your sword against your opponent. Believe in the truth. And if it helps, imagine the three of us are naked and sat on the loo."

Roberts suppressed an urge to giggle.

Sign continued. "Be calm. Don't go to the other extreme. Many cops are confident bullies. Don't be like them. Take the professional route. Be the man on the dojo." He glanced at Knutsen.

Knutsen nodded. "He's giving you good advice."

David hesitated. "The truth? The truth is I don't want to be a bully. I don't want to hide behind a uniform and rough people up. I want people like my Mum to make better decisions when they were younger."

Sign glanced at Knutsen and Roberts. "That is a good answer." He returned his attention to David. "You're no longer perspiring. Your voice now sounds confident. Your eye contact is good. My job is done. My colleagues will continue the interview. I will take my leave."

Knutsen and Roberts spent fifty minutes barraging David with questions. They also gave him hypothetical scenarios and asked him what he would do in such events. A mugger is stabbed with his own knife by the victim – do you first attend to the mugger or the traumatised victim? You witness a police officer, who once saved your life, steal cash from a drugs bust – do you report him to your superiors? An armed robber takes a hostage in an off-licence and you are first on the scene – do you request that you're taken hostage in exchange for the victim being released? A terrorist is about to blow himself up in a crowded location – do you kill him? The list of questions and scenarios were relentless. David didn't get all of the answers right. It would have been impossible for him to have done so without extensive police training and experience. And as every police veteran will agree, there are always situations that no police officer is prepared for. But that wasn't the purpose of the interview. What Knutsen and Roberts were looking for in David were thoughtfulness and swift decisiveness.

At the end of the interview Knutsen smiled. "David – you'll do an excellent job in your real interview. When you get home, hang your suit up and make sure it's free of fluff, wash and iron your shirt, polish your shoes, get rid of that goatee beard thing you've got going on, and – most importantly – be proud of who you are."

After David was gone, Sign re-entered the room and addressed Knutsen and Roberts. "General Vine has just called me. I know the limpet's name. He is Karl Hilt. He's a former Royal Marines commando and subsequently a Special Boat Service operative, before joining my lot and becoming a covert paramilitary operative. He left MI6 two years' ago. Now he works freelance."

Roberts asked, "What do you know about his character?"

Sign sat in his armchair. "Vine said he was an extremely effective operator in special forces. But, he's a psychopath; or a sociopath; or whatever label we can slap on him. That trait served him very well in behind-the-lines work, including with MI6. Regardless, Vine has told me to be very careful with him."

Knutsen asked, "What do we do next?"

"We hunt him down and make him talk."

CHAPTER 23

Four days' later Hilt checked into a hotel in Norwich. He felt grubby and exhausted. He'd walked and jogged one hundred and twenty miles from London to Norfolk and his only rest had been a few hours' kip in some ditches. He knew he couldn't go anywhere near his home, so he'd chosen Norfolk because there was a Cromer-based trawler captain he knew who might take him to Scandinavia. But the captain wasn't due back from his North Sea fishing trip until tomorrow and Hilt was on his knees. He needed a proper bed, But, in taking a room in the hotel, he knew that he was probably signing his own death sentence. In the bedroom, he showered and shaved, then sat in a chair, his gun on his lap. He stared at the door, desperately trying not to sleep, But fatigue started to overcome him. His head started nodding; eyes shutting and opening; nose sporadically snorting; and his mind was telling him to rest because he was too old for this lark. His gun fell off his lap as he slouched, deep in sleep.

Roberts ran up the stairs of West Square and hammered on Sign's door. Knutsen answered. Breathless, Roberts exclaimed, "We've got him! Hilt. He's checked in to a hotel in Norwich. He used his own ID. Must mean he doesn't have other ID. Hotel cameras picked up his face. There's no doubt it's him."

Knutsen ushered her in and called out to Sign.

Sign entered the living room. He was in a bathrobe. Roberts repeated what she'd told Knutsen. Sign said, "Norfolk will be the first stage of Hilt's escape route."

Knutsen frowned. "Escape?"

"Yes. Hilt's now of no use to the whisperer. He's been told to get out while he can. I imagine he didn't use any form of transport to get to Norfolk. He's tired and he's waiting for an asset to get him to," he looked at a framed map of the world, "somewhere. My guess is that his destination isn't the Netherlands or Germany – the crossings are too heavily policed. And if he wanted to take conventional ferries into Europe he'd have gravitated to Lowestoft. No. He's going to Denmark, Norway, or Sweden. And he's going there via unconventional transport. After that, who knows?"

Roberts was confused. "He'll have known that checking into a hotel might have blown his location. Why not check into a B&B where there are no cameras. It would have been far harder for us to trace him there."

Sign agreed. "He doesn't like you, me, and Knutsen. He's baiting us. He wants us to enter his room. Then he kills us and leaves."

Roberts pulled out her phone. "I'm calling SCO19. They'll arrest or kill him."

Sign shook his head. "It would take weeks for SWAT to rehearse how to take down a paramilitary spy. They're not trained for this."

"Then who is?"

"MI6. But they're not at my disposal." Sign rubbed his face. "Special forces could be an option, but there is a significant risk that they won't want to kill one of their own."

Knutsen asked, "What about foreign allies? Could they help? They'll be impartial."

Sign smiled. "It's a good thought but flawed. A foreign paramilitary unit would have to know what's at stake in order for them to risk a severe diplomatic row if they hit a UK national on UK soil. To get a foreign ally's help, we'd have to tell them that the next Chief of

MI6 is a murderer. That information would escalate beyond our control. We're looking for the whisperer. We are most certainly not looking to lose the allegiance of a partner country." Sign pointed at Roberts. "We take Hilt down ourselves. I've no time to tell you how. I'll be there. I'll do the thinking. Give me five minutes to get dressed. Then we get in the car to Norfolk. Bring guns. Also handcuffs or rope."

When he was out of the room, Roberts muttered, "Arrogant prick!"

Knutsen was shocked. "Sign? He gave you a place to stay after your husband was murdered. He helped you get back on your feet. He helped give me purpose. He helped David. For very little money, he's helping UK national security. He's not arrogant. He was the brightest star in MI6. He's gone into problem-solving mode. Don't mistake that for arrogance. He just thinks better than us. You want to slap a label on him then I'll give you one – he's lonely. No man is an island and all that. He's been adrift since his wife was murdered. And I'll tell you this – he'll take a bullet for us without blinking. He wants to be with her again." Knutsen stood. "Don't ever speak about my friend like that again!"

Roberts paled. "I... I hadn't thought about it that way."

"Then, don't think!" Knutsen knelt before her. "You've been through so much. Goodness knows how you've coped. Always remember who your friends are. Sign is the best of them." Knutsen smiled. "He can, however, be a pain in the ass."

As he stood, Roberts laughed and said, "He most certainly can. But you're right. He's done more for me than anyone else."

"Including your husband?" Knutsen looked aghast. "Sorry, that came out wrong. It was a dumb thing to ask."

Roberts looked at the floor. Quietly she said, "It's okay. Elliot and I worked. Good marriage. Barely a bad word between us. He remembered anniversaries and birthdays. He was charming with my family and friends. He never did anything bad to me. He was a very proper man. But..." her lips trembled, "but..."

"There sometimes is a *but*."

She raised her head. "It's hard for women. Sometimes, when the best thing is looking you in the face, you want something else."

"You cheated on him?"

"No. Nothing like that. I thought of him like a superb brother. Not a lover. Does that make sense?"

"Yes." Knutsen stripped his pistol, cleaned the working parts, and reassembled the gun. "We all have to forget the past. The next few hours will define our future. We have to put our faith in Sign. SCO19 might have been the best solution. Then again, I'm not a spy. I don't think like Sign. Nor do I have his training."

"You over estimate him."

"Maybe."

Sign entered the room. He was wearing corduroy trousers, hiking boots, and a green fleece jacket.

Hunting, shooting, and fishing in Norfolk was what immediately came into Knutsen's mind when he saw Sign's garb. "Do you have any clothes that are twenty first century?"

Sign laughed. "Would they keep me warmer than those manufactured in the last century?" He poured himself a coffee. "Clothing manufacture is about fashion, not necessity.

Still, people who need warmth within rugged environments are sucked in by alleged advances in clothing technology. It's a racket. Did you know in 1924 the British mountaineer George Herbert Leigh Mallory is probably the first man to scale Everest? He did so in clothing that by today's standards would be deemed nonsensical. It wasn't. I'm certain he reached the peak."

Knutsen was having none of this. "We don't know if he reached the peak. In any case, he died on the way down. His body was only discovered in 1999. I don't think his clothes were good enough."

Sign sat. "Or he was simply exhausted and suffering from altitude sickness." He smiled. "I've traversed Siberia during winter in little more than a shirt and trousers. I concede, I've never suffered altitude sickness. I did, however, have a pack of dogs on my heels. Men do what they have to do under the circumstances." His expression steeled. "I know what I'm doing. Clothes don't stop a bullet. If either of you think you know better, try swimming two miles in December from St. Petersburg to a British submarine."

Knutsen and Roberts were silent.

Sign said, "Now! Get dressed. Think like Mallory. We can ascend in whatever attire. But we may not make it back to base camp. We depart in five minutes."

John Smith watched Logan's home. He knew Logan was in there. It was Saturday. Logan had a rare day off. Given he had a six month old baby, that meant his wife would do anything to have a few hours respite from childcare. She'd be out of the house as soon as possible. Smith waited for ninety minutes. Logan's wife exited, holding a supermarket 'bag for life' and an umbrella. She looked tired but happy. Even an hour or two of buying baby food and other essentials would give her the head space she needed. Probably, when she returned home she'd feed her family, put her son to bed, and then collapse on the sofa. Smith waited until she was out of sight and then entered the house. He could hear Logan in the kitchen, washing dishes. He moved silently into the adjacent lounge. Logan had his back to him. His son was in a playpen, lying on his back while fiddling with toys that were too big to choke on. Smith stood by the playpen, staring at the child. He had no affinity to children. As far as he was concerned, they were not only a waste of time, they also produced emotions in their parents that ultimately messed with their minds and supplied them with an early grave. He knew that because his parents had worked themselves to the bone to support him. Like all children, he'd been selfish as a child. His highly educated and intelligent parents got through parenthood like any other mum and dad – they blagged it, taking each day as it came. Lack of sleep was a killer in the early days; so too lack of cash. In an attempt to keep things afloat, his dad had dragged his tiny family to tax havens around the world, every time telling his wife that his new job would make them millions. It never worked that way. His dad ended up bankrupt. His wife divorced him. Dad died of a broken heart. Mum killed herself. And before then, Smith had been schooled in Dubai, Isle of Man, Bermuda, and Vanuatu. Friends came and went. Childhood was a waste of time. Still, MI6 liked the fact that he'd had an unconventional upbringing. The organisation thought it made him well equipped for the work of a spy who had no connection to the normal world.

Smith pulled out a pistol and held it against the baby's head. "Mr. Logan! I urge you to desist from you chores."

Logan ran in to the room.

Smith smiled. "Hello Logan. The gun is loaded. If you don't do what I say, I will kill your son."

Logan's face flushed red. "Sign was right! There was always a killer!"

"We do what we have to in life." He placed the muzzle of the gun in the baby's mouth. It thought it was a toy. The boy gurgled. With his left hand, Smith withdrew a piece of paper and a pen and placed both on an adjacent table. "Sit down and write what I dictate. I'll stay here until you're done. Your baby's head will be mash if you make one error."

At midday, Sign, Knutsen, and Roberts stood outside the Holiday Inn in Norwich.

Roberts said to Sign, "The hotel concierge says Hilt's in his room. He has a 'Do Not Disturb' leaflet on his door. I've given the concierge your name and instructed him that you have police authority to approach the room. Are you sure this is a good idea?"

Sign shrugged. "Time will tell. But I don't think going in guns blazing will help. If anything, it will antagonise him and force him to keep his mouth shut. He'll stay silent out of principal. A more subtle tactic is needed. I want you both to stay outside in case he bolts."

Knutsen shook his head. "That will be a lottery. There are too many entrances and exits to cover."

"Try your best." Sign walked in to the hotel.

Knutsen muttered, "He's making a huge mistake doing this alone. He's unarmed. We can't back him up. All he's got is…"

"His brain." Roberts stared at the hotel. "This is what he does – going in to situations without a safety net. It's ingrained in him." She turned to Knutsen. "I'll take the north side of the hotel. You stay here. When he gives the signal, we move like fury."

Sign took a lift to the third floor and walked down the corridor. He knocked on a room door. "Karl Hilt, this is Ben Sign. You know who I am. I am alone and unarmed. But, I do have police officers surrounding the hotel. I'd like to talk."

There was silence for two minutes.

Sign spoke in a louder voice. "I know you're in there. And I know you're desperate. I have something that will help you."

The door opened a few inches. Hilt was there, his gun pointing at Sign. Hilt said, "If you've got others with you, you'll go down first."

"I agree to those terms."

"And it will be a head shot, in case you're wearing a bullet proof vest."

Sign patted his chest. "No vest. No wire. No recording device whatsoever. No pistol. No explosives. No tricks. But, I do have a piece of paper I'd like to show you." He pulled out a letter. "May I come in?"

Hilt fully opened the door, grabbed Sign by the back of his neck, flung him onto the bed, and stood with his gun in two hands. It was pointing at one of Sign's eyes.

Sign sat up. "There's no need for violence. I wouldn't be able to compete with you." He gestured to a chair. "May I sit there? I'd like you to sit opposite me. By all means keep your gun trained on me if you think it's necessary. I suspect you already know I can't hurt you. But I'll leave it to your intellect to decide whether I'm a problem or a solution."

Hilt hesitated, then nodded. "Get in the chair." He pulled up another chair and faced Sign. His gun was still in his hand but not pointing at Sign. "Why and how would you help me?"

Sign was calm. "You're in a bit of a pickle. No doubt you're here because you have an exfiltration route planed across the North Sea. If you haven't, that's bad luck because you've got nowhere to go in the UK. You've been hung out to dry by your paymaster. For people like us there's nothing worse than when you've been stabbed in the back by one of your own."

Hilt chuckled. "It comes with the territory."

"Yes. And I know you don't care about that. It's what you're trained for. Probably, abandonment is in your DNA. After all, your parents gave you up for adoption when you were four. But, you didn't get adopted. Instead it was foster care nearly every year until you were eighteen and enlisted in the marines. The commandos were the family you always wanted. The problem was that you could never really fit in with all the camaraderie and discipline. It was too late for you because you were a loner and had no trust. Nevertheless, you were top of your marine class and served with distinction. But, you wanted something different. Special forces appealed to you because you thought it might be a job where you could work alone. You made it through the excruciating selection process and were set to task for many years. Alas, you didn't find solace in the Special Boat Service. There was still a chain of command. And you had to work with colleagues. Family, you concluded, was not for you. And that's why we picked you up. MI6 gave you precisely what you always knew you had no family, nor any substitute families. You could now work alone."

Hilt was silent, though anger was evident in his face.

Sign crossed his legs. "It's not your fault that you are a sociopath. When a child gets no love – from parents, foster parents, teachers, social workers, aunts or uncles, siblings, anyone – as a result, they don't trust love."

"Thanks for the therapy session, *Dr.* Sign." Hilt waved his gun. "But, I'm a grown up. And I'm the one who can end your life."

"Yes, of course you can, dear fellow. This is the problem," He handed the letter to Hilt.

It took thirty seconds for Hilt to read the two page document. It was written by General Vine, was classed top secret, and had the word *Draft* printed at the top. Within the letter it said that Hilt suffered mental illness, was a coward in action, had allegedly slept with a fourteen year old girl, and was dishonourably discharged from the military.

Hilt tossed the letter aside. "These are all fucking lies!"

Sign smiled. "Of course they are. But who did you think you were dealing with?"

"Vine didn't come up with this! You did this!"

Sign said, "You're going to prison for the murder of Elliot Roberts. I would imagine the sentence will be approximately twenty five to thirty years. Here's the thing – prison officers and inmates respect courage. You'll get extra rations; you'll be treated well; you'll be able to run a fiefdom. But, if I put a copy of that letter into the system you'll be a nonce. Your life will be hell. So, I'm sat here wondering what to do. Letter or no letter? No letter means you'll probably be out on good behaviour in fifteen years. In court a brilliant defence lawyer will cite your appalling childhood, the traumas you've suffered in combat, and the fact you were paid to kill Elliot by a man who is infinitely worse than you. Alas, the letter will not go well for you."

Hilt stated, "If I do anything to you, a copy of this letter will go straight to the courts and prison."

"Yes." Sign looked out of the window. "You could shoot your way out of this situation. You'll die. The papers will say the police killed a paedophile. But if by some miracle you make it to a boat that can take you across the North Sea, know this – there is a British frigate sitting there, waiting to check every boat that heads out of East Anglia. And on the frigate are thirty marines. They won't like you at all."

Hilt frowned. "You're bluffing!"

Sign pulled out his mobile number and extended it to Hilt. "Vine's number is in my contact list. Call him. Ask him security passwords to verify he is who he says he is. Also in my contacts list are the Minister of Defence, the Foreign Secretary, the Head of MI6, the Metropolitan Police Commissioner, and the Prime Minister. Ask them if I'm bluffing."

Hilt didn't take the phone.

Sign leaned forward. "There will be no letter if I get a name. I want to know who in MI6 killed the competition."

Smith watched Logan write his signature at the bottom of the sheet of paper. Smith withdrew his gun from the baby's mouth and looked at the sheet. It read as follows:

To whom it may concern

My name is James Logan. I am a senior official in British Intelligence. It was probable I would be the next chief of the Secret Intelligence Service. But, to attain that post, I knew I was up against strong competition, as well as external forces. The other men on the shortlist for chief are Mark Archer, Arthur Lake, Edward Messenger, Nicholas Pendry, and Terry File. All but Messenger and Pendry were killed by my hand. I would have killed Messenger and Pendry but my identity has been discovered by former MI6 officer Ben Sign. My tactic has failed. I also confess to instructing a subordinate to kill Elliot Roberts, the husband of a Special Branch Detective who has been helping Sign, and murder Colin Parker, a high ranking counter-intelligence officer. I'm writing this letter under duress. Ben Sign is pointing a gun at my child. He is forcing this confession out of me.

Nevertheless, I will accept whatever punishment is owed to me.

James Logan

Smith grinned as placed the muzzle of his handgun back against the baby's head. "Him? Or you?"

"You bastard!" Logan was sweating.

"Live with what you might see for the rest of your life, or end the pain. You choose!"

Logan shook his head. "How could you do this?"

Smith cocked the gun. "Bye bye baby."

"No! No!"

Smith walked to Logan and shoved the gun in his mouth. "That was the right decision." He pulled the trigger. Logan was instantly dead.

Sign called Roberts. "Bring one of your colleagues. He's ready to come in. He won't hurt you. I have the name."

Knutsen and Roberts were in the room within eighty seconds. Both trained their guns on Hilt.

Roberts' stomach knotted as she looked at the man who'd killed her husband. "Why did you let us find you?!"

Hilt smiled. "I didn't want to run anymore."

"Liar!" Roberts stepped forward,

Hilt tossed his gun onto the bed. "I'm sorry about the loss of your husband. Life ain't fair, is it? If it's any consolation, pretty much everyone I know is dead. All I have left is a job. The jobs usually include bullets or knives. That's my path. Shit happens." He looked Roberts directly in the eye. "I came here because I want to reach the end of that path. I was going to get on a fishing boat tomorrow. But, then what? More of the same old crap. Reinventing myself. No ID I can use. One day being caught out and smashed up in a prison cell in Moscow or Beijing. I could have done that ten years ago. Now, I'm not so sure. See, the thing is I've got a bit of a medical situation. Only found out three months ago." He looked away, his smile no longer on his face. "If you're a betting person, don't put a wager on me making it past the next few weeks. Lung cancer's a fucker. I've never smoked. Probably it's all that nuclear, biological, and chemical training they put SF through. Respirators aren't faultless. Guess I got some filth in my airways." He stood and then laid on his front with his hands behind his back. "It's muscle memory. Leg it to an escape and evasion route. Get to Scandinavia. Go on foot and other means across Europe. End up in Thailand or similar. Then you realise you're not that person anymore." He looked over his shoulder. "Get it done!"

Roberts put her foot on his back and attached handcuffs. "You're under arrest for the murder of my husband." She looked at Sign. "How did you know?!"

Sign clasped his hands. "I didn't know about his cancer. But I deduced he'd come here because it was his last stand and a cry for help. It's like an old wolf who wanders from the pack because it knows something is wrong with its health. It chooses a place to die." Sign stood and walked out of the room while saying, "Do your police thing and get Hilt to a secure facility. He won't try to escape."

Ten minutes later, police were on the scene. They escorted Hilt to Norwich police station where he was placed in a cell. The custody sergeant refused the Metropolitan Police's request to transfer him to a London police station, on the grounds that Hilt might do severe damage to the officers transporting him. The Metropolitan commissioner tried to object, but the sergeant told him that custody sergeants can only be overruled by the home secretary. Hilt was to be kept in Norfolk, awaiting trial. A doctor and nurses visited him in his cell and did tests on him. They concluded he'd be dead before a court verdict was issued.

When Sign, Knutsen, and Roberts were back in London, Roberts received a phone call. After she ended the call, she said to Sign, "James Logan has written a letter stating he did the murders. Then he killed himself. His wife found the body. Logan wasn't the name Hilt gave you. The limpet lied."

Sign looked distracted as he strolled alongside his colleagues into West Square. "He didn't lie. The whisperer cast him aside, like a rabid dog. He wouldn't protect him now." He stopped and turned to Roberts. "By all means slap me if you wish, but I do feel sorry for Hilt – his upbringing and adult life have been hell. It would have been good if we could have turned back the clock and given him a proper family."

Roberts stared at him. First, she looked angry. Then sad. "Yes. I know all about living with grief. It corrupts the soul."

Knutsen said, "We all know how that feels." He placed his hand on Sign's arm. "What next?"

266

Sign stood outside the entrance to the apartment block. "Logan isn't the whisperer. Nor did he commit suicide. He was executed in the same room as his baby. What I would have done if I were the whisperer is tape bin bags to my arms so that I could dispose of cordite residue on my forearms, wear gloves, plastic shoe covers, hold a gun to the baby's head, and force a false confession out of Logan. When he'd finished the note, I'd have placed the gun in his mouth. Logan would have put his hands around the weapon, out of fear. I'd have pulled the trigger, knowing that Logan's prints were now on the gun and that cordite would be on his arms. Police forensics would see the case as cut and dry. And there'd be no trace of an external party in the room."

Roberts asked, "How do you know this stuff?"

"Life and death." Sign looked at Knutsen. "I need you and your skills today. You and I aren't going in to the apartment. However, Mrs. Roberts is going into her flat."

Roberts looked furious. "Don't leave me out of this!"

Sign leaned toward her and whispered into her ear. "I cannot compromise you or your profession. Knutsen and I are unconventional. But you have a career and life to protect. You can argue with me as much as you like, dear lady. But, on this matter I must hold fast." He patted Knutsen's arm. "Let's finish this awful affair."

Sign and Knutsen spun on their heels and walked away.

They traversed London via tubes and a taxi. On arrival, the residential house before them was where the whisperer lived. It was seven PM and getting dark. Tbe house had internal lights on. The whisperer and his wife were easily visible in their dining room.

As they stood on the street, Knutsen asked, "What are we going to do about his wife?"

"We need her as a witness. There are two scenarios: she's either complicit in what the whisperer has done; or she's not complicit, in which case we need her to hear what's happened. Either way, she won't want prison. Regardless, here." He handed Knutsen a recording device the size of a cigarette lighter. "This is state of the art MI6. Turn this on as soon as we enter."

Knutsen laughed. "You spooks are so out of touch with technology. We could have just used a mobile phone to record everything that's said. It can be saved to Cloud forever."

Sign looked puzzled. "I've no idea what that means." His expression steeled. "Onwards."

Sign rang the front door bell.

The whisperer's wife opened the door.

Sign said, "We're colleagues of your husband. There is urgent business to attend to. May we come in? We're sorry if we are intruding on your dinner."

She answered, "The dinner is in the oven. Casserole. It won't be ready for a couple of hours." She called out to her husband. "Two men are here. They say they know you. I'm not letting them in unless you say it's okay."

The whisperer appeared in the hallway and asked, "What do you want, Ben Sign?"

"I need to talk to you about Logan. He's killed himself and confessed his direct involvement in criminal matters that affect national security. My investigation is now closed. But, I need you to hear from me what has happened."

The whisperer nodded. "Come in. And congratulations on a job well done."

Sign and Knutsen entered the house.

CHAPTER 24

The whisperer gestured Sign and Knutsen to the dining room table. The whisperer sat opposite them. He was wearing the suit he'd worn to work. He asked, "Would you like my wife to leave the room?"

She was leaning against the wall, watching the three men.

Sign faked a gentlemanly smile. "That won't be necessary. She's security cleared to know all about your work."

"She is. So let's get on with it. I need to shower and change into more comfortable attire before dinner."

Sign nodded. "I quite understand, dear chap. And once again, sorry for the intrusion. We're here because we want to protect you. When MI6 learns tomorrow of Logan's betrayal, it will be in a mess. Henry Gable won't be able to control that mess. He's not up to the task. The Metropolitan Police has no jurisdiction over the intelligence agencies. It can't step in to keep a steady ship. MI5 are a bunch of quasi-cops. They don't understand espionage. The announcement about Logan will have to be made to all MI6 staff. But the announcement will rock the morale of the service."

"Cambridge Five springs to mind." The whisperer's tone was calm and precise.

"Exactly. It took decades for us to get over that sucker-punch. During the Cold War, we couldn't afford that catastrophe. Now, the world's a more dangerous place."

The whisperer sighed and drummed his fingers on the table. "Spare me a lecture on the obvious."

"We need leadership. You can give that. So can the only other candidate left alive for the post of chief. One of you has to step up to the plate."

The whisperer was more benign as he answered, "I'm ready for the challenge."

"I feared you would be."

Knutsen's handgun was hidden from view under the table and pointing at the whisperer's stomach. Everything being said was being recorded by the electronic device in his jacket.

In a louder voice, Sign said, "Logan didn't kill Mark Archer, Colin Parker, Arthur Lake, and Terry File. Karl Hilt killed Elliot Roberts. Hilt is now in custody. He has a fatal illness and has nothing to lose. You employed him. *You* are the serial killer. You are what I call the whisperer. You are Edward Messenger."

Messenger laughed. "This is the stuff of fantasy!"

"No, it's not. Hilt has confessed."

Messenger shook his head. "This man Hilt has been briefed by Logan to give you my name. Probably Logan knew Hilt had cancer. It was Logan's parting shot."

Sign glanced at Messenger's wife. "Mrs. Logan. You're a nurse. Can you tell me how many fatal illnesses there are?"

She went pale. "Tens, hundreds, thousands. It depends on the quality of the treatment, how far advanced the disease is, the age of the patient, their immune system, and other factors."

Sign's expression was cold as he returned his attention to Messenger. "Thousands of possibilities. I didn't tell you Hilt had cancer. But he does."

Messenger breathed in deeply. "An educated guess. My wife and I have an agreement not to talk about her day job. My parents are dead. It's stressful to know what my wife goes through every day."

"Rubbish!" Sign slapped his hand on the table. "You've seen more death than she has. And you've dealt it out throughout your career. You understand death as well as me. You're not squeamish. But, you are stupid. There's no possibility of you knowing Hilt had cancer unless you knew Hilt and you knew his condition. Hilt will testify against you to get a lesser sentence. A resourceful man like him would never have trusted a Machiavellian man like you I guarantee you he'll have concrete evidence of your contract together and he'll have kept the evidence hidden from you Who knows? Photos; recordings; bank transfers; phone calls; evidence in a closed court of where your paths crossed in MI6. You put him out to an unsavoury pasture. Now, he's doing the same to you. He'll crucify you in court."

Knutsen said, "I'm a former police officer. But, I still work for the police. What you say next will be used in court."

Messenger was silent but let out a groan after his wife walked up to him and slapped his face.

"How could you?!" She said to him. "How could you?!"

Slowly, Messenger raised his head and rubbed his face. He looked at his wife, then Sign and Knutsen. He bowed his head and said in a quiet voice, "Pendry is going to die."

Sign frowned. "You're going to jail. You won't be able to touch him."

Messenger rubbed his eyes and smiled. "I'm not, as you describe, stupid. I'm smarter than you. It's all about chess. The others had to be dealt with expediently. But after I got Logan to confess, I had to deal with Pendry differently. I saw him for a cup of tea yesterday in the MI6 canteen. When he wasn't looking, I placed a liquid nerve agent in his tea. The agent was designed at Porton Down. It's ingenious. Under our instructions four years' ago, the boffins constructed a deadly liquid that assaults the body. But it was crucial the effects weren't immediate. It means you can have a Russian, or whoever, visiting the UK, be infected with the nerve agent, fly back to Russia and not start getting ill for a few weeks. As a result, no one can categorically trace the poisoning to the UK, even if there are suspicions from other states. Ergo: bad guy dies; no diplomatic fallout." Messenger retained his smile. "Pendry is a dead man walking. He'll feel fine now. But soon he'll start frothing at the mouth. Not even Porton Down can reverse the effects. Our most lethal scientific research and development facility has created a poison that they cannot counteract. There's an irony there."

Sign was motionless. "Pendry will die, but you will not be made chief. You'll go to jail for multiple life sentences."

Messenger looked resigned to his fate. "I'd have made an excellent chief. The others on the shortlist weren't a patch on me." His expression turned menacing as he looked at Sign. "You too would have made a superb chief. But, you took yourself out of the equation. So, it was down to me to step up to the plate. And sometimes in life we have to do rough things to allow the little people to sleep peacefully in their beds."

"Serial killing to obtain power is *not* part of the job description of an MI6 officer." Sign looked at Messenger's wife. "Did you know anything about what your husband has done? Or, did you have any suspicions?"

She was tearful as she replied, "No. No… I never knew what he did at work. This is awful. Edward – how could you have done this? We were happy. We didn't need you to get a pay rise. I didn't need you to be chief."

Messenger looked at her. "You weren't enough for me. I needed a mistress. The position of chief was my mistress." He smiled and returned his attention to Sign. "I won't spend the rest of my life in prison. So, how do we resolve this situation?"

Knutsen gripped his handgun.

Messenger was calm as he said to Knutsen, "You're pointing a handgun at me, under the table. Did you expect me not to anticipate that? And did you expect me not to be doing the same to you? I believe they call it a Mexican standoff."

Sign snapped, "If you kill anyone in this room, it will go bad for you."

Messenger pulled his hand out from under the table. He placed his pistol on the table. "For the sake of the recording device that no doubt one of you has on his person, I employed Karl Hilt to watch you and kill Katy Roberts' husband and Colin Parker. I forced Mark Archer, Arthur Lake, and Terry File to commit suicide. I shot James Logan after forcing him to write a false confession. I made that murder look like suicide. And I poisoned Nicholas Pendry. I did all of this because I wanted to be the only remaining candidate for the top job in British intelligence." He picked up the gun.

Knutsen shouted, "No!"

Messenger blew his own brains out.

Three hours later, Knutsen and Sign were back in West Square. In the lounge, Knutsen lit a fire. "I'll get Katy," he said.

When she entered the bachelor pad, Roberts was fully clothed. "What happened?"

Knutsen explained everything.

She looked at Sign. "Will you take over as chief of MI6, even if briefly?"

Sign was in his armchair. "No. I like this job. I like working with you both."

Roberts touched his hand. "I'm moving to New Zealand. It will be a new life. You and Tom will be on your own." A tear fell down her cheek.

Sign gripped her hand. "Damn right you should go to New Zealand." He smiled. "Don't look back."

"Never."

Sign rose and kissed her on the cheek. "Knutsen and I will be alright. You'll be alright." He walked to the window and stared through it. "It's what's out there that worries me." He turned rapidly. "Mr. Knutsen, if you please! Three glasses of calvados immediately. Tonight we celebrate. Tomorrow may bring ills. I've received a letter. Knutsen – you and I have a new case."

THE END